I waited an... ...ing to hear
anyth... ...s location.

...my ankles
into j...
O... ...go.

I stopped and crouched up against the inside wall of the staircase. Just earsplitting silence. Gathering myself, I summoned whatever semblance of courage remained in my trembling body.

A second later, my brain issued the command. *Okay—it's go time.*

I lunged up toward the last stair, propelling myself into the loft.

At least that was the plan.

My leading foot caught the lip of the top stair, sending me crashing down. The pepper spray sailed across the room as the elbow of my outstretched arm slammed into the wood floor. I didn't hear the dispenser hit anything, so either the killer caught it, or it landed in the pile of clean clothes on the floor. Either way, not good. Worse yet, the raised bat fell backward, its barrel cracking me on the back of the head before bouncing and rolling down the stairs.

Disarmed and face down, I lay sprawled between the top step and the floor of the room. Before the killer could react, I scrambled to my feet and hit the light switch.

And there he was, his intensity palpable.

I stared into his piercing eyes.

Praise for B. T. Polcari

Semifinalist in the ShoreIndie Contest

~

Against My Better Judgment

by

B. T. Polcari

A Mauzzy and Me Mystery

Against My Better Judgment

Cover Art by *Debbie Taylor*

The Wild Rose Press, Inc.
PO Box 708
Adams Basin, NY 14410-0708
Visit us at www.thewildrosepress.com

Publishing History
First Champagne Rose Edition, 2020
Trade Paperback ISBN 978-1-5092-3276-5
Digital ISBN 978-1-5092-3277-2

A Mauzzy and Me Mystery
Published in the United States of America

Dedication

To Maria and Mary,
without whom this book would never have been possible. I am forever grateful for your inspiration, constant encouragement, and countless manuscript readings, comments, and edits. Thank you for being there every step of the journey. You cannot imagine how much your support kept me going.

~

To Mom, for encouraging me at a very young age that I could do anything if I put my mind to it, including becoming an author. This book is all about perseverance, on so many levels.

~

Thank you to Cynthia Luna and Jeni Chappelle for teaching me the ropes and providing tremendous developmental editing input. With your help, the story went from having potential to being published.

~

Finally, to Mauzzy, the only real-life character in the book, thank you for providing me with so much material and agreeing to be part of the book and the series. I also appreciate your eventual agreement to being a co-protagonist instead of the main character. It made the story much easier to write. And yes, I'll honor our agreement: one treat for every book sold, provided you don't eat them all in one day.

~

Roll Tide.

Chapter One

What the...

As far back as I can remember, people said I could be stubborn and hardheaded. I prefer the word passionate. I just do and see things my own way, which at times created a few—minor—issues with my parents. And teachers. And boyfriends. But it's me being me. Not stubborn or hardheaded. Just being true to myself. Passionate. In time, Mom embraced my independence, as she preferred to call it, and said I would make a difference in the world. Now, I'm wondering what kind of difference.

My name is Sara Donovan. I'm a second-semester freshman at the University of Alabama, navigating my way as best I can. But because of this blessed passionate independence, I'm facing an ever-decreasing chance of returning for sophomore year. Flunking out isn't the concern. That's not an acceptable outcome, even to me. The issue I'm having is the result of a deal I made with the devil, as in Dad, to go outside Maryland for school. Once he realized the cost of out-of-state tuition, and after he gagged, we negotiated. At the end of freshman year, I needed to have a GPA of three-point-five or higher, otherwise I was coming home for school. Oh, and not to mention another—issue—I'm dealing with this semester not entirely of my own making. So yeah, I'm thinking hard about making some changes in my life. Fast. Starting with ditching that fricking independent drumbeat of mine and taking up something else—like the glockenspiel. Otherwise, kiss 'Bama goodbye and say hello to living back home with my parents. And the exciting life of a commuter student.

****

"Thanks, Dad. It's working."

"Good. Get back to studying."

"Okay. I love you."

"Love you too. Bye."

Talk about fun. That call was precisely twenty-two seconds of small talk and sixty-eight minutes of setting up a new printer. And apparently reversing a few things I might have done to my laptop prior to calling my father. Although it's not a personal record for the longest "Nine-One-One Tech Call" to him, it's definitely top five. What good is a plug-and-play printer if it doesn't *play* when you *plug* it into your laptop? In my limited defense, I attempted fixing everything before making The Call. And now I've learned not to delete computer drivers because they're kinda important.

Normally, Dad is good-humored and quick with a joke, overall a pretty cool guy who's fun to be around. However, if he had a task at hand or a job to finish, the man became beyond driven. So, whenever I called him to solve a computer problem, things usually got complicated. Fast. Like today.

Despite the past hour, I turned this Thursday in early April into a very productive day. Two online French lessons completed—one computer crash. Three pictures hung—two smashed fingers and one teeny hammer hole. Six light bulbs replaced—screwdriver needed. One ten-minute walk—Mauzzy sprawled out and snoring in his child recliner, little dachshund legs straight up in the air. Finished studying at Harmon & Harmon bookstore—"HH" to us cool kids—and bought a new edition of *Pride and Prejudice* because it had a new cover. Purchased ink cartridges for the printer. And—the freaking printer itself.

I snagged a vanilla yogurt from the barren refrigerator and in three steps was in the living room of our cottage. The off-campus place made tiny living grandiose, although it had a very cool loft bedroom with a slanty ceiling. And no doubt, Mauzzy believed he shared his mansion with me. The little genius understood without him, I was in the dorms. With all those germs. A veritable CDC treasure trove.

Dropping on the couch, I used the revived laptop to bulldoze space on the coffee table for the yogurt. I needed to get back onto a semester-long research project about the growing antiquities black market for my Egyptology class. I was way behind and had less than three weeks to finish. It represented sixty percent of my grade and replaced the final exam. Kinda important. Worse yet, I had to present it to Professor Sawalha in a sixty-minute face-to-face session. That one-on-one session loomed large on the horizon. I can't even give an anonymous confession to a priest sitting behind the confessional screen.

A wailing siren outside caused Mauzzy to stir. He remained upside down, head hanging sideways off the front of the chair. With one eye he gave me a quick check, yawned, yawned again, and resumed snoring.

Definitely a college dog.

My phone's *Pretty Little Princess* ringtone sang as I was mid-gulp with a half-spoonful of yogurt, the other half having dripped on the laptop. I answered after a quick glimpse at the caller ID. "Hello?"

"I believe you have something of mine." The distorted voice sounded tinny, almost electronic.

"Who's this?" I checked the phone display again. It read *No Caller ID*. "Is this JT?"

JT Bridges occasionally repaired my laptop when I had issues and didn't feel like making The Call. He was a nice enough guy, but not really my type—a tad too geeky, bordering on weird. At the beginning of the semester, I bumped into him outside the library. After we exchanged insurance info, he asked me out and ended up fixing more than just my laptop. Even though the next day I told him it was just one time, he calls every now and again to ask if I have anything that needs "fixing."

"My dear, you have something of mine. And I want it back," the voice growled.

"Look, I know it's you. And—no, my V-card is mine. Like I've told you before. You're not getting the goodies."

A long pause ensued, punctuated by an exhale. "My dear, I am not—JT." The tone was firm. Controlled. "I do not want your—V-card? You have—"

"What else would you want besides messing around?"

Rising irritation crept into the voice. "I do not want to—mess around. I do not want your V-card. I do not—"

"Then why are you calling? Drop the act. I can tell

it's you and—"

"*Stop*," the voice commanded, followed by a long, heavy sigh. "So bloody cheeky."

"Whatever. I gotta go. And you need to get back to work. I'm sure the Geek Patrol is just the Patrol without your presence."

The voice lost total control and boiled over into rage. "I want my—"

I tapped off, flipped the phone on the couch, and addressed the little recliner where my miniature red dachshund continued to lounge. "Interesting, huh, Mauz?"

No response, but I didn't expect one. He was comatose. The perfect study-buddy.

After opening the resurgent laptop, I spent the next thirty minutes browsing the Internet for more information on the antiquities black market. The project was for course number CL201, but I just called it Egyptology. And I found some crazy stuff out there. Private collectors paid obscene amounts of money for antiquities and primitive art. Some assessments placed the antiquities black market as the third largest illegal global activity, only behind drug trafficking and arms smuggling. One estimate claimed it to be in the seven-billion-dollar range.

I clicked on a link about a famous statue of Queen Nefertari called the *White Queen* when my phone chirped. It was Edna Martin, assistant manager for the Dauphin Museum's gift shop. I worked there most Wednesday and Friday nights, and on weekends.

That's what my negotiating skills got me with Dad. A part-time job in Birmingham and a miniscule cottage in a housing complex that, according to JT, featured weekly on the police scanner. I called the complex Sketchville because…it was sketchy. Simple. And a little uncomfortable. Although, the guy across the parking lot owned several guns, so I had a safety net there. Granted, when I needed him to get the drug addict off my front deck last night, he was in the shower. But I just call that poor timing.

"Edna? Everything all right?"

"Absolutely not." Unless you showed up late for work, my boss was dry and unemotional, a direct opposite of her current tone. "I just got off the phone with Karen. She's furious with you."

Karen Allen was the weekday cashier at the gift shop.

I jumped off the sofa, sending a seismic tremor through the coffee table. "Furious? With me?"

"Mrs. Bagley called the shop this afternoon to say she couldn't get in before the weekend to pick up her packages. When Karen told her she only had one package, an Anubis statue, she blew up, yelling something about a missing funerary mask."

Edna's snitty mood now made sense because Mrs. Bagley, a local sixth-grade teacher, was one of our best customers.

"That's impossible. I put two boxes for her in Karen's bin, including a funerary mask."

"Are you sure, because it's not there. She needs it by Monday for a new segment she's starting. She's waiting for a call back."

"Positive. The box was like the one mine came in."

"Yours?"

"I ordered the same item a little while back. It arrived in Saturday's shipment, too."

6

I picked up my newest souvenir and surveyed it. It had a gold face with a big headdress over huge black oval eyes, thick arched black eyebrows, elephant-like ears, and a full-lipped smirk. All together I found it very colorful. It may have been gaudy, but something about the colors made it pop. I set the mask down. Even in the middle of a crowded coffee table, it stood out. And in my book, that was a good thing. When I discovered it in the shop's catalog, I had to buy it. In fact, I would have bought it even if I didn't have my well-used employee discount.

"I see. Why did you ship it to the gift shop and not your home address?"

I let out a little snort. "Where I live is not the best part of town. I don't trust packages being left on the front deck."

"Mmmm, yes," she said under her breath, before erupting in frustration. "Where could that thing have gone? They're both livid."

"You can have mine if…wait…why don't you pull one from inventory? We received ten others in the shipment. Just give her one of those."

Edna took a moment to respond to clearly an obvious solution. "I guess with all the drama and confusion, I didn't even think about that. How stupid of me. Sorry for bothering you."

"It's okay. Just glad I could help."

"I'll let you go. I have to make some calls."

"I'll see you tomorrow night." Silence. I looked at the display and collapsed on the couch. "Okay, then."

With my research mood broken, I decided to redo my toenails since the polish and remover also sat on the quite popular coffee table. I unscrewed the cap from the bottle of acetone and stretched for a bag of cotton balls on the far side of the table.

Crap.

The first thing I saved from an acetone tsunami washing across the coffee table was the laptop. After making sure the beleaguered machine did not require electronic CPR, I turned my attention back to the table to rescue additional survivors. Miraculously, my phone lay on the couch beside me, sparing it from a disastrous end unlike so many of its predecessors.

Not so miraculously, my new souvenir lay in sixteen ounces of acetone. Melting.

Melting?

I seized the stricken mask, raced to the galley kitchen, and grabbed a dishtowel partially burned from an earlier firefighting incident. After a few seconds of wiping and blotting like a crazed ER nurse, the thing became useless from sticky goo gumming it up.

"Dang it."

I flung the towel toward a sink full of crusted crockery, only it stuck to my flailing hand. Using the defaced mask, I worked to scrape the glued cloth off my hand. Until I noticed—

"What the…Mauzzy, get over here and look at this."

Chapter Two

Is it? Or isn't it?

Mauzzy jumped off his chair and met me at the couch. We both sat on an end cushion, and I placed the disfigured souvenir on the middle one. He scrutinized what was left of the face, hazel eyes studying it from multiple angles. After a few sniffs, he licked around a small hole melted in it. With a frown, he flicked the mask over with his pointy nose, clearly disgusted with the bourgeois taste of acetone and plastic. Then he—

I snapped it away. "It's not a chew toy."

He snorted, sneezed on my bare leg, and retreated to his recliner.

"That's rude."

With another snort, he pivoted and laid down, his fat butt facing me.

"Way to use your words, Mauz."

I assessed the damage. The ears were blobs of gray, the nose was gone, and in the center of the red smirk was a hole smaller than a dime and a quarter-inch deep. I activated my phone's flashlight and studied the tiny hole. The surface beneath appeared to be metallic. Maybe brass. Or...

I tapped the flashlight off and called Zoe, my best friend. She lived near me in Annapolis for five years before her family moved back to Tuscaloosa after our junior year in high school.

"Hey, Sara."

"You gotta get over here and see this."

She sighed. "I'm studying, which is what you should be doing. What'd you burn this time?"

"Melted."

"Dishwasher issues again?"

I huffed. "They shouldn't say dishwasher safe if it isn't. That's false advertising."

"How many times I gotta tell you? That's what the top rack is for. What melted?"

"A souvenir from the gift shop. You gotta—"

"You put it in the *dishwasher?*"

"Why would I do that?"

"How do I know? I'm not Sara Donovan. Why are you calling me?"

I slipped over to the front door and peered out the side window. "I don't think it's a souvenir. I think it's gold or something."

She chuckled. "That's hard to believe. Unless you're Sara Donovan."

It appeared all quiet. For once. I backed away from the door and retraced my steps toward the living room. "I'm serious. I think I have something."

"I really need to study. Finals are just around the corner."

That girl always worried about upcoming tests. Finals weren't for three weeks. That meant we had two weeks before cramming started.

"Just please come over and look at this thing?"

Zoe exhaled into the phone.

"I had a strange phone call, too. I think it's tied to this mask."

"Every call with you is—"

"Please?"

Another exhale. "Fine. I'll be there in fifteen minutes. But this shit better be good, and not another one of your effed-up theories."

"You're the best."

"See you in fifteen."

I set the phone down and glanced at the King Tut wall clock across the room. Nine-fifteen. "Mauzzy, let's go—"

My pouting roomie spun, launched himself off the chair, and shot to the front door before I could even stand.

"—outside before Zoe gets here."

I got him leashed up, and we stepped out onto the small wooden deck that served as the front porch and gateway to all that I call Sketchville. The housing complex "boasted" a decent pool that only sometimes closed because of broken bottles in the water. And after a while, police sirens and gunshots just became another form of white noise. Our robust perimeter security consisted of a rusted three-foot chain-link fence with an interwoven hedge of weeds running behind the last row of cottages. Somehow, it remained standing no matter how far the thing listed against the lone oak sapling dying behind my cottage. I suspect the weeds had a helping hand in keeping the fence halfway upright. It was the only thing separating my place from what I'm sure were crack houses on the other side.

Like I said. Sketch.

An uncomfortable stillness filled the air. No sirens. No subsonic woofers bouncing cottages off their foundations. Not even a single gunshot. My right hand instinctively tightened on the pepper spray key chain and leash, keeping my phone at the ready in the left.

A slight breeze wandered through the muted parking lot. The nearby dumpster announced its disgusting presence with a pungent stink that made my kitchen, melted plastic and all, smell lemony fresh. We meandered around the edge of the parking lot toward the complex's grass clearing, reluctantly closer to an overwhelming bouquet of rotting fish. Despite my maternal coaxing, Mauzzy stood firm and refused to pee.

I sighed and gave him my very best "Really?" look. He stared back, unblinking, smugness splashed across his needle-nosed face.

"Dude, we're not going in until you do it."

The little guy called my bluff. He faced away from me and sat.

Obviously, I needed to work on my authoritarian voice. And my fierce look. "All right, mister, but this is it for the night." I gave the leash a good tug. "Let's go."

He popped up and with nose in the air trotted along the upper sidewalk toward the walk leading to my cottage. When we got to the front steps, tires grinding asphalt and a squealing fan belt sounded behind us. While we waited on the deck, Mauzzy looked away the entire time. Whatever.

Petite little Zoe bounded up the sidewalk, green eyes shimmering and pink streaks in her black tousled hair gleamed as they caught the moonlight. We were best friends and complete opposites. I stood just over five-eleven. She might have been five feet. I had curves. She was beyond wee and wiry. I tended to be polite to a fault. She was flat out feisty.

"Okay, what's so important to pull me away from studying for our GBA380 final?"

The course name was Strategic Analysis in the Global Business Setting, and it was as difficult as it sounds. Most freshman course schedules were cake, full of various intro courses. Zoe and I were not most freshmen. We both received over twenty credits from AP tests last year, making us sophomores in terms of credits. And since we wanted to graduate in three years, to save our parents' money, this second semester was shaping up to be a cross between a Venti Double-Dirty Chai Latte and—shudder—instant coffee. On the good end was Egyptology, which I loved more than bingeing my favorite shows. Although I'm drawing the line at coffee.

On the butt end of things sat GBA380, also known as Satan's Spawn. It was the one class I needed to pass in order to get into the University's uber-prestigious business school and hit the GPA I'd "negotiated" with Dad. Kinda important.

"You gotta see this."

"I bet," an unenthused Zoe replied, following me inside.

After closing and bolting the door, I unleashed Mauzzy, who scampered for his chair. "It's over there on the couch."

She bopped over to the couch, picked up the mask, and examined it. "You sure fucked it up. What'd you do?"

I placed the pink retractable leash on a small table next to the front door. "Spilled nail polish remover on it."

She rotated it over and back in her hand several

times before shaking her head. "What am I supposed to be seeing?"

"Don't you see the melted surface?"

"No shit."

I pointed to the hole. "Look at that. What do you think that is?"

She held it close to her face and squinted. "Looks like melted plastic. No way it's gold. Smells like your dishwasher."

Mauzzy snorted.

Ignoring her accurate statement and my gloating roommate, I activated my phone's flashlight. "Use this."

She took it and lit up the surface. "Just melted plastic shit."

"It doesn't look like metal?"

She shook her head slowly. "Probably resin or something."

I took the mask back. "It's strange. Just as a test, I put a little remover on one of my statuettes, and nothing happened. But on this thing, it's like there's some kind of plastic coating that melted away."

Zoe shot her hands in the air and stuck her neck out. "Like I said, plastic shit. I'm still not seeing what's strange. You fucked up a souvenir. You spill things all the time. You burn things all the time. Now, you melt things too, without using a dishwasher. All in the life of Sara Donovan."

I examined the hole. "Doesn't it look kinda darkish yellow—metal maybe—underneath?"

She crossed her arms, dropped her head, and eyeballed me through the top of her eyes. "You honestly think this is gold?"

"I don't know. But if it is, I'm not supposed to have it. That's for sure. It would explain the strange phone call."

Her expression softened. "Yeah, what about that, girl? JT chasing after you again?"

I placed the mask on the couch, far away from the rogue bottle of acetone. "I'm not sure. It was only a couple hours ago."

"Hold on. Hold on. Is that the real world's definition of a couple, as in two? Or the Sara Donovan couple, as in three to five?"

I made a face and threw up two fingers. "He disguised his voice, but I really thought it was JT."

" 'Strange phone call' sounds like him. What'd he want? As if I even have to ask."

"That's just it. He said he didn't want the goods. That's why it feels off."

"If he didn't want the goods, that wasn't JT. Definitely a local call?"

I shrugged. "No caller ID."

"I bet he used star-sixty-seven on your ass."

"I'm afraid to ask."

"You don't know about star-sixty-seven?"

I shook my head.

"If you type asterisk sixty-seven before making a call, it'll block the caller ID info. I bet that's what the creep did."

"Never heard of it."

"What'd the asshole want?"

"He kept saying I had something of his and he wanted it back."

"Did you take something from someone?" Zoe's hands flew to the sides of her head. "Shit. Did you toss

15

some drug dealer's stash when we helped out last week at the clinic?"

My eyes widened. "Really? A dealer's stash?"

She gave me one of her patented wiseass smiles. "How the hell should I know? Remember who I'm talking to."

"Ha. Ha."

"Did he say what you had of his?"

"Uh-uh. I ended the call."

"He call back?"

"Nope."

She waved a diminutive hand. "I bet it was JT."

"I'm not so sure. I get this strange mask and phone call within days of each other. That's too coincidental."

"I can hear your dad now."

"Sara, there's no such thing as coincidence," we said together in deep voices, our forefingers wagging in unison.

Zoe headed for the door. "It's going on ten. I gotta go."

"What about my mask?"

"What about it? You've got a ruined souvenir. Throw it in the box with all the other stuff you've"— she giggled and counted off her fingers—"burned, broke, drowned, driven over, smashed, mashed, stepped on, dropped in the disposal, and now—melted." She finished with an over-the-top smile of brilliant white teeth.

I scrunched up my cheeks and made an exaggerated face. "Hilarious. I still think there's something different about it, and I'm gonna find out what."

"Don't stay up too late. We're working out

16

tomorrow morning."

"Ugh. Don't remind me."

She opened the door and leaned back in my direction. "And if I were you, I'd spend my time tonight studying for GBA380 and not traipsing across the Internet. Unless you wanna go to community college next year."

I waved a dismissive hand. "I've got three weeks. Plenty of time."

"Ooookay. See you at the gym."

"Thanks for coming over, Zo."

"Sure thing."

When the door closed, I hit the couch and jumped on the Internet. Two hours later, I found a newspaper article from six months ago in the electronic archives of *The Birmingham Bugler*. As I read it, my mouth went dry and my chest tingled. "Mauz, I knew this mask was different."

He jumped out of his chair, trotted over, and hopped up next to me.

I moved the laptop to the couch. "See for yourself."

Mauzzy put his nose close to the display, peering at it from different angles. He looked back at me, back at the screen, and sneezed.

"That's disgusting. Oh my God, stop licking the screen."

I shoved him out of the way, snatched a disinfectant wipe from a tub on the coffee table, and cleansed his germs away. Then I read the article again, just to make sure I wasn't jumping to conclusions. Apparently, according to some people, that was a bad habit of mine.

The Birmingham Bugler

U.S.-based smuggling rings suspected of looting ancient Egyptian tomb

Global investigation zeroes in on U.S. shipping ports

BIRMINGHAM—The FBI and INTERPOL are working closely with U.S. law enforcement authorities and increasing customs controls in response to a tip that a major antiquities smuggling operation may be based in the U.S. A recently discovered tomb dedicated to King Akhenaten in the Valley of the Kings, near the southern city of Luxor, has been the most recent known victim of looting. While authorities are still assessing the loss, estimates are running in the hundreds of millions of dollars.

According to an FBI spokesman: "We're collaborating with several federal departments, including ICE, to address the growing illegal import and sale of looted antiquities."

"This is yet another worrisome example of the expanding global black market for antiquities," said Dr. Mahmoud Sawalha, a noted Egyptologist and tenured professor at the University of Alabama, who recently visited the site. "Regrettably, before the team could properly catalogue and remove the items, gold bejeweled funerary masks and other treasures went missing. Indications are the tomb was dedicated to Akhenaten, the father of King Tut, and dates back to the 18th Dynasty, or from 1543 to 1292 BC, which is the most famous of ancient Egyptian dynasties," continued Dr. Sawalha.

In a statement addressing stolen antiquities ending up in reputable museums, Dr. Roger Gwynne, Director of the Ancient Egypt and Byzantine Empire Collection at Birmingham's Dauphin Museum, said, "Before acquiring any piece, the Dauphin employs a thorough due diligence process to review the piece and its provenance. On the rare occasion we find an anomaly or an item reported stolen, we immediately contact the authorities."

A source at Egypt's Ministry of Antiquities, who spoke on the condition of anonymity, said U.S. law enforcement will continue investigations in the southern states, including Alabama and other states with key ports of entry.

I read the article three more times, and became more convinced I was onto something. I couldn't wait for morning to arrive so I could tell Zoe. Well, technically it was already morning. And this might be the first time in my entire nineteen years that I looked forward to getting up early the next day.

What's happening to me?

Chapter Three

ROTC boys

It was the crack of dawn on Friday morning. Actually, not even the crack of dawn. More like the dark of night, with no cracks whatsoever. Anywhere. With slitted eyelids I negotiated the turn into the witch-black parking lot of the University's Student Recreation Center as the dashboard clock ticked over to six-twenty. I swerved around a parked pickup with a lift kit and huge tires, a standard accessory in Alabama, almost clipping the bottom of its bumper. With a scowl for good measure, I cranked the wheel and knifed into an open space.

Country music flowed from the car radio. I don't know why, but when I left Annapolis for 'Bama, occasionally I listened to country music. And when driving, even singing along at the top of my lungs.

Right before I shut off the engine, the radio crooned, *"Baby, like I tell ya each and every day, I love ya more than my hound in every way. But when it comes to my Lord, my guns and my pickup truck, I reckon, baby, best not press your luck."*

Religion, dogs, trucks, and guns all in one song. I loved the South.

There was only one good reason for going to the gym at such a terrible time of day. Although it didn't hurt that I was still basically asleep, making my body incapable of registering the pain and misery coming soon. And it was a bonus the skinny sorority skanks were sleeping off their hangovers or making the walk of shame because it meant they weren't here. But the real reason? ROTC boys. Yep—that's right—military. However, I have one caveat. I don't care how hot military boys are—I still wasn't putting on mascara.

During the fall semester, Zoe and I worked out together two or three times a week. Usually early in the morning. And I mean adult early. Like six o'clock. Ordinarily, no way I would ever subject myself to such physical abuse before the sun even rose. But on that very first day, I realized this workout rainbow had a pot of gold at the end. And it had nothing to do with getting fit, staying healthy, or any other Surgeon General stated benefit.

Nope. It was ROTC boys.

Well proportioned. In gray fitted t-shirts and swishy workout shorts. Doing jumping jacks. All in a row. With nice, tight, round butts.

After some investigation, I found out the ROTC program included predawn daily workouts. And it worked out perfect that around the time we left, all the no-neck behemoths started arriving. Except for the dark-of-morning before the crack-of-dawn part. Apparently, ROTC boys were all the motivation I needed to fall out of bed before sunrise and go transform into a sweaty, panting mess.

Zoe waited at the front entrance, her pixie-like body electric with energy.

"Hey," I said, grim-faced.

"Hey yourself, bitch," she said with a dazzling

smile. "We ready to rock?"

She was too damn perky for this time of morning. "No. No. No. So not ready. My legs are already getting tight."

"Great. Let's get into the building and get those legs even tighter."

I clumped, and she bounced, up the five stairs into the massive structure. We entered through two sets of glass doors, showed our university ID cards to the non-caring, half-asleep student, and stepped into a cavernous space with a soaring ceiling and running track balcony ringing the upper floor.

Detecting a faint hint of chlorine from the pool along with bleach, I breathed in deep through my nose and savored the scent. It smelled delicious. Like an exotic perfume. Only better. To the right stretched rows of torture equipment, lined up like plebes on a parade ground.

And speaking of delicious, there were the ROTC boys. All gleaming and toned. Working away on treadmills, weight machines, and stair-steppers. I marveled at their rounded butts, glistening arms, and tapered backs. Sweet mother, they were hot.

"Sara." Zoe's voice yanked me back from my intoxicating vision.

"What?"

"You didn't hear a word I said. Every time you step in here, you space out. You working tomorrow?"

"Yeah. Tomorrow's…Saturday," I uttered, a little distracted. Okay. A lot distracted.

"What's the matter, girl? Stay up too late? I warned you."

And just like that, my ROTC Boys High was—no

longer.

"Two-thirty."

"You're nuts."

"I prefer the technical term. Pistachio."

She wrinkled her cute little nose and threw a quick head shake.

I stepped past her. "It was worth it." Stopping in front of the hand-weights station, I took a glimpse around. Other than the ROTC boys and us, nobody else was crazy enough to be here this early. "I found an article from the *Birmingham Bugler*."

"Yeah, so."

"About a tomb looting six months ago." I worked out a small baggie bulging with disinfectant wipes from my shorts pocket, extracted a wipe, and sanitized the heck out of a weight until it shimmered. "King Tut's father."

Zoe clambered onto an elliptical next to the weight station. "And now you think this phony fucked-up mask is from that tomb."

"Yup."

"What a surprise."

I did a right arm curl. God, it was heavy. I so needed to build my arm strength for an upcoming dodgeball tournament. "The article alluded to smuggling rings operating in the southern states, including Alabama."

"Alluded?"

With a death grip on the one-pounder, I breathed in deep, blew out, and hoisted the second rep. "It said law enforcement investigations continued in the South, or something like that. What does that tell you?"

"Our tax dollars are hard at work."

"Our? You don't even pay taxes." *Three*. Pant.

"Whatever. I'm just saying that article doesn't mean shit."

"After I found the article—" Gasp. "—I went back and made the hole a little bigger."

"Uh-huh?"

"There's definitely some kind of dark yellow metal underneath."

"*You mean it's gold?*" She was flying so fast I half-expected her little body to flip right over the front of the machine.

I finished the third rep, blew out, and glared. "Shhhh. Keep your voice down."

"Sorry," she whispered back. "It's gold?"

"I don't know. It could be brass. But it could also be…" I mouthed the word *gold*.

Foouurrr. Oof.

"So it's real?" an oscillating Zoe blurted from the whirring elliptical.

I dropped my right arm with the weight, set my jaw, and slammed my left index finger to my lips. "I don't know. I haven't removed the rest of the coating. If it's real, I don't want to damage it."

Fiiiivvvvve. Blow. Pant.

"Then go to the cops," she mouthed.

I rattled my head no. "If it's gold, why send it to me? If I can't explain it to myself, how can I explain it to the cops?" I rasped. "Gotta sort this out first."

The girl wasn't even breathing hard. Ridiculous. "Yah, I'm not so sure that's a good idea. I love you dearly, but you worry me when you get these hunches. You always take them too far, and you end up in the shit. Remember the Air Marshal Incident?"

That flight home didn't go too well. You out one air marshal as a gun-packing hijacker and he gets all shades of pissy. If he had only said yes when I first asked, things wouldn't have escalated. I just wanted to thank him for his service.

"How can I forget? It was just last month."

Neither could Mauzzy. Without him, I'm sure they would have hauled me off in cuffs. Who would have believed a big powerful armed dude like that would have an affinity for dachshunds? He let me go with a very serious reprimand, and a vigorous chin scratch and kisses for my wingman.

"All I'm sayin' is, you get going on something you think you saw, and you take it too far. Only to find out it wasn't what you thought. After it's too late. Just be careful because you don't know who or what you're dealing with."

As the weight fell to my side, I grunted, "No…worries."

"Uh-huh. JT call you back?"

Halfway home to ten reps, my arm began begging me to stop. I paused to wipe matted hair out of my face. "Nope. And after finding that article, I'm thinking it ties the caller to the mask. It wasn't JT."

"I've been thinking about that, too. Why don't you get one of those phone tracking services?"

"Sounds like it costs money."

"Any call you get with the ID blocked, they can track it and find out the name, number, and sometimes the address of the caller. You just have to decline the call."

I sucked in and hefted the weight. Come on…siiiiix. "How…much?"

"Three or four bucks a month."

"Don't…know. If Dad found out…"

"Don't tell. That's why you're working, right? If it's JT, you got him cold."

I exhaled hard and let the weight down. "And if it isn't?"

"You still got him."

"I'll check it out." O…m…g. Sevvvven.

"I'll help you find—"

I didn't hear the rest of what Zoe said. My right arm fell, wisely letting gravity do the work. The ROTC boys were in full swing, and they were awe-inspiring. When they did crunches? Mmmm. Or the pull-ups? Oh God, the pull-ups. Or the—frick. *What rep was that? Eight? Nine?* No matter. I'm saying ten. I gladly switched arms. I had no shame standing there doing my little weights. It was six-forty in the freaking morning. And heaven forbid I overexert at such an ungodly hour.

Mmmm, the super-hot boys were flexing with their free weights. I must admit, the only time I felt shameful doing my little weights was when—

"Excuse me, dear," a soft female voice floated over me from behind.

I twisted my head around, left arm still pumping iron. Right on cue.

"Oh, Sara," the voice rejoiced. "I thought that was you. How are you, dear?"

"Fine, Mrs. Majelski," I said politely, motioning to the rack of hand weights. "I guess you need to get by me here." I stepped to the side to clear the way.

I first met Mrs. M at the gym at the beginning of last semester. Now I water her plants whenever she goes on vacation. Why retirees need multiple month-long vacations, I have no clue. And yet she still had time to fit in night classes, which is why she could use the rec facilities.

"Thank you, dear."

She shuffled past, her walker gliding silently toward the weight rack. The wrinkly old lady was in her eighties but so could be one hundred years old. And she was so short, maybe four-feet-eight, that her arms stuck straight out holding the walker. When she eventually got to the weight rack, she used both hands to pick up a five-pound dumbbell and placed it in a pink-flowered basket strapped to the front of the walker. Thirty seconds later, she got to a bench four feet from the weight rack, perched on its edge, and began jacking the five-pounder.

Just as I finished the tenth rep with my left arm, Mrs. Majelski piped up. "You know, I couldn't help but overhear you talking with your little friend."

I narrowed my eyes at Zoe before turning back to the iron-pumping octogenarian. "Hear what?" I asked, as innocently guilty as possible.

"Exactly," she replied, putting an index finger from her free hand beside a droopy nose while mid-rep with the fiver. "My great-nephew is a Tuscaloosa cop. If you need his help, just let me know. His name is Rhett Preater, but we just call him Billy."

I smiled appreciatively. "Um, that's okay. Everything's fine."

"Okay, dear. Just remember it." She put the five-pounder down and angled toward me. The laughing eyes and sweet face of a grandmother vanished, replaced by a piercing, hard-edged visage. She scanned the room before cupping a gnarly hand to her mouth.

"And if you need muscle, you come find me. I'm sorta the bouncer at Sunny Time's Stein Room. Those Bar Belles, especially Madeline and Ida, can be quite the rowdy group of gals. That's why I work out."

I gaped back, dumbfounded.

Her countenance got even harder. "You know, dear," she said, her icy-gray eyes drilling into mine. "For your protection."

In that instant, I totally forgot about the ROTC boys.

Chapter Four

Scotch or oil?

Fricking Universe. If navigating parking garages wasn't bad enough, finding Professor Sawalha's office in Garland Hall rivaled searching for the Lost City of Atlantis, El Dorado, and the Garden of Eden, all on the same road trip. For twenty minutes I roamed a puzzle of dim hallways and stagnant staircases. It gave me a greater appreciation how the ancient Greeks felt in King Minos' labyrinth. Except my Minotaur was the professor, waiting to devour my late butt.

I made it to the top of the narrow stairs on the fourth floor a little out of breath and a lot panicky. I was ten minutes late, my quads burned, and the mild perspiration that blossomed on the second floor was now in full bloom. My legs admonished me over wearing heeled clogs after doing fricking wall sits this morning at the end of my workout. Straining to see down a stuffy hallway that smelled like a gym locker room, something—squeaked? This had to be it, since I've been to every other fricking floor in the entire damn building, including both basements.

As I edged down the hall, floorboards creaking with each uneven step from aching legs, a shaft of light spilled into the dark corridor. Another ten agonizing steps and I reached the source. I peeked around the doorframe. For so much light pouring into the hall, only a floor lamp and a small desk light illuminated the room. A massive wooden desk against the far wall and stacks of books *everywhere* made the cramped office even smaller. On the floor. On the desk. On the visitor's chair. And despite three bookcases lining the left wall, none held any books. Instead, Egyptian statuettes, painted burial masks, stone head busts, miniature gilded sarcophagi, and colorful jewelry all competed for attention.

Hunched behind the desk in an ancient wooden chair with a slatted back and rollers sat Professor Sawalha, wearing a tweed jacket with brown leather elbow patches. The same one he wore to every Egyptology lecture. Seriously, the man needed to work on his wardrobe. The last remnants of gray hair shot out from both sides of his head in a very Einsteinesque manner, rendering his former balding head to just being—bald.

I tapped twice on the door. "Excuse me, professor?"

He swung around. The chair protested profusely with a high-pitched squeak that launched a shiver down my spine. No wonder his hair defected in all the wrong directions. Or maybe the heavy cologne he'd recently showered in caused some kind of weird chemical reaction to his totally frizzed-out follicles. Why do men always think more is better? About anything and everything. That Y-chromosome carries some pretty messed up code.

"Ah, yes. Miss Donovan. Come in, come in." He gestured to the visitor's chair piled high with books, then hauled himself up and took a step toward the overloaded chair. "Let me just throw these on the floor."

After three armfuls of books went flying, I placed my backpack on the floor and sat facing the professor, who returned to his unruly chair. Another squeak led to another shiver.

OMG. It's called multipurpose oil.

"So," he said smiling, "have you brought me my bottle of scotch?"

"Excuse me, sir?"

"Ha," he exclaimed, clapping in triumph. "Just a little icebreaker. I find it helps in these one-on-one sessions with students."

"Oh…okay."

He stuck out a downturned hand, his wide, olive-complexioned face wrinkling into a grin. "The joke, I mean. Not the scotch. There is no scotch. Although, that might have helped some of my students in these situations."

I swallowed. Great. These situations. Am I in a situation? Because I'm ten minutes late? What did he expect from me? This was just supposed to be me disclosing the topic for my semester-ending presentation. For his approval. Nothing more. Am I supposed to make an actual presentation of the research topic—for my presentation? Is that why he advised me this was a situation? Which scotch could help? That I didn't have.

"I'm sure of that," I said, trying hard to pull myself together. I motioned to the crowded bookcases. "You have quite a collection. Those aren't real, are they?"

"Goodness no. They're all just replicas," he said, gesturing around the room. "I have some pieces from digs during the seventies, but I would never keep that collection here. Too valuable for this place."

I jumped on an opening to get things back on track and rectify the apparent *situation*. "Right. The seventies. Because before 1983, people could legally take anything out of Egypt."

The professor's forefinger tore at the air. "Well done, Miss Donovan. Well done, indeed. Law 117, enacted August 6, 1983. It's also called the Antiquities Protection Law. Simply put, this law instituted stringent regulations declaring all antiquities found in Egypt after the law's enactment to be government property. It further stipulated removal from the country of any such artifacts without official government approval constituted theft, prosecutable under Egyptian law. And if somebody brings these items into the United States, that is also a prosecutable offense under Federal law." He eyed me with raised eyebrows.

Did he know about the mask? I didn't even know about the mask. Maybe I could ask him to examine it, determine if it's real. Because if it wasn't, I could pitch it and move on. But if it was real, I've—

"Miss Donovan, I didn't discuss Law 117 in your course. How do you know about it?"

I gave him a no-big-deal shrug. "I learned about it in my Master Art Thieves of the Twentieth Century class. We just finished antiquities smuggling. Now we're starting major museum thefts. I thought taking it would be a good complement to your class."

Okay, so I didn't tell him the real reason I enrolled in the course. The Registration Incident was none of his business. And it wasn't so much lying. More like polishing the apple. Or in the professor's case, delivering him a bottle of scotch.

He slid silver wire-frame glasses up over the hook on his nose and—s*queeeek*—sat back in his chair. "Excellent, Miss Donovan. Excellent. Okay, what can I do for you?"

"I'm here to run my presentation topic by you."

His head jerked back. "It's April seventh. I required your topic by mid-February. Semester-long research means just that—semester-long."

The perspiration machine cranked up as my stomach dropped to my knees. "You did?"

He nodded once.

I shifted in my chair. "Um, is it too late?"

Another nod. "It could be. If I don't approve your topic." He tapped his lips with a forefinger. "Yes, yes, it certainly could be."

I swallowed. Trepidation filled my quavering voice. "Would you like to hear it?"

Squeeeek. He propped an elbow on the chair's arm and rested his chin in his palm. "Perhaps. What do you have for me?"

I wished I had a scotch for me, that's for sure.

Plucking a spiral notebook from my backpack, I flipped it open and scanned my notes one last time. *Breathe, Sara. Just throw it out there. You have nothing to lose.* I inhaled a deep breath of cologne-saturated air through my nose. "It's kinda funny we were talking about Law 117 because my topic is antiquities smuggling in Peru, Mexico, China, and Egypt, starting when it was lawful to remove and sell antiquities from each. Before they passed laws to protect their national treasures."

I made eye contact, trying to gauge the reaction. He

made a rolling motion with his hand.

"It's a good place to start because that's what makes today's antiquities market so murky," I continued. "Since each country had a time when people legally removed and sold artifacts, legitimately acquired pieces are in private collections and museums all over the world. Criminals take advantage of this by forging provenances for illegally obtained items and date them prior to the enactment of a country's protective laws. From there, I—"

Up went a hand. "Very good. Very good, indeed. This is an excellent topic for your project. Albeit a late one. However"—he pointed a finger to the ceiling in a cautioning manner—"full disclosure, Miss Donovan. I must warn you—" A muffled ringtone from his jacket cut him off. He took out a phone and squinted at the display. "Excuse me. This won't take a minute."

I went to stand, but he motioned me to sit. Nice. I hope the cologne doesn't short circuit his memory. It's never good when your professor wants to warn you about something, especially regarding a research project representing sixty percent of your grade. After being almost two months late giving him the topic. I wriggled back into my seat.

"Hello, Valerie, how are you doing today?" he trumpeted into the phone. The chair went s*queeeek* as he tilted forward and nodded. "Good, good. Glad to hear it. Yes, yes, everything is fine." He studied the floor with narrowed eyes. The man was either in deep academic concentration, or he finally caught a whiff of his cologne. "Uh-huh. Is it possible that…pardon?" For the next minute he listened intently, with an occasional frown or head bob being his only input. "Hmmm, I see.

Yes, yes. You are correct. That is quite significant. Yes, indeed."

I noticed he loved to repeat his exclamations. Did he think we didn't hear him the first time? Perhaps a byproduct of his cologne use? I've been breathing his cologne for a few minutes now. Was I destined to repeating myself? Was I?

Squeeeek.

The professor put his back to me, his voice lowered. "Mmmm hmmm. Absolutely. I can come up Monday. How many again? Three?" He listened, the back of his head bobbing, rebellious stray hairs riding the disturbed air. "Mmmm hmmm. Right. FBI?" he mumbled. "Okay. Not a problem. We'll sort it out. See you at three. Right." He tapped the screen, and—*squeeeek*—swiveled back.

Slipping the phone into his outer pocket, he sat up and gawked at me for a moment, lost in thought. Or maybe just lost. Respect the power of The Cologne Effect. "I'm sorry, Miss Donovan. The Dauphin wants…ah, yes…wants a second opinion on some items the museum just received."

"Cool. Do you know I work in their gift shop?"

"Good for you. Wonderful institution. Tremendous collections."

"I love it, too. Sir, you were saying something. Before your phone call?"

His gaze drifted off. "Oh?"

Crap. The old pregnant pause cliché. I was having grave concerns about The Cologne Effect when his eyes lit up behind rectangular frames as he slid them back up his nose. Again. "Ah, yes," he said with way too much delight. "I was about to warn you, hmmm?"

"Um, yes," I croaked. After the last ten minutes, pretty sure I've sweated all bodily fluids into my shoes, blouse, and good luck underpants I affectionately named *Sorbet*. I hope there's still some residual luck left in those babies.

"Yes, yes," the professor said, his voice laced with glee. "Full disclosure, Miss Donovan. Full disclosure." His index finger shot into the air, stirring the air like a swashbuckling musketeer brandishing his sword before striking the deathblow. "I want to warn you—the study of antiquities smuggling is one of my specialties." He watched me over the top of his glasses that were back down at the end of his hook. Only now he had a smirk like a fricking Cheshire cat.

I'm not sure what that meant, but I could guess. This man just mumbled "FBI" over the phone with his back to me. I was so not telling him about the mask.

Chapter Five

It's go time

It was almost twelve-thirty Saturday morning by the time I got back to my front deck from Gorgas Library. For some reason, Edna gave me the evening off. Normally I work at the shop from five to nine on Fridays and close on my own. But she called this morning and said she would cover for me. Go figure.

So, with Professor Sawalha's warning from today banging around in my head, I dashed home from Garland Hall to take care of Mauzzy and then skedaddled straight to Gorgas. I was deep in the fourth-floor stacks all night, doing research for my project, with the occasional foray researching stolen antiquities that could be my mask. It kinda fit my research project, so why not? I became so engrossed in smugglers' tactics that I lost track of time. Until the lights flickered, followed by a PA announcement that it was eleven fifty-five, and all patrons had five minutes to check anything out and leave. It had been almost eight hours.

I turned the key to the cottage door's deadbolt, but nothing happened. Strange. I know I locked it. Next to Dad, I'm the most security-conscious person on the planet. Although with my earlier excitement today over having the night off and getting to work on my project, I might have forgotten to lock the deadbolt.

I jiggled the doorknob. Still locked. That must have been it. Over-excitement. Like that's ever happened before. I unlocked the door and pushed it open.

"Sweet Handsome, Mommy's home."

A black stillness engulfed the room. I clicked on the overhead light. "Mauuuuzzzzzy."

His pink blanket lay on the recliner beside the abandoned couch. I tiptoed over and lifted a corner of the blanket. Nothing. Something was wrong. He never failed to greet me. Never.

The cottage was stone quiet. I retreated across the floor and grabbed a baseball bat leaning up against the wall beside the couch. Dad's suggestion, after he got a load of the neighborhood. With my pepper spray key chain in hand, I inched toward the loft stairs.

I'm coming, Mauzzy.

As adrenaline surged through me, I sounded like Mrs. Majelski after she got off the treadmill. I'm sure my wheezing alerted the intruder, who likely had Sweet Handsome tied up and muzzled. Poor little guy probably had sweat cascading like the River Nile. To keep the element of surprise intact, I decided not to turn on the upstairs lights.

At the base of the stairs, I stopped to regain control of myself. *You're fine. You've taken self-defense classes. Pepper spray to the eyes. Bat to the knees. Grab Mauzzy and get out, screaming like hell.* I prayed Gun Guy wasn't in the shower and brought the heat. Otherwise, the only other option was to rely on my blazing Sara Speed to get away. Which barely qualified as an option.

I crept up the stairs, bat raised high in my right hand, pepper spray at the ready in my left.

Crrreeeak.

I froze.

Crap.

I forgot about the third step. I remained frozen in place, arms and legs on fire. If we got out alive, I needed to take my exercise program more seriously. One more quick prayer. *I promise, God, it'll no longer be just about the ROTC boys.*

I waited another ten seconds, straining to hear anything that would give away the intruder's location.

Still nothing.

I forged ahead, the snail's pace turning my ankles into jelly.

One more step to go.

I stopped and crouched up against the inside wall of the staircase. Just earsplitting silence. Gathering myself, I summoned whatever semblance of courage remained in my trembling body.

A second later, my brain issued the command. *Okay—it's go time.*

I lunged up toward the last stair, propelling myself into the loft.

At least that was the plan.

My leading foot caught the lip of the top stair, sending me crashing down. The pepper spray sailed across the room as the elbow of my outstretched arm slammed into the wood floor. I didn't hear the dispenser hit anything, so either the killer caught it, or it landed in the pile of clean clothes on the floor. Either way, not good. Worse yet, the raised bat fell backward, its barrel cracking me on the back of the head before bouncing and rolling down the stairs.

Disarmed and face down, I lay sprawled between

the top step and the floor of the room. Before the killer could react, I scrambled to my feet and hit the light switch.

And there he was, his intensity palpable.

I stared into his piercing eyes. The pounding of my heart could not rival the ferocity of my rising fury.

"*Mauzzy.*"

That vindictive little—bastard—was on the bed. Sitting. Glowering at me. No killer. No intruder. No perp. Just him. Waiting. In the frigging dark. For at least five hours because he can't climb the stairs at night if the lights are out.

"Damn it," I cried in exasperation. "What in the hell are you doing?"

He hardened his countenance before twisting his head away toward the far wall. After a dramatic pause, his head swung back, an even more defiant leer on his face.

"Don't you be angry at me, mister. And drop the guilt trip," I said, wagging a finger. "I'm sure you slept the whole time."

His expression didn't change. I stomped over and picked him up. "C'mon. Time to go out."

We descended the stairs, cautiously stepping around the felonious bat on the landing. Digging into his wardrobe crate full of shirts, jackets, coats, and tuxedos, I selected a pink winter coat with faux fur edging. It was a little cool for early April, and I didn't want the spiteful little bitch to freeze to death. If that happened, he would never let me forget it.

I put the coat on a seething Mauzzy, and as I gathered his leash and keys from the hall table, I caught something out of the corner of my eye. My mouth flopped open.

I swore his recliner was to the left of its usual spot, a little closer to the kitchen. There was no way he could budge that chair. It weighed at least twice what he did. Plus, in its current location, he couldn't see the TV. And if he couldn't watch *Animal World*, he got beyond pissy. That meant...

I wheeled about, charged out the front door, and raced to my car. As I ran up the sidewalk toward the parking lot, I had my hand out front, frantically mashing the unlock button on the car's key fob. The hatchback's lights flashed my urgency to the entire parking lot, which was probably not the smartest thing. I popped the hatch, unbolted the spare tire, and hoisted up its front edge so I could see underneath. The void was dark. With the other hand, I groped around until my fingers wrapped around the mask. I raised it close to my face. Yep, there's the hole. They didn't find it.

I replaced the mask in the void, bolted the tire back in place, and activated the alarm. With a quick glance over each shoulder, I hustled back into the cottage. That was a great snap decision to hide it this morning before leaving for the gym. Normally, my snap decisions are not the best. Things were on the upswing. Although now I had a smuggling ring after me.

Maybe.

Chapter Six

Highly observant—or just snooping?

After checking the hatchback, it was almost one in the morning. Bedtime called to me because I had to be at the shop by eight tomorrow morning and Mauzzy still needed to go out. He didn't think so, but I said he does. It had been over eight hours since he last went out. And I had yet to finish my end-of-the-night routine.

Before dealing with him, I opened the cabinet beneath the kitchen sink, took out my trusty pink rubber gloves and an empty gallon-sized freezer bag, and placed them on the counter. Snapping the gloves on like a surgeon preparing for the OR, I opened my purse and removed my OCD Tissue System, patent pending by Sara Donovan. The system consisted of a gallon-sized freezer bag for its heavy-duty construction. It served as the "container of containers" and held two baggies. One was a sandwich baggie stuffed with clean tissues and a full travel-sized bottle of purple hand sanitizer. The second was a quart-sized freezer baggie, again for its heavy-duty construction, to hold all the grody used tissues. Proper Sara Donovan biohazard disposal procedures called for replacement of this second baggie in its entirety at the end of each day. Or worse, earlier, if it was full before the end of the day. Ugh.

I picked up the empty gallon-sized freezer bag

from the counter, sealed the waste baggie inside it, and threw the bag into the trashcan. After peeling off the rubber gloves, I placed them back under the sink where they stayed until the next kitchen crisis or the removal and discarding of the following day's waste tissue baggie. Whichever came first.

My stomach reminded me I had eaten nothing since early afternoon, so I scarfed down my last two strawberry-banana yogurts, followed by a chaser of cold coffee from a mug sitting on the counter. I ate the yogurts so fast I rivaled Mauzzy with my speed of consumption.

And now the time arrived for the final ritual, or battle, of the evening. "Come on, Sweet Handsome. Let's go outside."

Still wearing his pink coat, Mauzzy had taken his usual spot on the recliner. He rolled over and hung his head off the front of the chair, watching me upside down. Staring, but no other movement.

"Let's go. Mommy needs to go to sleep."

Nothing. His indifference signaled he knew something I didn't. But no surprise there. He probably stood a better chance at passing GBA380 than I did.

"Not tonight, mister." I picked him up from his throne, leashed him, and tramped out the door.

To my left, a car started up. A dark-colored sedan sneaked out of the parking lot with its lights off and headed left down the street. Just another day in Sketchville.

As we moseyed down the sidewalk, I cocked an eye over my shoulder at the empty parking space where the mystery car sat just two minutes ago. Even for Sketchville, there was something about it…

Mauzzy was doing his usual refusal-to-pee routine when I noticed the cottage to the immediate right of mine had the lights on. A guy moved in the front room, but I couldn't quite tell what he was doing. He must have moved in earlier in the day.

I sidestepped to get a better vantage point. Tall and dorky. Just my type. He had on a gray t-shirt and well-worn jeans with—a fine butt. Oh yeah, definitely my type. I made a mental note to introduce myself tomorrow after work. Pretty young. He just swigged from a bottle of water, so no way a college student. No beer or shots visible. Not much furniture in the room. A clunky TV. Not a flatscreen. Definitely not a college student. One floor lamp. A love seat and a—I took a few steps and craned my neck to get a better angle—yes, one end table with the varnish peeling off. What appeared to be—uh-huh—a footlocker coffee table with the lock busted off. And a small eating table with two wooden chairs.

He probably should put up drapes.

A hacking cough rose from below. Mauzzy stared up at me with a heavy dose of condemnation.

"What?"

He rolled his head away, then back up at me. We've *so* been down this road before. My actions disgusted him. No doubt he disapproved of my snooping. Which, for the record, I wasn't doing. That was just his limited definition of my superpower of observation.

"I don't snoop," I whispered emphatically. "I'm just curious. And highly observant."

He took two steps, lifted his leg, gave me an unconvinced mug, and put it down.

I hissed. "Seriously?"

The snooty expression on his face said it all. *Until you stop snooping, we're not going anywhere. This behavior will get you in serious trouble one day. And I shall not be a part of it. I have a reputation to uphold.*

He could be so high and mighty sometimes. Standing there in his pink fur coat. Please. Like he didn't snoop.

"Dude, let it go."

Mauzzy gave me a loooooong stare of reproach.

"C'mon, Mau—"

Apparently, my scolding had ended as he finally addressed the matter at hand. And point taken. Maybe.

Upon conclusion of the matter at hand, I slunk back for one last spectacular peep. I mean, after all, the guy was hot.

What the...

Risking discovery, I stuck my head closer, adrenaline surging. It wasn't there five minutes ago, but now a black handgun lay on the footlocker.

This was Alabama, and I lived in the middle of Sketchville, so guns were pretty much standard-issue. But something didn't feel right. I eased away from the window, and we headed back toward the cottage. We hadn't taken five steps when my stomach lurched so much, I almost heaved yogurt and coffee on an unsuspecting Mauzzy. Could my new neighbor be after the mask? Or was it just coincidence last Saturday I got this mask, and now I had a new neighbor? With a gun? I wasn't waiting to find out.

"Let's get inside. Quick."

I hustled the startled, and quite fortunate, little guy toward the cottage before stopping so abruptly the trailing Mauzzy accordioned up into my legs. Was the snobbish Mr. Bloody Cheeky who called yesterday and his henchpeople watching me? Since they didn't find their treasure in my cottage, was their plan to kidnap and torture me to find out where I hid it?

Without a word I bent down, scooped up a bewildered Mauzzy, and raced down the hill to the cottage. I fumbled with him and the keys, throwing looks over my shoulder, before finally getting the door unlocked. Shoving it open with my shoulder, I jumped inside and kicked it shut. After throwing the deadbolt, I put Handsome down, unleashed him, and immediately implemented the Sara Donovan Emergency Security Protocol, which consisted of a five-layer security system.

Mauzzy implemented his own emergency protocol. He tore upstairs. Pink furry coat and all.

I rushed to the kitchen for the pointy chef knife that stayed in the top drawer specifically for this purpose. Wielding the knife like a manic hibachi chef, I zipped from window to window securing all locks. Check. From behind the bathroom door, I retrieved the security bar designed to prevent a door from being kicked in. Fitting the open end under the front door's knob, I jammed the other end's rubber foot into the floor. Double check. First layer of security—in place.

With the cottage perimeter locked down, I deployed the second layer: the Sara Donovan Intrusion Deterrence System—patent application pending if I survived this mess. With a great deal of apprehension, I put the knife down, stretched behind the couch, and hauled out Mauzzy's useless furniture-proofing mats with spiky things. I bought them when I moved in to keep him off the furniture when I was gone. The fact they stayed behind the couch and not on it signified the Little Professor easily defeated their purpose. But they fit beautifully into my emergency security protocol. Unfolding the mats, I positioned them under each window, including the ones in the loft, because one could never be too vigilant. Ninjas were real.

After placing the last mat, I pounded down the stairs, darted to the cabinets under the TV, and dragged out a stash of small plastic air cushions that came as packing material in Dauphin vendor shipments. On top of each mat, I strategically placed several air cushions. The genius behind this two-level system is if the intruders are ninjas or ninja-lites, they will be barefoot or wearing thin booties. When they step or jump through the window and onto the mat, their feet will slip off the bulbous air cushions and become impaled on the spiky things. But if the intruder is wearing shoes, which is most probable, he will step onto the air packs and pop them, alerting me to the intrusion. Second layer of security—in place.

The third layer consisted of selective weaponry staged where a breach might occur. I hurried to the kitchen and swept an almost-empty can of roach spray off the counter. Reversing course, I sprang toward the front door, snagging a lighter off the coffee table as I blew past. After positioning the redneck flamethrower on the small table at the front door, I snatched the pepper spray from my purse and thundered upstairs, placing it on the nightstand. If they snuck through the loft window when I was upstairs, in which case it would be a ninja, I had the pepper spray within my reach. Along with the aforementioned chef knife, which stayed with me during lockdown. My deployment of the third layer was complete.

The fourth layer was redundant, but I preferred to include it in the security protocol. It entailed keeping my trusty phone in hand at all times, including when sleeping. Yeah, that made for some uncomfortable butt dials.

Which brought me to the fifth layer. While upstairs deploying the third layer, the fifth and ultimate layer of security was nowhere to be seen. I suspected the Fifth Layer went into hiding. Under the bed. Head down. Paws over eyes. Butt up.

A muffled whine emanated from beneath the bed.

I placed the knife on the nightstand and sighed.

Chapter Seven

A clue

The next morning, Dr. Roger Gwynne, who oversaw the gift shop in addition to his role as Director of the Ancient Egypt and Byzantine collections, stood inside the front door with hands clasped behind him when I arrived. Roger was a tall skinny man who reminded me of a goateed Ichabod Crane with impeccably trimmed, short black hair, parted to the side. Only uglier, if that's possible, and way better dressed. Today he sported a charcoal-gray pinstripe suit with a starched white shirt and dark-red tie. On a fricking Saturday. During the week, he was even spiffier.

"Good morning, Miss Donovan." He glanced at his watch, then returned his hands behind his back. "You appear to be late, hmmm?"

"I'm sorry, sir. I think I hit every light on the way in."

"Mmmm, yes. I'm sure you did. Ms. Martin had something come up so I will be your supervisor today."

"Is everything okay?"

"Most certainly." Roger unclasped his hands, tugged at each sleeve of his jacket, and moved toward the front door. "However, with that said, I have paperwork waiting for me upstairs. Do call if you need assistance, hmmm?"

"Yes, sir. But I think I can handle it."

He tugged the door open and shot through it, calling over his shoulder, "Very well then."

With the shop empty, I seized on an opportunity. I dumped my stuff in the back room, fished out a small bottle of nail polish remover from my purse, and whisked out to scout the main lobby through the glass walls of the shop. Just a couple people at the elevators. I had a few minutes, which was all I needed.

I wandered over to the display with the same masks as mine, straightening boxes and other merchandise to throw off suspicion if someone entered the shop. When I got to the display, I picked up a box and zipped over to the checkout counter. My hands shook as I unscrewed the bottle and painted the smirking face with the liquid, my eyes flitting up and down as I kept a watchful eye on the front door.

Thirty seconds and a half-bottle later, I examined the unlucky souvenir. Nothing melted. Instead, the garish colors vanished. Just a lump of gray material with a nose and ears sat on the counter. No holes. No dark yellow color beneath. Mulling over the ruined mask, I realized I made a thirty-dollar mistake. Why in the heck did I apply acetone to the face? I inspected the back. Paint was missing from a spot smaller than a dime, exposing the same gray subsurface.

My ruinous experiment confirmed the mask I hid in the hatchback was not like the ones in inventory, but what could be under its surface? If I used the acetone to dissolve the remaining coating, I risked ruining a possible artifact.

I ran through the limited options. Go to the cops?

The grim-faced air marshal popped in my head. Uh-uh. I needed to be one hundred percent sure. The professor? After that meeting yesterday, no fricking way. Call Dad? Double no fricking way. Mom? Maybe. After reconsidering the situation, I knew the answer. I needed more evidence before taking it to anyone.

I stashed the faceless test subject and remover under the counter and took in the shop. Desolation continued to reign supreme, just like any room following one of Mauzzy's farts. It was as good a time as any to wipe down the counters, since this year's flu season has been the longest in a decade. And working in a retail store, especially during flu season, was a constant biological hazard. This peril became even more dangerous in a museum gift shop where runny-nosed kids came in and sneezed and hacked all over the place without covering their mouths. And they had to touch everything. Every single fricking thing they could get their little, germy, snot-encrusted hands on. To combat this germicidal onslaught, I kept under the first register several tubs of disinfectant wipes marked as *Mine—Back Off*. I also, as best I could, identified and took sick people or those with spewing children to the far end of the counter and used the last register. I referred to it as my retail quarantine protocol. And, using at least two wipes per targeted item, I sanitized the crap out of all phones, keyboards, screens, counters, staplers, cash drawers, handles and knobs of any kind, and writing implements.

As a standard personal line of defense, I carried an array of hand sanitizer sprays and gels to offset the continual parade of sniffles, coughs, sneezes, and blowing of snot. And they got such a workout during flu season, I doubled the number of containers with me as they didn't last long. And running out of sanitizer was not an option. I used the sprays for surfaces when I wasn't in immediate reach of disinfectant wipes. And I kept travel-sized sparkly purple containers of gel both in my purse and attached to my backpack for quick access, because seconds counted.

After completing my biosafety Level Four containment precautions, I hurried into the back room, stowed the nail polish remover in my purse, placed the ruined souvenir in my storage bin, and nuked some chicken soup. Minutes later, I finished lunch. Actually, I didn't so much finish lunch. It more like ended when I dumped it on my phone. Direct hit. And so far, my precious lifeline was still working. Good thing I let the condescending bastard at the phone store shame me into finally buying a premium phone case. Now they can add soup-proof to its advertising claims.

I caught sight of Edna's desk, piled with folders. And it gave me an idea. She did all the purchasing. Somewhere she had the vendor file for the souvenir funerary masks.

I strode over to her desk and the filing cabinets behind it, loaded myself up with as many folders as I could carry, and lugged them back out front to the counter. Picking through the pile, I quickly zeroed in on an overstuffed file for a company in Cairo called All Things Egyptian, Ltd. It was by far the thickest one. I spread it out on the counter. The majority of the documents included orders, receiving reports, and packing lists for all kinds of items we carried in the shop. As I sorted through the paperwork, I noticed Mrs. Bagley ordered a good number of items. She may be our best customer, but I didn't realize how much she bought through the shop.

Our cash registers were computers tied into the mainframe, so I accessed her account. At the end of a long list of order transactions was—only the Anubis statue? No funerary mask? But I remember putting one addressed to her in Karen's bin.

Switching back to the vendor file, I pored over the paperwork for last Saturday's shipment. The packing list included a funerary mask for Mrs. Bagley, but I couldn't find a corresponding entry in the shop's purchase order or in her account transactions. Like a master spy on a covert mission, I took a picture of each page from the last four shipments, including Saturday's, and printed Bagley's order history for the past three months. Now I had something to go on, including an address and phone number for All Things Egyptian. It was past eight in the evening, Cairo time. I would have to call the company in the morning.

"Where is everybody?"

My head shot up as my phone clattered on the floor. "Dr. Gwynne." I scooped up the papers I was working from, shoved them in the folder, and closed it. "It's slow for a Saturday."

He angled his head to see what I had my hand over. "Yes…" His eyes darted to the mass of files strewn across the counter. "It appears the number of patrons is on the sparse side."

I threw the All Things Egyptian folder under the counter. "Maybe because it's such a nice day outside. That usually keeps people away."

His bushy eyebrows arched over slitted eyes. "What might you be working on, Miss Donovan?"

With a little flip of my hand, I said, "Just some boring clerical stuff. I figured with it being so dead here, I would help getting ready for inventory next month. You know, get the vendor paperwork all properly sorted."

He considered me for a few seconds. "Mmmm hmmm, I see. Yes." He checked his watch. "I really must be off. I have a late lunch with a dealer on the far side of town. I popped down to see if you're able to close by yourself if I gave you the keys."

"Yes, sir. I've closed before. It's no biggie."

"You have keys?"

"Yes, sir."

"Hmmm, I wasn't aware."

"Edna gave them to me when I started working Wednesday and Friday nights." I winced. "I need the money."

"Mmmm, of course you do." His brow furrowed. "Tell me, how long have you been working here? In the gift shop."

"Started in August. I was lucky to find this job so fast."

"Yes. I'm sure you were."

"And Edna is terrific."

He assessed the haphazard pile of files and shrugged. "I suppose. Well then, I'll be on my cell if you encounter any difficulties today." He patted the counter two quick times with his hand, spun about, and headed for the door.

Despite Roger being Roger, I recognized another opportunity. Something at the museum smelled way worse than the grody dumpster in Sketchville. I had to widen the investigation. "Dr. Gwynne?"

With one hand on the door, he corkscrewed around in my direction. "Yes, Miss Donovan?"

"Would you have some time next week to meet with me?"

Roger dropped his hand off the door handle and faced me fully. His eyes widened. "I'm sorry, and the subject is…"

"I'm working on a research project for my Egyptology class. I read an article about a tomb linked to King Akhenaten being looted. The *Birmingham Bugler* quoted you about the Dauphin's due diligence process for acquisitions. I'd like to discuss that process with you, if that's okay."

He studied me.

"I'm analyzing the antiquities black market," I added quickly.

His return smile was as dull as the man himself. "Mmmm hmmm. Interesting." He slipped a phone out from his inner jacket pocket and tapped it. Another tap. Two swipes with his finger. "Two o'clock Monday."

"Excellent. Thank you, sir."

"Mmmm, yes. See you then." And with that he disappeared into the main lobby, his heels clicking smartly on the marble floor as the door glided closed.

I had a solid lead, so I gathered everything up off the counter and hauled the folders back to Edna's desk and filing cabinets. After returning to the front register, I jumped back on the computer and delved into Bagley's account. There was something susp—

"Excuse me?" a voice croaked.

Chapter Eight

Mayday!

A tired lady of about forty in a colorful lightweight jacket stood in front of me with an ashen face, red nose, and blonde hair pulled back in a thick ponytail.

"Yes, can I help you?" I asked in a pleasant tone tinged with caution while scrutinizing her for telltale signs of influenza.

She was short and squat. Not fat, but definitely broad with a lantern-jawed face. And she wore no makeup, which was a shame because her pale blue eyes and blonde eyelashes begged for attention.

"I hope so. Karen left a message Monday that my order arrived. I called her back Thursday to say I tried but just couldn't make it here before the weekend to pick it up. I was a bit under the weather. The—"

Mayday. Mayday.

"—flu really hit the classrooms hard. And so late in the year. It must be a nasty strain because it even got me." She squinted at me with a hard smile chiseled into her pallid face. "And I just never get sick."

Her last words exploded like a biological WMD. I stole a glimpse at the quarantine register at the far end of the counter. It was miles away. I needed to wipe everything down. I just finished with Level Four decontamination procedures and now had to do it all over again. Once I got rid of Patient Zero.

"Um, Mrs. Bagley?"

"Yes," she said, extending her hand. "I'm sorry. Where are my manners? Mary Bagley. I don't believe we've met."

The back of my neck prickled as I sized up her germ-infested hand. May-fricking-day. "That's correct. We have not," I replied in a measured tone, an internal debate raging over the next course of action. It quickly became apparent I couldn't offend one of the store's best customers. And a lady with some mighty suspicious transactions. Bit by bit, I extended my arm and shook her hand. Oh, my God. It was so—moist. "I'm Sara Donovan." I let go of her hand. "Pleased to meet you, ma'am."

I was such a liar. If I could pick one thing I didn't want to do today, or any day, it would be shaking hands with a moist petri dish. Who just got released from the ICU. After having the plague. I would rather fish my phone out of the toilet again, this time with ungloved hands, than stand here getting up close and personal with Mary and The Microbes.

I wanted to dash to the back room, grab both hand sanitizers out of my purse, and empty them into my hands. But I couldn't do it. That would be rude.

I struggled to hold it together, but my tumbling stomach mirrored an Olympic gold medal gymnastics routine. My embattled brain issued a frenzied call to battle stations, but nobody was listening. I no longer had a right hand because it was having an out-of-body experience all on its own. And my feet already bugged out, dragging leaden legs to the safety of the back room, leaving the rest of my body to fend for itself.

"Very pleased to meet you, too, Sara. It seems I only ever see Karen and Edna here."

"I work most Wednesday and Friday evenings, and the weekends." Fleeing legs kicked the door closed, leaving my torso stuck at the counter as a disembodied right hand floated behind Typhoid Mary. "I believe you come on Tuesdays to pick up your orders."

Little bugs snaked their way up my arm, invading my sans-sanitizer defenseless body through unguarded pores. Treasonous legs removed any option for a strategic retreat. My Fight or Flight Command Center implemented emergency defense mechanisms by filling up the moats in a last-ditch effort to flush the enemy and save the castle. But I was not optimistic.

"That's right. My planning period is at the end on Tuesdays so I can sneak out early and beat that awful traffic on Sixty-Five." She finished with a cute little mischievous smile that belied the infected squat bruiser breathing all over me.

"Your packages. Let me go check. I'll be right back." The sooner she left, the quicker I could implement Level Five decontamination protocol. In the last minute, we blew way past Level Four.

She let out a little giggle. "That would be terrible, wouldn't it? If I left without getting my package? It was the only reason for coming here."

Sure. She could laugh. She had the antibodies.

I race-walked to the back and headed straight to my bin. First things first. I fished a bottle of sanitizer from my purse and squeezed multiple streams of the lifesaving liquid into shaking hands and all over my arms. In seconds, the apprehensive right hand reunited with my body. After a subsequent thorough wipe-down of the purse and the hand sanitizer bottle itself, because one can never be too cautious when dealing with biohazards, I was ready to address her request.

Karen's storage bin contained several packages wrapped in brown paper, including the one containing Mrs. Bagley's statue, right where I placed it last week. But not a second package with her name. I guess Karen didn't get around to wrapping a replacement mask, which was odd considering she told Edna that Mrs. Bagley needed it by Monday. Grudgingly, I trudged to the front counter. "Here's your statue."

She took the package and placed it in a blue cloth shopping bag slung over her arm. "Thanks so much. When I placed the order, I worried it wouldn't get here in time. We study the Middle Kingdom next week, so I just had to beat that flu. Chicken soup. That's the secret."

I did my best to smile. Chicken soup of all varieties make claim to mysterious flu-killing properties, provided you ingested the stuff and not bathed your phone with it. Somehow, I suspect chicken soup also wielded phone-killing properties. After today's abbreviated lunch, I guess I'll find out soon, if I lived long enough.

Her swollen eyes lit up. "I made up a big batch and ate it by the quart because I just had to get down here this weekend. For the children. I know it's only a cheap replica, but the children will be so excited on Monday. Have a great weekend."

"Thanks. You too."

She turned and chugged toward the door.

I rushed out from behind the counter. "Ma'am?"

The teacher stopped and turned around. "Yes?"

I legged it over to the display, snagged a box as I passed, and approached her with it in my outstretched hand. "This is for you."

She took the box and dropped it in her bag. "Oh, yes. My gift. I totally forgot. That's sweet of Karen."

"Gift?"

"For being so ill this week. She called yesterday to tell me it was compliments of the shop."

"Um, I know nothing about that." I gestured to her bag. "That's for the funerary mask you ordered. I told Edna she could give you one from—"

Her jaw jutted, and straw-colored eyebrows drew together. "Excuse me? This isn't my gift?"

"No, ma'am. It's the mask you said was missing from your order. On Thursday."

"What"—Mrs. Bagley's face scrunched up like she had a brain freeze from eating a popsicle too fast—"mask?"

I pointed back to the display. "You know. Like that one."

Her eyes narrowed, emitting an intense, almost menacing, attitude. She could be an army drill sergeant staring down some unfortunate cadet on the parade ground. "No. I do not know. I believe you are mistaken, Miss Donovan," her guarded tone infused with a hard edge. She raised the shopping bag for me to see. "I'm sure this is my gift. Otherwise, I'm not paying for something I didn't order."

"Oh. I guess you have no idea what I'm talking about."

She shook her head in a very slow and deliberate fashion. "None. None whatsoever."

"Sorry. I must be misremembering. I'm coming off

a crazy Friday night of crafting. Hot glue gun and beads. Woot woot," I said, trying to throw a little humor into a surprisingly tense situation.

Mrs. Bagley scrutinized me, a thin smile on her face. "Enjoy your day, Miss Donovan." With a toss of her ponytail, she did an about-face and lumbered out of the shop, her squat legs and square frame marching through the door in a very determined fashion.

I exhaled and clutched the tub of disinfectant wipes. As I observed her in the lobby heading for the main entrance, deep within, my slumbering intuition stirred. Soon it was wide awake and screeching at me like a banshee. I hated when that skank got like that. Bad things usually ended up happening. To me.

Chapter Nine

Child prodigy. Or something?

After Mrs. Bagley left, customers flooded the shop. It was two hours of chaos that left me exhausted and removed any chance to continue sorting through her account. I was driving home and just wanted to binge shows on the couch. I needed to study, but all afternoon I dreamed of having a lovely evening with Mauzzy, coffee, and Colt Chance, a sweeeeet blue-eyed blond-haired set of abs and butt who starred in my favorite TV series, *The Mysteries of Chance*. It featured a former investigative journalist turned consultant who helped the feds unravel money laundering operations, art counterfeiting rings, and high-end cons. I would try to identify the perps and their schemes before Colt did, but I always got it wrong. Still, it was exciting and fun to watch. And so was the show. My favorite—

I yanked the hatchback's steering wheel hard to the left. "Whoa."

Crunch.

Frick. I just clipped a car backing out of a parking space in the lot outside my cottage. I scrambled out of my seat and raced up to the exiting driver. "I'm so—"

He smiled and swatted at the air with his hand. "Hey, it's okay. Let's see what the damage looks like."

We circled around the merged vehicles, stopping

where the right corner of my bumper rested up against the rear side panel of his car. He bent over and focused on a small dent among several preexisting ones.

I, on the other hand, remained upright and focused on his butt. In well-worn jeans. The same glorious butt I marveled at last night at my new neighbor's cottage. Because I just hit—my new neighbor.

He straightened and faced me. "It's all good. You didn't break the taillight. That was my only concern. I just—"

At least I think that's what he said. If this guy wanted the mask, he could have it. And me. Because this guy was fireman hot. Just younger than what I expected. For the first time, I drank him in not looking through a window, and yum. He stood about six feet two inches tall with broad shoulders and a wiry, almost-but-not-quite athletic frame. As he talked, he whipped his above-the-shoulder black hair out of breathtaking beacons of blue brilliance. Sorta in a hot-surfer-boy-with-brains kind of way.

He stuck out a hand. "Connor Reed. You okay?"

"Oh, um, yeah." Without hesitation, I shook his hand. No way a guy this gorgeous could have germs. "Sara Donovan."

"Nice to meet you, Sara." He chuckled and nodded at our still-touching cars. "This neighborhood has quite the welcome wagon."

My cheeks burned hot. "I'm so sorry."

He flashed a warm smile of perfect white teeth. "Don't worry about it. As you can see, this isn't the first for me."

"Same here."

He stuffed his hands in his front pockets and took

stock of the hatchback. "Yeah, I can see that."

And there we stood. Staring at each other. Connor rocking on his heels. Me concentrating on breathing.

He broke the silence. "I saw you leaving this morning. I guess we're neighbors."

"Oh? I didn't know that," I lied.

"Moved in Friday. I just landed a teaching gig."

"What? You're a teacher?"

"Why the surprise?"

I twisted my face up. "You're kinda young."

Another captivating smile of radiating warmth. "How old do you think I am?"

"I don't know. Nineteen. Maybe twenty. Way too young to be a teacher. That's for sure."

"You're close. I'm twenty-one."

"Ah, I get it. You graduated last May and are teaching elementary school or something."

He wagged a finger. "Now there you're not so close. I'm here as a teaching assistant finishing up my doctorate."

"You're a TA? In what?"

"Egyptology."

I stood there, slack-jawed. "That's my favorite subject. What are you, some kind of genius or child prodigy or something?"

Connor shrugged. "Or something, I guess. Finished high school at fifteen. College at seventeen. Masters at nineteen."

"Wow. I'm nineteen and just a freshman. You *are* a genius."

He reddened. "I just wanna get my doctorate wrapped up so I can start giving back."

"Ha. And I'm just hoping to finish the year with a

three-five GPA."

He nodded. "That'll work. Should get you on the Dean's List."

"Operative word there is *hoping*."

He waved an unconcerned hand. "You seem like a smart person. I'm sure you'll be fine."

"Tell that to my dad."

"Just study and everything will fall into place. If you ever need a helping hand, let me know." With an easy smile, he hooked a thumb toward his cottage. "I'll be right next door."

Oh, I could so use a helping hand from you. Shirtless. In those jeans. We would—

"Sara? Hello, Sara?"

"Um, yes?"

"I have to leave. Can you move your car, please?"

"Right. Ha-ha. I guess I should do that."

"Thanks." He extended a hand and smiled at me with riveting blue orbs of hotness. "It was a real pleasure meeting you, Sara Donovan."

I took his hand and held it, masculine yet sensitive. Caring. Stirring. "Me too," I breathed.

He retrieved his hand and got into his car. I got into mine, backed up, *carefully* maneuvered around his, and parked.

Connor lowered his window, and with a wave and a smile, said, "See you around." Then he drove off.

Chapter Ten

Roll Tide

It was ten-thirty Sunday morning. Before I delivered the shop's weekly reports to the executive offices for Monday's management meeting, I called All Things Egyptian.

"Marhaba," a deep male voice said.

"Hello, this is Sara Donovan from the Dauphin Museum Gift Shop. I'm calling from Birmingham, Alabama in the United States."

"Na'am," the voice growled.

"I have a few questions about a recent order from our shop. To whom am I speaking?"

After a few seconds of dead air, he said, "Mansour."

"Hello, Mr. Mansour. We recently received a shipment containing a dozen painted funerary masks. Your packing list included one for Mary Bagley, but we never ordered one for her. Can you check your records to see if someone made a mistake?"

Static was the only response before the voice replied, "Mafi...English."

The line clicked dead.

I debated calling back but realized I would get nowhere with the man. He lied about not understanding English since he answered my first question. That told me everything.

After delivering the reports, I spent the remaining time before the shop opened unpacking a shipment from a supplier in Mexico City. No sooner had I unlocked the front door and began wiping down the counters when in cruised Hot Neighbor Bad Boy. Also known as Hot Teacher Guy. Also known as Connor Reed. Yummmmy.

Why was he here? Did he follow me? I hadn't forgotten he was possibly an armed smuggler waiting to get his mask back. Or perhaps, after our connection yesterday, he came here to see me?

"Hey," I. said happily, making eye contact with those cool blue pools of hotness.

"Wow. Hey, Sara. What are you doing here?" he asked with absolute puzzlement in his syrupy-smooth voice.

Or not.

"I, um…"

A nervous laugh escaped Connor. "I guess that's a stupid question, isn't it? You work here."

My cheeks were so hot I must have resembled an over-rouged cabaret dancer in a seedy burlesque club. With an awkward smile, I attempted to quell quivering insides and regain some self-control. "Wednesday and Friday evenings, and weekends."

"Hey, good for you." He took in the store. "I've never been here before. There's some nice stuff here."

"You mean to the gift shop, right? Because I'm sure you've been to the museum, with you being an Egyptologist and all."

For a brief moment, he stiffened. "First time for both."

"Oh?"

"I'm from the Washington, D.C. area. It's all new to me down here."

"Cool. I'm from Annapolis."

"Really? Nice area." He shifted his weight and double-tapped the counter with a finger, leaving a smudge. "I finished my master's at George Washington and couldn't find a teaching position while I pursued my doctorate. Nobody wanted a TA who looked younger than the students. Then out of the blue, Professor Sawalha called about a sudden vacancy, and here I am."

I plucked a disinfectant wipe from the tub under the counter and a tissue from a box next to the register. "You know I have a class with him?"

"Awesome. He's one of the best."

I attacked the counter smudge. "Kinda late to be starting now though, isn't it?"

"I know it's only for the last couple weeks, but he said I could have the position going forward into next year. I really got lucky."

"Makes sense. I mean, about you staying on into next year. Not about getting lucky."

Unless you wanted to get lucky, you very bad boy.

I continued with my verbal disgorgement. "I mean, I'm sure you're quite qualified. I don't think you got lucky. About getting the position. Although it does sound pretty amazing this late in the year." I wanted to stop talking, but I couldn't. Any regained self-control was no longer.

Connor stared at me—stupefied.

"And…uh…no southern accent. Um…you have no accent." *Smooth, Sara. Real smooth. Time to roll out the old standby line. Desperate times*...I arched my eyebrows and gave him a coy smile. "Roll Tide?"

"Um, Roll Tide. Gotta get used to saying that around here, huh?"

"Yup. It's kinda like a southern aloha, only much more. It can mean hi, bye, yes, no, thanks, even sorry and condolences for your loss."

His eyes reached deep into my soul. "Roll Tide."

I locked in on his sparkling blues. "Roll Tide." We were connecting. It was electric. We were talking without speaking a word, like we—

"Can you help me?"

I so could help you. Starting with—

"Hello? Sara? Can...you...help...me?"

A hand waved in front of me. Whoops, he *was* speaking to me. "Okay. I mean, maybe. What do you need?"

He dug in his pocket and took out a slip of paper. "Someone from the gift shop called the professor on Friday. A Karen Allen? She said there's been a package waiting for him. He went out of town earlier in the week and after returning had to get caught up on some things this weekend. He asked if I could pick it up."

"Hang on a sec. Let me see if I can find it in the back."

I sashayed to the back room, working it for all it was worth, and hoping all that damn stair-stepper work was paying dividends. I lifted a heavy brown package from Karen's bin with the professor's name typed on a label and nothing else. Strange. We normally didn't get big items like that, and I didn't remember unpacking it. Hugging the package to my chest with both arms, I scuffed out to the front, carefully setting it on the counter. "Here you go, but good luck carrying it out. I hope you have a close parking spot."

"Why's that?" Connor picked up the package and fumbled with it as the weight caught him off guard. "Now I get it." He grunted as he shifted the unwieldy package in his arms. "I guess no need for push-ups today. Thanks, Sara."

I gave him my very best you're-so-welcome-your-hotness smile. "No problem," I said with a flick of the hand. "Glad I could help. See you around."

Mmmm—push-ups. I wonder how he would fill out ROTC gear?

He tipped his head, and his butt headed out of the shop. I assume the rest of him made it out, too.

Mansour's voice reverberated in my head, cutting my reverie short and reminding me I had investigative work to do. I logged into the system, pulled up the All Things Egyptian account, and compared the shop's orders over the past three months against the packing list photos I took yesterday. On February eleventh, we received six King Tut busts, including one for Bagley. But in the system, I could only find five on the corresponding purchase order Edna sent on January sixteenth. And all five went into the shop's inventory. I scribbled the info on a notepad. On February twenty-fifth I found another set of six busts being received, with one for Bagley, and again the shop only ordered five. I carried on, my excitement growing with each find. The work was painstaking, bouncing back and forth between my phone's pics and the computer, but a pattern soon developed. When I finished, my notepad showed the shop received nine items for Mrs. Bagley that nobody ordered. I was certain she never ordered them either, but I pulled up her account anyway, just to be sure.

I combed through the account for each of the excess items. Despite an extensive order history, not one over the last ninety days matched the nine I found as being received for her. That wasn't a quirky series of mistakes. Something was going on and it included Mansour, but I needed proof.

Chapter Eleven

Sweet mercy

"Okay, Starshine, rise and shine," an enthusiastic melodramatic gay voice sang out.

It was my multiple-personality alarm clock. For alarms, it used randomly selected dialogues from ten different personas, including a theatrical gay guy, a mafia dude, and a very pissed off drill sergeant. It once ranked as the backup alarm across the room, but I gave it a recent promotion to the bedside tray table. Its predecessor broke when it hit the living room floor after I launched it out of the loft one afternoon. That was a tough Friday.

Mauzzy, taking exception to the early morning ruckus, rolled over and stuck his abundant butt in my face, encouraging me to get out of his bed so he could get back to sleep. After all, he spent half the night scratching and licking. Meaning, I spent half the night listening to his scratching and licking.

As I lay there exhausted, I realized bingeing shows until one in the morning was not one of my better ideas. Unfortunately, this Monday morning I had to meet Zoe at the gym at six-thirty. Even the prospect of ROTC boys couldn't get me to budge.

Just bite the bullet, Sara. Think of what's waiting for you. If ravenous ROTC rapaciousness can't motivate you, then—

That did it. Fifteen minutes later, I arrived at the Student Recreation Center parking lot. When I rolled out of the car, Zoe was there to meet me, her wee little body hopping around me like an over-hyped boxer in the middle of that thing with the ropes. I refuse to call it a boxing ring because—it isn't. It's square. Men.

"Hey, bitch," she said, her eyes shining as bright as her hair's flaming red streaks that replaced last week's pink ones. "We ready to kick some ass? The dodgeball tourney is this weekend and we gotta get you ready."

I gave her a look.

"Hey, what's with the eye roll?"

"We do this every time. You know the answer. No, no, and no. Just let me sleep 'til we get to the door. Pleeeaaasse."

She danced all around me as I dragged myself through the parking lot. I half expected her to coldcock me with a right hook or something. "What's up, girl?" she asked, bouncing side to side off each leg.

"Mauzzy."

Zoe snickered. "What'd he do? Pee on your head again?"

I frowned at the memory. He was beyond pissed that night. We passed through the inner glass doors and navigated toward a line of long-armed monsters. I savored the breathtaking bouquet of clean. "Nope." I stopped in front of an elliptical, took out a wipe, and savaged the handles. "Remember that new neighbor I told you about?"

"The one with the butt and gun?"

I climbed onto the sanitized waiting beast. "That one."

She scaled an adjacent elliptical before staring at me, mouth open. "Ah, shit. What'd you do? He catch you peeping?"

"Really? You think I'm a peeper?"

"If the shoe fits."

"I don't peep. I'm observant. And a little curious."

"Just a bit. Your neighbor?"

I punched some console buttons and the monster sprang to life. "I bumped into him Saturday night in the parking lot and then yesterday he shows up at the gift shop. His name is Connor Reed, and he says he's an Egyptology TA." I leisurely pumped my arms and legs.

"I'm hip to Sara Donovan Code. By bumped…"

"It just left a small paint mark on my bumper," I fired back. "And he didn't mind the dent on account of all the other dents on his piece-of-crap car."

Zoe's machine hummed happily, her arms moving in a rhythmic fervor. "That's my Sara."

I picked up the speed. She was making me look bad in front of the ROTC boys. "I don't know. After he left Saturday night, I went to check for the—"

"You peeped on him."

"He wasn't there, so that doesn't count. And he left his light on."

"Semantics. What'd you see?"

"Nothing. I think he took the gun with him."

"Maybe he locked it up?"

"Where? He's hardly got anything in that place to lock it in."

"So, he's packing. Big deal. Conceal carry licenses are easy to get in 'Bama."

"Why does a TA need to carry?"

"You seem to have forgotten, I've seen your

neighborhood."

"I'm not entirely convinced he's a TA. He's way too young. He said he's twenty-one. But he looks even younger."

Still working away, Zoe tilted her head in my direction and sized me up with one eye. "Where you going with this?"

"He's cute and all, but there's something…I can't put my finger on it. He's different. Like he doesn't belong in Sketchville."

"You still on that smuggler kick?"

I sucked in a much-needed breath and dropped the speed. ROTC boys would be useless to me if I had a broken neck. "Yesterday at the shop I found some strange transactions over the past three months."

"You forget, what's strange to you is normal to the rest of us."

"It doesn't mean I'm wrong."

"Uh-huh. Keep thinking that, girl. I'm surprised you haven't dropped this whole thing by now. Your max attention span is only about forty-eight hours."

"Very funny."

Zoe gave me a triumphant smile as she bobbed up and down.

I rattled my head as I concentrated on keeping my limbs halfway coordinated. "It's strange is all. I have this weird mask. The shop has been receiving stuff it never ordered. Then a supposed Egyptologist shows up next door. With a gun. It's getting to be too much. And Dad says there's no such thing as coincidence."

No comment from her. She just picked up the pace, her arms flapping like some crazy bird lady.

"I took your suggestion," I offered.

She flipped me a smile. "Wow. For once you listened to me?"

"I always listen to you."

"Good to know. Which excellent suggestion?"

"The phone tracker thingy. I set up a subscription last night. Four-ninety-nine a month."

"Good for you. It'll stop JT in his tracks the next time he star-sixty-sevens you."

"Or the smuggler."

"Sure."

"Excuse me, dear," said a bodiless voice.

Two machines to the left, parked behind an elliptical, was a walker with a small pink-flowered basket strapped to the front. A second later, Mrs. Majelski's jowly face popped up from behind the machine and a bulky stair-stepper standing between us. She beamed at me as the rest of her emerged above the torture devices. After a brief stop to gauge the distance, she spryly stepped from the top of a stepstool over onto the elliptical.

"Hi, Mrs. Majelski," I wheezed.

"Good morning, Sara." The retired relic mashed some console buttons, stretched up for the giant arms, and cranked away. "I couldn't help but overhear you talking with your little friend."

This little old lady possessed hearing like a bat. How long was she standing behind those machines?

"Pardon me?"

Her slate-gray eyes twinkled. "You know, dear. Your neighbor."

"Oh. Him," I panted.

Mrs. M was already dominating me on the elliptical. I picked up the pace but got so out of rhythm

I resembled a seventh grader at her first dance.

"Yes. Him. I can check him out. I have—" She winked at me. "—contacts."

I slowed down and found my rhythm again. "Seriously? How?"

"I have my ways," she chimed. She wasn't even breathing heavy. "I'm former—well, you know." Another wink.

No. I didn't know. My mouth opened, but nothing came out.

Mrs. Majelski gave me a reassuring smile. "Don't worry, dear. I'll see what I can find out."

"But…you don't even know where I live."

"Perhaps," she replied with a knowing inflection in her voice. "Perhaps not. You just watch yourself with all that snooping around. Some might call it stalking." She smiled sweetly, her pistons and guns whipping the poor helpless machine into a frenzy.

"I don't snoo—"

A booming cadence pounded the air. The ROTC boys were doing push-ups. Sweet mercy.

Chapter Twelve

What the...?

While showering after my workout, and later walking with Mauzzy, I ran things through my head. Someone or some group was using All Things Egyptian to smuggle antiquities disguised as souvenirs through the gift shop. At a minimum, Mrs. Bagley was dirty, because Mansour kept sending her items the shop never ordered, and he pretended not to understand English right after I mentioned her name. Plus, she reacted suspiciously on Saturday when I raised the subject of the mask. Karen had to be involved, too, since I always put the orders for Mrs. Bagley in her bin. And Roger showed quite an interest in the All Things Egyptian file when he came into the store. It made sense someone with his background had a hand in it because otherwise how would they know the value of the stuff they stole. I read somewhere that many times art smugglers were art historians gone bad. Since I had a meeting with him in the afternoon, I planned to sniff him out.

After another thoroughly unproductive walk with Mauzzy, I took off to catch a campus bus to class. Driving to the bus hub, I kept thinking about Mrs. Bagley, Karen, Roger and the call with Mansour. There was—

A roar washed over me as a sudden rush of wind

buffeted the side of my car, knocking me onto the shoulder. As I gained control of the hatchback, the diesel slipstream of a passing University bus latched onto it, sucking me forward.

I have a hot-cold relationship with the bus, aka the Bane of My Existence. Mostly cold. More like absolute zero. I swear the damn thing sits at the curb until it spies my little hatchback turning into the parking lot. It politely waits for me to get out and start running for it, and then slowly—slowly—slowly slips away. Leaving me shouting with arms flailing and things tumbling to the ground.

Wait. The bus?

I was back in the moment, my rumination of recent events a fading memory. I fired up all four cylinders and sped past the evil beast. Tearing into the parking lot, I caught sight of my Nemesis in the rearview mirror. It was approaching fast, black smoke shrouding it like an executioner's hood.

I threw the hatchback into a primo space right next to the stop, the front tires smacking up the low concrete barrier before rocking back. In that instant, the bus hurled a fiendish guffaw at me, once again heralding my impending defeat.

"Not this time, you bastard." Fumbling with my phone while seizing backpack and purse from the passenger seat, I leaped out the door.

"Oomph."

Only my legs made it out the open—ouch—semi-closed door. My shoulder was bent back like a carnival contortionist, and my airborne phone landed somewhere outside the car. A quick assessment of the situation revealed the backpack's strap caught on the automatic shift knob, laying me out like the victim of a carjacking gone bad.

I disentangled the backpack from the shift knob and struggled to sit up, the door holding my feet down like Zoe in the gym when I did my five sit-ups. An image of Mrs. Majelski banging out Russian twists with her ginormous medicine ball popped in my head.

Where the heck did my—it was ringing. I shoved the door off crushed shins and zeroed in on the singing phone in the abutting vacant parking space. It was the ringtone for an unknown caller.

A burst of red ripped past me.

"Nooooooooooooooo."

Too late. My phone stopped ringing. Forever. Although a premium hard case can protect a phone from many things, the list did not include a jacked-up four-wheeler. The right-side wheels of a mud-encrusted SUV just stomped all over my baby, flattening it beyond flattened. Dead at the scene.

I shouted to the bubba. "Hey, dude, you just—"

He didn't acknowledge me, shooting out of the SUV in a dead sprint toward the bus stop before I could even finish administering last rites. I crawled out of the car and fixed with an open mouth on the nearby bus stop. My Nemesis pulled up, collected the bubba, and raced away.

I gathered up pieces of phone and put them in a baggie I carried in my purse for this very purpose. Long story. Bad ending.

Thirty minutes later, with shards of phone in my purse, I arrived early for my Egyptology recitation, which was a class Professor Sawalha's doctoral candidates ran. The University referred to them as teaching assistants, but everyone just called them TAs. For courses with large lectures, like Egyptology, they added an extra class into the weekly schedule. It allowed TAs to go over the previous week's lecture material in more detail with smaller class sizes. I loved it because it meant more Egyptology every week.

Since recitation didn't start for another twenty minutes, I took out my textbook to read chapter eight again. Despite concerns over Mrs. Majelski, Bagley, Karen, Roger, Mr. Bloody Cheeky, Mansour, *and* my gun-packing TA neighbor rattling around in my head, I still enjoyed the chapter. I was halfway through it when the classroom door burst open, followed by the sound of a backpack or something heavy being dumped on the teacher's desk. A mild rustling morphed into a growing commotion behind me. I threw a look over both shoulders before realizing the distraction came from the front of the room.

What—the—what the heck? What the heck was he doing there?

Chapter Thirteen

Where's Mona?

Standing at the front of the classroom, staring at me, was my neighbor. Not Crazy Cat Lady. Not Gun Guy from across the parking lot. It was the dorky-cute guy with the butt. He wore faded blue jeans, a coral-and-white-striped button-down shirt, and scarred brown shoes. And a toothy white smile.

"Good morning, everybody. My name is Connor Reed. I'll be your TA for the rest of the semester." He chuckled. "Or the next two weeks. Whichever comes first."

A muffled response of uncomfortable laughs rippled through the room.

With raised shoulders, he turned his palms upward. "I guess this is where I say Roll Tide."

The classroom intoned "Roll Tide" like a congregation repeating an intercessory prayer.

His resplendent crystal-blue eyes set off an amused smile as he stared at me. "I'm new here but I recognize one or two faces."

Damn. Screw him being a crook. He was *fine*.

His voice drifted around me, but it sounded like he was talking through a pillow. I forgot all about my former TA, and that this guy might be a very bad dude. Were bad boys posing as teaching assistants hands off to libidinous college coeds? They were just grad students, not professors or anything, so no real ethical—

A melodious voice broke my trance. "Any questions before we finish up?"

Whoa, where did the time go? I raised a hand. A few students voiced complaints from behind, and someone said "curve buster" under his breath. So rude. The dude was probably an art major.

Connor motioned toward me. "Yes?"

"Thank you, Mr. Reed. Will—"

He raised a hand and stopped me. "Hold on. I'm sorry, Sara." He raised the other hand and addressed the room. "Everybody, no need for my last name. I'm a student, just like everybody else. The only difference is, I'm a grad student here to help you out with Professor Sawalha's lectures this week and on your presentations." He fixed back on me with a big loving smile. Well, to me it was loving. "Now, you had a question?"

"Um…yes…uh…"

Geez, Sara, you've never had a problem talking before. Dad droned in my head—*speechless is not in Sara's well-used vocabulary.*

My voice lifted with excitement. "Will we have any special reserved readings for this week's lectures?"

More bitching.

"I went through Mona's class plans and there are no special readings necessary to follow the last set of lectures."

Dang it.

A girl's voice came from the back of the room. "Why isn't Ms. Barth here anyways?"

"I should have mentioned this at the start of class. My apologies. Mona Barth is on emergency medical leave. I don't have many details other than it was serious."

The room erupted. Another concerned voice rose above the din. "Is she going to be okay?"

He raised his arms and voice and reassured the tumultuous class. "Please, she'll be fine. She caught a nasty virus and just needs some time to get her strength back."

My hand inched toward the purple-sparkly hand sanitizer dangling from my backpack.

As the class calmed down, Connor attended to the chalkboard. For a class all about antiquities, I thought it fitting that our classroom had probably the last chalkboard in the entire world. Despite all the wonderful material we covered today, I sat back and waited for the most enjoyable part of the recitation. Mona was a distant memory as his cute little butt, pooched in faded jeans, wiggled just enough as his arm arced in large semicircles, erasing the chalkboard. His broad shoulders and upper back, tapering down to a firm, trim waist, flexed wonderfully through his shirt with each glorious sweep of the eraser.

Job complete, he placed the eraser on the tray and faced the class, wiping his hands on the back of his butt. Oh, my gah, to be so lucky. Scanning the room before sitting at the desk, he dug into his backpack.

I leaned forward, waiting for a gun to fall out.

Instead of a gun, out came an electronic tablet. "Okay, we have about fifteen minutes left. If there are no further questions on the Thutmosid kings, late Eighteenth Dynasty, and Amenhotep III, I'd like to go through the class and have each of you tell me your research topic. Since you have only two weeks before presentations, I want to know what you're working on so I can point you in the right direction if you need last minute help. Okay?"

The class responded with murmurs of assent and a few head bobs.

"Let's start over here," he said, motioning to the far-left front of the class. "We'll just go right down each row."

For the next ten minutes, Connor typed with the speed of an amped-up court reporter as each student announced his or her topic. He sometimes asked a clarifying question or raised a little angle for a certain subject, but usually he just popped his head up to call on the next student. Tutankhamen themes and hieroglyphs nonsense were the most popular, embarrassingly amateurish and so cliché. I was dying to announce mine.

Finally, my turn arrived. "Sara?"

Folding my hands, I threw my shoulders back. "I'm examining the smuggling of antiquities. Since this is an Egyptology course, I'm concentrating on Egypt, but I'll also include Peru, China, and Mexico for comparison."

His head jerked up. "Go on."

I continued, but he stopped typing and was studying me. "I'll start with the history of the antiquities market and then center on the smuggling aspect. Who are the buyers? How lucrative is it for the smugglers? Who are they and how do they get these artifacts out, some of which are massive statues and sarcophagi? I'll conclude with what law enforcement is doing, and what additional tools they need to be more effective. This will include Interpol, the FBI, and the Homeland Security Investigation Directorate."

"The professor approved this?"

"He loved it. Said it was a specialty of his."

"Can you stay for a few minutes after class? This is a complicated topic you're tackling."

I threw him a little shrug of nonchalance. "Sure."

"Good, thanks. Okay, let's continue. Maria?" he said, motioning to the girl next to me who's been squirming so much the last ten minutes I swear her bladder was about to burst.

When class ended, I stayed in my seat as the room cleared. Soon it was just the two of us. Mrs. Majelski's cryptic appearance this morning seemed eternities ago.

Connor stood and edged around to the front of his desk. He half sat on a corner, one rounded cheek nestled on the fortunate desk. The other hung delectably off the edge, like an oh so sweet piece of ripe fruit waiting to be squee—picked. "What made you come up with this theme? It seems to me, with so much ancient Egyptian history, there's a wealth of subjects you could research that are more pertinent to this course."

I erased all images of butt cheeks and sweet fruit, like last semester's reformatted library hard drive. That huffy librarian was beside herself.

"Is there a problem? Like I said, the professor approved it. In fact, he said—"

He held up a hand. "Hold on, hold on. There's no problem. I'm just curious. You heard everyone else's topics. Maria's may be a tad unusual, but yours is the only one way outside the mainstream. So—" He leaned forward, his stare penetrating me. "—I get curious.

Why is this student going overboard and bringing in things outside the study of Egyptology, including law enforcement? It just struck me as strange."

"I'm taking a class, Master Art Thieves of the Twentieth Century. It had a segment on antiquities smuggling. Just a couple lectures. But really fascinating. I thought it would be cool to research it for this class."

Connor slouched, folded his arms, and said nothing for a moment, his lips pinched together in a thoughtful pose. "Tell me what Sawalha said."

I scrunched my face. "Not much other than he loved it. And he warned me it was a specialty of his." I thought it best to leave the whole scotch thing out of the discussion.

"He warned you?"

"Not threatening or anything."

"What else?"

I visualized the meeting, fighting to get past that fricking squeaky chair and stifling cologne. That was some strong stuff if it could still overwhelm me from three days ago. "Not that it matters, but he had a phone call from the Dauphin Museum. Something about a second opinion needed. That's about it."

"Very good. I've gotta run. If you don't mind, I'd like to talk with you more about this at another time. That's because, coincidentally"—he hopped off the desk with a wry smile—"the doctoral dissertation I'm working on is an analysis of the economic infrastructure of the antiquities black market."

Coincidentally? Another coincidence?

Crap.

Chapter Fourteen

Dauphin double-dealing?

After recitation, I hurried to the campus bus stop. I was on a tight schedule and still needed to get to the phone store before my meeting with Roger Gwynne this afternoon. One missed bus, a Mauzzy pee break, and an hour later I arrived at the mall.

Inside the store, a tall skinny man skulked toward me with an extended hand of long beckoning fingers. Unfortunately, I knew all too well this soul-sucking demon coercing me for my heart. He stopped in front of me and unleashed a cold, unfeeling black stare. I shuddered at this loathsome man, this condescending Purveyor of Death.

I took a half-step back from the Grim Reaper's bony hand.

"How's my best customer doing?" His face was all gums and crooked teeth. With that smile, I call into question the whole "Grim" part. It's bad when you can transform the Grim Reaper into the Happy Harvester.

I rummaged in my purse and produced the phone remnants baggie. "Not too well."

He recoiled. "Ouch. How?"

"A bubba and an SUV. Bad combo."

He warily took the baggie from me and held it out with thumb and index finger, like it was the waste tissue baggie from my OCD Tissue System, patent pending by Sara Donovan. "Mmmm, that's a new one."

"Aren't they always with me?"

"Only with you, Ms. Donovan," he sang. "Only with you."

I squeezed out a smile.

"Well, I know you have insurance. In fact, you're killing us in that department. I have your phone number memorized, so you know the drill. I'll be back in a few minutes." He vanished into the back with the phone shards as quickly as he materialized.

I wandered around the store, looking at nothing in particular. Glancing out front, I noticed an older man standing in the doorway of a store on the other side of the atrium, staring at me. He wheeled around and disappeared into the store before I could catch his face, but it might as well have been his face. I was staring at brown leather elbow patches on a tweed jacket and a balding head with gray frizzy hair.

I took off after him.

A voice rang out from behind. "Oh, Miss Donovan."

I stopped and spun around in the voice's direction.

Coming out from the back, the Prince of Darkness held out a lump of plastic and broken glass in his claw.

I checked over my shoulder. The man got away. I slumped to the rear of the store where Dr. Doom waited for me.

Without a word, I took the electronic carnage from him.

The Dark Angel drew in a breath, judging me with obsidian orbs. You'd think I was a baby killer or something. "You're very fortunate you listened to me. I believe just last month? If you didn't back everything up to our cloud, well..." He ended with several clucks of admonishment. "We'll be able to have everything transferred over. Can you wait?"

"Sure."

While waiting, I scoured the mall for Professor Sawalha with no success. An hour later, I was racing the clock to get to the Dauphin for my two o'clock with Roger.

When I made it to his office, it was ten after two. I poked my head in the door.

He glanced up and waved me in. "Miss Donovan, you're late."

"I'm so sorry, Dr. Gwynne. I needed to get a new phone, and it took longer than expected."

"Mmmm, yes, well—" He consulted his phone. "—you now have fifteen minutes. I have a two-thirty with Dr. Mitchell."

"Thank you for taking the time from your busy schedule to meet with me."

He nodded, and with two fingers stirred the air, signaling me to get on with it.

I pulled a notebook and pen from my backpack and flipped it open. "I'm doing a research project on the antiquities black market. Can—"

"Yes, so you said earlier."

"Can you describe how the museum goes about determining if a piece is legitimate? Also, if you found any illegal artifacts coming to the Dauphin?"

"Legitimate how? Authentic? Stolen? Forged provenance?"

"Everything."

For the next ten minutes, the esteemed Dr. Roger

Gwynne pontificated. Some stuff I understood, such as an analysis of the provenance for a piece and any original documents associated with it. Most stuff I didn't, such as using various non-destructive techniques like Raman spectroscopy to analyze chemical components of a piece. While he talked about that techno-thingy, all I could think about was a nice steaming bowl of ramen. So far, this meeting was useless. I needed a more direct approach.

"Since the *Bugler* quoted you in the article about the King Akhenaten dedication tomb being looted, are you aware of any pieces from it showing up in the marketplace?" I hesitated. "Or here?"

His beady eyes studied me. "Here?"

"Just curious."

Roger rested his chin between thumb and forefinger, his elbow propped on the arm of the chair. He let out an emphatic sigh. "Miss Donovan, if any artifact from that tomb became available for acquisition, we would have reported it to the authorities."

"Oh, for sure."

"Why would you ask a question with such an obvious answer?"

"I was more wondering if you've heard of pieces from that looting surfacing anywhere?"

He considered me, eyes becoming slits. "For someone looking at the entire antiquities black market, you're quite fixated on that particular tomb."

"I just figured you might know, since you were in the article and all."

"Only as an informative source from an acquisitions standpoint. If you want to talk to someone who has firsthand knowledge of that tomb, I suggest you interview Dr. Sawalha at your school. Not me."

"But have you heard of any pieces—"

"If I recall, the dig team had not finished the cataloging process before the looting occurred. So, it's highly likely items were stolen that nobody knew existed. Therefore, it stands to reason, some of those pieces have made their way into museums or private collections with forged provenances." He paused, observing me. "But not here."

"Oh, I would never expect—"

He stood. "Time is up, Miss Donovan. I trust this was helpful."

I stood, and he ushered me out of his office. "Definitely. Thank you again for your time."

Riding the elevator to the main lobby, I ran back the last fifteen minutes. When I addressed the Akhenaten looting, I couldn't tell if Roger was being his normal obnoxious snobby self, or if he was hiding something. My brand-new phone signaled a text arrived. I opened the message as the doors opened and—

"*Oof.*"

I fumbled with the phone to keep it from disappearing forever through the yawning gap between the elevator and the floor landing. In a surreal act of dexterity, my left hand pinned it against the right as my shoulder and cheek sank into a doughy midsection of cologne. Using the bushwhacked torso to steady myself, I fought for a breath of fresh air. "Professor—" Cough. "—Sawalha? I'm so—" Deep inhale and exhale. "—sorry."

The professor stepped back and adjusted his

glasses. "Miss Donovan, what a...pleasant surprise. Yes, yes, a pleasant surprise."

I crammed the phone in my back pocket, lungs scratching at the noxious air for anything resembling oxygen. "We were—" Wheeze. "—just talking about you." I pivoted from the closed elevator doors and took two steps away from him and the chemical cloud engulfing his space.

"We?"

"Dr. Gwynne and I."

He tilted his head. "Really? Why?"

Two deep glorious breaths liberated my flailing respiratory system. "He suggested I talk to you about the Akhenaten dedication tomb being looted."

"Yes, yes, quite a shame. Quite a shame indeed. Why your interest?"

"For my research project."

His smile was flat, sly even. "Ah, yes. Your project. Now that would be an inappropriate discussion, it would seem."

"You think so?"

An elevator door opened, and the professor stepped into the cab and punched a button. "Absolutely. I really must run. Dr. Mitchell is waiting for me." He grinned. "Good luck with your project." The door slid closed, leaving me standing alone in the lobby.

Roger said he had a meeting with her, too. Were they all meeting together, or was someone lying? And if they were meeting together, why? They're all professionals, so it could be nothing. But then again...

On my way toward the main entrance, I passed the gift shop and thought it would be nice to pop in. "Hi, Karen."

She was straightening a display at the end of the front counter. Her head snapped up with an instant frown. "What are you doing here?"

So much for being social. "I had a meeting this afternoon with Dr. Gwynne. Thought I would say hi."

Her eyes narrowed. "Dr. Gwynne? Why?"

"For a class project. Hey, I'm glad you're here. Mrs. Bagley came in this Saturday—"

Edna emerged from the back room. "Sara, I thought I heard your voice."

She was medium height, middle-aged, with round wire-frame glasses, and a head of short gray disheveled hair, almost in a scholarly I-don't-care look. But that had to be a pure accident on her part because she was no more scholarly than me. I just don't think she had any idea what to do with her hair, or her wardrobe. The woman had no fashion sense. This afternoon she wore a navy pleated skirt with a crazy red floral pattern gallivanting in all directions, a pink chiffon blouse, and black clunker heels. So wrong.

Edna marched up to me. "Were you into my filing cabinets over the weekend? When I came in this morning, everything was out of order, and I can't find the All Things Egyptian file."

The perspiration machine cranked up. If she found out I messed with her stuff, she would kill me. And then fire me. I needed to play it cool. I threw a casual shrug. "Nope. Not me. But Dr. Gwynne was here Saturday. Maybe he was looking for something?"

She scowled. "Why would he be rummaging around in my files?"

"I don't know. He *is* your boss."

"So he is. Karen, have you seen it?"

"I work the retail space," she huffed. "Why are you asking me?"

"Answer the question."

Indignation swept over her face as her arm waved around the counter. "You see anything here?"

Edna stepped behind the counter and disappeared below it, her muffled voice saying, "Let's find out."

"It won't be under there," Karen said, her derisive tone insinuating her boss was an idiot.

A few seconds later Edna stood, holding the overstuffed folder in one hand. "Found it."

Karen's face flared red. "But...how'd...I don't know how that got there."

"Well, I'm glad you found your file," I said. "See you Wednesday."

I took off out of the shop before anybody could respond. Behind me, the two were going at it. The skank deserved everything Edna gave her.

Chapter Fifteen

Beyond ingenious

Just ahead, a knife of yellow radiance severed the hallway's somber darkness. I rapped on the open door.

Squuuuueeeeeeek.

Seriously, by now the old guy must be hearing impaired.

"Sir?"

"Miss Donovan. Come in. You're right on time. Please sit." The high humidity today made the professor's hair especially frizzy. Or the Cologne Effect was working its diabolical magic because a suffocating musky sweetness dominated the air.

I remembered the drill. I took an armful of books from the visitor's chair and placed them on the floor beside his cluttered desk. "Thank you for taking the time to meet with me."

"If I can't make time for my best student, then I don't deserve to be teaching." He gave me a heartwarming smile and a wink. "What's on your mind?"

"After seeing you and Dr. Gwynne yesterday, it got me thinking. I can't put a finger on it, but I feel like I'm missing something big with my research."

The professor furrowed a protruding brow, further darkening eyes already resembling black coffee beans.

"I don't have any problem with that, Miss Donovan, but it is rather odd at this late juncture in the semester. You realize I scheduled your presentation for—" He swiveled to his desk.

Squeeeek.

I flinched.

Mental Note—instead of scotch, take a can of multipurpose oil when you make your presentation.

Shoving even more books and a few folders out of the way, he picked up an appointment book stuffed with papers. Yellow sticky notes poked out in every direction, like an office supply porcupine. "Ah yes, here you are—" He swiveled back to face me.

Squeeeek.

I think I just performed a mental hara-kiri.

"—on April twenty-fourth at four o'clock." He eyed me over his glasses, which hung by a thread from the end of his nose. I don't know how those things didn't just slide off the ski slope once they cleared his nose's hook. But somehow, they got to the end and stopped.

"Yes, sir. Thank you." I spent the next ten minutes running through my presentation outline, stopping intermittently to respond to a question or comment. When I finished, the professor remained quiet. "Do you think I'm missing something?"

He tapped his pale lips a few times and gave me an academia nod. "Mmmm hmmm. How big is the market?"

"Huge. Some experts believe stolen art and antiquities make up the fourth largest black market in the world. There are other assessments that only drug trafficking and arms smuggling top it."

"Incredible, isn't it?"

"It is."

He squinted at me. "What measurement tools are the experts using to gauge the size of these criminal markets?"

The old man wasn't about to serve up the answer. He used the Socratic Method in his lectures, and apparently also in his face-to-face sessions. A trickle of moisture wound its way down the small of my back toward—I got it.

"Money?"

"Precisely. What does that mean?"

I gave the room a once-over. A garish funerary mask similar to my melted piece sat on one bookcase.

"Miss Donovan?" *Squeeeek.* The professor bent forward and tilted his head sideways. "What does that mean?"

"Um…" I couldn't stop thinking about Mr. Bloody Cheeky and the whole motley crew of suspects. Including Connor. And now this guy. Friday, he talked to Dr. Mitchell about the FBI. Yesterday, he followed me and showed up at the Dauphin to meet with her at the same time Roger, a suspect, was meeting with her. And suddenly that mask appears on the bookcase?

"How much money?"

"It's…uh…estimated to be…in the billions of dollars annually."

"And with that much money from ill-gotten means passing hands, what does that lead to?" The professor surveyed me, his deep-set eyes trying to coax the answer out of my seized-up brain.

I blinked once. Then again. My cerebral cortex stirred. "Money laundering?"

He sat back, his eyes smiling proudly. *Squeeeek.* "Correct. Money laundering."

I snapped my fingers. "I get it. With that kind of money and law enforcement's tools for tracking financial transactions, smuggling rings have to launder the money."

"It's another whole submarket."

"Wow. I've got less than two weeks. I better get cracking."

He raised his eyebrows and nodded briefly.

"Thank you for your time." I stood but stopped at the door and spun around. "Um, sir?" I pointed to the last bookcase. "Is that a new piece? I don't recall seeing it before."

He twisted toward the bookcase. *Squeeeek.* "Which piece is that?"

"The funerary mask there. It's very colorful."

"Ah, that's a replica of a princess' death mask from the Middle Kingdom." After a second, he added, "I've had it for some time now."

I pursed my lips. "Huh. Never noticed it before. I thought I saw it somewhere else recently."

The professor swung back.

Squeeeek.

Stamped on his weathered features was a stoic smile. "That's possible, but it would be a replica. Like that one. The original is worth a small fortune. It's stored in an Egyptian government warehouse."

"I'm sure of that. Thank you again for your time." I closed the door.

Navigating the dark hallway, I pictured the bulky package Connor picked up Sunday at the gift shop.

I stopped.

An epiphany struck me like a macchiato with an extra shot. Karen purposely made the package he picked up bigger and heavier to throw off suspicion. The professor was part of the ring. And he hid the stolen artifacts among his collection of reproductions. Right in plain sight. Some of those pieces on his bookshelves were real. Nobody would search for looted antiquities in the open, and definitely not in the office of a world-renowned Egyptologist. Beyond ingenious.

I clomped down the stairs but another thought exploded in my head, stopping me cold on the first landing. Connor's curiosity yesterday about my project sure seemed—it couldn't be. He couldn't be. Could he? Was I right about his reason for carrying a gun? He and Mrs. Bagley were the ring's mules.

I rushed out of the building, all the while trying to banish a rising swell of suspicion from my mind.

Chapter Sixteen

Niagara Falls Donovan

After a day full of classes and my meeting with the professor, I spent six hours doing research for my project in the stacks at Gorgas Library. Once again, I lost track of the time until the library staff kicked us out just before midnight.

The night was miserably wet, cloaked with an inky-black cover of heavy dank air. I hit the bottom of the library steps only to see the Bane of My Existence ease away from the library's bus stop on Capstone Drive. I decided to catch a bus at another stop across the Quad near Denny Chimes rather than wait for the next one to come to the library.

Water dripped everywhere from an earlier thunderstorm that also flooded the surrounding paths of the Quad Outer Trail. The only way to avoid the underwater walkways and get to the other stop meant going down Capstone Drive to Sixth Avenue. And then all the way down Sixth to University, a trek of something like eight or nine blocks. Or I could take a shortcut through the Quad to University. With no umbrella, I didn't want to take any chances on getting caught in a downpour, so I took the shortcut.

I passed Rotunda Plaza and trundled halfway across the Quad in the pitch black because my one-day old phone's flashlight broke this morning after Mauzzy vommed on it. Well, I'm not sure if it was his vom or the full bottle of travel hand sanitizer I unleashed afterward on the unfortunate phone. Either way, it hasn't worked since. No doubt my immediate future held yet another new pho—

Splash. Splash.

Excellent.

A deep puddle washed over my shoes. More like a pond. A taunting vision floated past of butterfly-embossed rain boots sitting next to my front door, right behind the pile of clean clothes waiting to go upstairs. As I tiptoed out of the rippling lake, my socks soaked up half its water. Soooo grody. I slipped and almost fell back into the puddle, but somehow regained my minimal balance. It's funny. When you don't have much of something, such as balance in my case, it's not as difficult to regain if you lose it.

Since I made it halfway to the other side, might as well finish my brilliant shortcut. I resumed the trek, but with each step taken, sodden shoes issued a squishing censure. Like I so meant to drown them.

Despite the dark, I sized up the situation. Mud covered my shoes and the lower half of my pants, totally like when Elizabeth Bennet walked from Longbourn to Meryton to care for Jane with her dress six inches deep in mud. Although not six inches deep, I still had a ways to go before reaching the stop.

While sloshing and splashing across the Quad, I gave up trying to keep from getting wet. Mainly because—I was wet. I just wanted to get on the damn bus. And the first one better be mine. And it better be heated. I pictured my warm cottage, heartwarming ginger tea, and Sweet Handsome patiently waiting in his chair.

Ever conscious of my personal security—*complacency will get you killed*—my pepper spray led the way as I floundered toward University. Denny Chimes loomed in the distance.

Internal alarm bells reverberated, putting me on ultrahigh alert.

A silhouette slinked around the front of the tower's base, moving in my direction. More shadowy shapes lurked behind the first while muffled voices carried over the oppressive air. My grip tightened on the pepper spray.

Who in their right mind would be out on a night like this, let alone sneaking around in the shadows behind Denny Chimes? Frat Row was just a few blocks away. Were the idiot Greeks up to another of their stupid pranks?

I took a few more cautious steps.

Squish. Squish. Squish. Squish.

Frick. The only people I could sneak up on would have to be deaf and blind.

Those four splattering steps got me a little closer, and I made out three people. One tall and kinda lanky. The second was nondescript, except for a fuzzy head reflecting the stray wisps of light from University Boulevard. The third, just a short blob. The hushed voices grew louder. One sounded like a woman, but I couldn't be sure. I needed to get closer.

Squish. Squish.

Wonderful.

Niagara Falls Donovan just spooked them. The tall one dashed around the front of the tower and ran across

University. The bald one put up an umbrella, shielding any facial features and hustled up University. The third, the shadow blob, raced down University toward Graves Hall.

I kicked up the pace to a power walk in pursuit of the clandestine group. A streak of movement exploded ahead and to the right on University. The short squat person scurried down the street, a light-colored jacket catching the occasional wash of mist-shrouded streetlights. Frantic legs fired like overworked pistons while a blonde ponytail protested wildly.

By the time I reached University, everybody was gone. I hurried across the street because, after that lovely bath in the Quad, the last thing I needed was my Nemesis to leave me dripping at the curb. But as fate would have it, things were improving because a bus appeared and opened its doors. Just for me.

After slopping up the stairs, I squished-squashed down the aisle toward the rear. Before I sat, the driver gunned it, throwing me headlong into the side of a seat. I caught myself, steered toward the back, slid into a seat, and squirmed out of my backpack. Remarkably, the bus was empty.

I wiggled off my shoes and poured out the consequences of my shortcut. After peeling off both socks, I wrung out my remorse for that fricking decision. I pictured the person with the ponytail shooting down University. Did I see Mrs. Bagley, or someone who looked like her? Maybe best to sort that out later, under more arid conditions. With a deep breath, I tugged the throttled socks back on my feet and crammed them into waterlogged shoes. I just wanted to go home to a warm cottage. And a welcoming Mauzzy?

Hopefully.

****

Fortunately, I was the lone passenger, and my stop the last on the route. Otherwise, I'm not so sure the driver would have come back to wake me when we got to the bus hub. Although it's not like it hasn't happened before. Several times in the past I made multiple round trips on the route just to reach my destination. Tonight, I got lucky.

When I finally got home, my soaked cold feet weighed twenty pounds and seemed five sizes too large for their shrunken shoes. Connor's car sat in front of his dark cottage. As I carried myself up the outer deck stairs, a faint noise like a cooling engine came from the parking area. I dropped my stuff, sloshed back down the steps, and slid over to his car. I touched the hood.

It was hot.

Chapter Seventeen

Zoe goes postal

I stopped short at the steps leading into the Student Recreation Center this early Wednesday morning, made even earlier by my getting home late after wading across the Quad. "Dang it. I forgot my University ID."

Zoe headed up the steps. "So? No biggie."

"It kinda is. I can't get in the rock-climbing room without it."

She whipped around midway up, bulging eyes overtaking her dainty little face. Just two green traffic lights and a button nose. "Nobody's gonna arrest you. Now c'mon. Just act normal and walk on by the desk." She motioned with her head and bounded up the last three steps.

Act normal? Was that normal-normal or my normal? Or her normal? What was normal anyway and who determined normality? And if that determining person or entity wasn't nor—

"*Sara.*"

"Okay. Okay. Coming."

Anxiety built as I trudged up the steps because invariably, it's us good girls who get busted for breaking the rules. Not ever the cool kids like Zoe. Never fails.

I hit the top landing. "Act normal?"

"And not your normal. Just be a typical Alabama dumbass student for once. K?"

"Hey, you lost the color streaks. When did you do that?"

"Yesterday. Now quit stalling. We're going inside, and nobody's arresting you." She got a little mischievous smile and a twinkle in her eye. "At least not today."

I took a deep breath. "Okay, let's go."

We entered through the double-glass doors. I ducked my head and shot past as Zoe flashed her ID to the indifferent student slumped at the desk. We exited the lobby and hung a left down a wide corridor toward the rock-climbing room. The closer we got, the more my stomach danced and tumbled like an overzealous tyke in her first gymnastics class. A routine likely repeated when I take my GBA380 final. In twelve days. I had not even started studying. For the single course capable of transforming me from a successful business school candidate at Alabama to just another commuter student living at home. Utter brilliance.

Too soon, the moment arrived. We were outside the rock-climbing room. I half-expected to find Mrs. Majelski with her walker parked at the bottom of the traversing wall, and her hanging from a single handhold. The old lady was ridiculous.

I took one last glorious whiff of chlorinated air from the lap pool across the hall and made my move. "Hey," I said, striding past the check-in desk. The two girls sitting there, tapping and swiping like crazy on their phones, barely noticed us.

Inside, the room was empty. No Mrs. Majelski. Yes.

I breathed out. "Way too easy."

"Those girls don't give a shit. They remember you."

"I feel like a felon. Hopefully, they're not calling the University cops on me because, you know, we have a—history."

"Ya. I know. You ready?"

I inhaled deep and let it out slow. Three different twenty-foot high climbing walls encased the space. Each wall provided a separate challenge, allowing climbers to choose from top-rope, traversing, and bouldering. Every time I entered this room with its soaring ceilings and colossal walls, a feeling of insignificance overtook me. I wonder if Zoe experienced this all the time. It explained her feistiness. She looked up at everyone. Well, except Mrs. Majelski. They were about eye level.

"Yep." I took in the top-rope wall. It was so fricking high. I turned away from the wall and locked in on Zoe. "Before we get started, I gotta tell you about something from last night. On the Quad."

She groaned. "I've seen this face before. Don't do it. Let's just climb. Please?"

"I've been giving this a lot of thought since I got that mask. And I've been digging into things at the museum. I keep coming back to the same conclusion. Something crazy is going on around here. I've gotta talk to someone. You're my best friend. So?"

"Fine. Let's hear it. What do you think you saw last night?"

I leveled my gaze. "Remember last night, when it rained ridiculously hard?"

She tipped her head to the side and winced.

"Yeah."

"I had to cut across the Quad 'cause the rain flooded all the walkways. That's when I saw them."

"What, two people making out? You see, when two people love each other, they—"

"I'm serious. This is serious."

"Sorry. Who'd you see?"

"Professor Sawalha. Some other guy I couldn't recognize. And a regular customer from the gift shop, Mrs. Bagley. It—"

"Mrs. Bagley? Mary Bagley?"

"Uh-huh."

"Sixth-grade teacher? Looks like a short blonde drill sergeant?"

"How did you know?"

"She was my favorite teacher. Everybody loved her."

I forgot Zoe didn't move to Annapolis from here until the seventh grade. "Yeah, I'm not so sure she's on the up-and-up."

"What the hell are you talking about?"

I told her everything.

"So far, I've only heard Sara-crazy over-imaginative stuff. People can order shit. And people forget things, too." She jabbed an index finger at me. "You even said it. Poor Mrs. Bags was just getting over the flu. And you always think you see somebody who turns out to be someone else." A short, sardonic snort. "Remember Carter? You chased after him because you thought he was Kurt? Remember his embarrassing social media post? Remember?"

I screwed up my face. "Okay. That was bad. But I'm not wrong about this. I just know it."

Zoe wrinkled her nose. "I'm smelling what you're stepping in. I'm so smelling it."

"Don't forget about the mask I received."

"Girl, you *bought* that piece of junk. You didn't *receive* anything."

"Stop. Listen to me. I think there's an antiquities smuggling ring here. And I think Roger, the professor, Connor, Karen, and Mrs. Bagley are all a big part of it. In fact, I think Roger is the guy who called me last Thursday. I've thought it all out. That's what—"

"I told you. Mrs. Bags is just a teacher."

"Hear me out. Please?"

She crossed her arms, clenched her jaw, and slapped on a fake smile.

I paced back and forth as I laid out my case. "The professor, Connor, and Roger use their contacts in Egypt to find and hold artifacts they buy from local looters. Karen alerts Roger when Edna is preparing the next order for All Things Egyptian, a discount souvenir company in the purchasing system as a preferred vendor. Just as important, she tells him *what* is in the order. Roger informs his Cairo people of the pending shipment, what artifact he wants sent, and what souvenir disguise to use based on her info. They use plaster or something to build it up like the target souvenir, a King Tut bust is the most popular, put a plastic coating on it, and paint it up. Then they have this guy Mansour at the vendor, who they either bribe or he's part of the ring, address it to Mrs. Bagley and add it to the packing list. It eludes close inspection by the authorities because it's part of a bunch of cheap souvenirs." Stopping in front of the bouldering wall, I whirled and faced Zoe. "And that's why I got this strange mask. Because Mansour made a mistake. He meant to send it to her, not me. I also think to throw any suspicion off her, this past Sunday they switched things up and used Connor to pick up a package from the museum." I watched for a reaction.

"You finished?" she asked calmly.

"Yes. I—"

"You're fucking nuts. You need to stop and reel it back in. I know Mrs. Bags. She's not a crook. Especially not some international smuggler. It's crazy. You're crazy. This is little 'ole Podunkville, USA. We don't have international art smuggling rings here. We have rednecks night-poaching deer. Not art thieves stealing old Egyptian shit." She thrust her arms in the air. "And Mrs. Bagley? No way. No fucking way."

We fell silent for a moment.

"Why did my mask melt? It could be gold underneath."

"I don't buy it. It's a cheesy souvenir. That's all. And it's no big deal you melted it. It's some kind of cheap plastic or resin. It should melt." Zoe stuck her neck out, gave me a mocking smile, turned away, and sized up the top-rope wall.

"But I tested anoth—"

She froze for an instant before spinning around. "I've heard this shit all before." Her index finger slashed at the space between us. "This is another one of those crazy schemes you've concocted in your head. There's nothing there. Just like when you called the cops last semester on your neighbor. You thought he was dealing drugs out of his house."

I took a step back and crossed my arms. "Okay, maybe not dealing drugs, but he got busted later for running a gambling operation."

Her hands bounced through the air. "But not drugs. You were wrong about that. And what about the guy you swore you saw throwing library books out the window in the stacks? The windows were screwed up tight, and they found no books in the bushes. But you swore you saw it. It was just another mirage."

"But I did—"

"And how 'bout that Air Marshal Incident? How'd that work out for you, hmmm?" Zoe's eyebrows rose as she rocked back and forth on her heels, hands on hips.

My cheeks flushed. I returned her smirk with my fierce look. "But I was righ—"

"Seriously, Sara," she said between belly laughs, "you can't even scare Mauzzy with your killer stare." Her hysterics subsided to a light chuckle before she was back to being serious. "You were also wrong. Every time you act on one of these feelings, you end up being wrong and create real problems for yourself. Real problems. Do yourself a favor. Leave it alone. Mrs. Bags is only a sixth-grade teacher. That professor of yours is just that, a nerdy college professor. Roger is a snobbish museum dork who couldn't mastermind knocking off a kid's lemonade stand, let alone run a smuggling ring. And Connor is a boy-genius who quite correctly recognizes he needs a gun in that shithole you call home. There's nothing going on. Forget about all this bullshit. Focus on passing GBA380 and getting into business school. Okay? Please?"

I stared back at pleading eyes and let my arms drop. "Okay. GBA380. No smuggling conspiracy."

"Good. You'll thank me later. Now let's climb."

I stepped to the wall and harnessed up. As I

grabbed the first handhold, the room's door behind us banged open. A shuffling sound followed by rolling wheels entered the room.

"Excuse me, dear."

Zoe twirled around while I pirouetted like a giant marionette, bobbing and bouncing as a hidden puppeteer played with my harness.

"Hi, Mrs. Majelski," we droned together.

"Good morning, Sara. I couldn't help but overhear you talking with your little friend here," she said pleasantly, motioning with her snowy white head in my spotter's direction.

"Overhear—what?" I asked.

Her sweet smile contorted into a crooked grin. "I've been standing outside the door, dear."

My head tilted. "For how long?"

"Mmmm, let's just say long enough." The multitude of wrinkles in her face dissolved into one big smile. "Long enough."

I opened my mouth to respond, but she extended an index finger from a brawny hand. Man, I need to start working out with Mrs. M.

"Now, you seem to have an interesting, hmmm, theory."

"My...theory?"

"Yes, your theory. Remember Monday I promised to check your new neighbor out?"

Without breaking eye contact, I gradually nodded my head. This iron-pumping, elliptical-riding, treadmill-running, and now apparently, mountain-climbing ancient wonder, was freaking me out.

"Take a little advice from an old lady who knows a thing or two. Nothing is as it seems, dear."

"There you go, Sara. Even Mrs. M agrees with me," crowed Zoe.

"That's not what I said, sweetie," Mrs. Majelski snarled, shooting a searing sideways glare without turning her head from me. She edged up close. "It seems...well...I'd be *very* careful with that mask, dear." She studied me with steely gray eyes. "I suggest giving it to someone for safekeeping." A wink.

I gaped back.

After a second or two, she rolled past me and toward the climbing walls, singing, "Do you mind if I take the bouldering wall?"

The banshee continued to scream in my head. Only louder. And way shriller.

Chapter Eighteen

They're all in cahoots?

Right after I got home from climbing, my phone chimed. The caller ID read "unknown," so I declined the call like the tracking service instructed me to do. Seconds later I received a text with a name, phone number, and address in Birmingham.

After showering, I picked out dark-gray dress yoga pants with a black empire-waisted blouse and three-quarter length sleeves. It was proper stakeout attire. Loose and comfortable, yet professional for work later in the day. While getting dressed, the Universe signaled me it would be a good day. The signal? When I wriggled into my underpants, my fitness tracker hit ten-thousand steps.

With renewed energy, I charged downstairs, powered up the laptop, and searched the name I got from the tracking service, Thornburn Gallery of Antiquities. Henderson Thornburn opened the business three years ago. What kind of first name is Henderson? Sounds English and hoity-toity to me. This could be Mr. Bloody Cheeky from the phone call that started this whole mess.

The gallery's very minimal website said it specialized in the acquisition, sale, and brokerage of legitimately acquired antiquities, with a focus on ancient Egyptian pieces. A statement emphasized they would only handle pieces with strong provenances capable of withstanding the highest scrutiny. I found it odd they had no pieces posted to the website as being for sale, as if they wanted to keep their listings secret. Just some basic information and a "contact us" button. Maybe that's typical for the antiquities dealer business, but to me it made no sense. The only other thing I could find was from a business database search engine saying the company had one to five employees and annual revenues of between one and five million.

I browsed the Internet for Henderson Thornburn and sifted through the data. He was between forty-five and fifty-five and used to be an art history professor at Knighton University, just outside London. Knighton was right up there with Oxford and Cambridge. Scholars considered their fine arts program one of the best in the world. He left Knighton ten years ago and came to the States to work as—score—a curator for the Egyptian collection under Dr. Roger Gwynne at the Dauphin Museum. My pulse quickened. Three years ago, he left the Dauphin when he opened a gallery in Birmingham.

I just found Mr. Bloody Cheeky. And a connection back to the Dauphin and Roger.

I grabbed my purse and phone. "Okay, Mauzzy, I'm off to Birmingham. You need to go out before I leave?"

He raised his head from the recliner, yawned, licked his lips, and rolled over.

"I'll take that as a no." Ordinarily, I wouldn't let him get away with that flippant attitude, but I had to get on the case. I had a hot lead and limited time today to run it down. "I work tonight so I won't be home until after nine. Don't do anything in the house."

The only reply, a sigh and a fart. What a surprise.

I exited the cottage, locked the door, and headed toward the hatchback.

Fifty-five minutes later I was slouching in my car across the street from the gallery. I couldn't decide between going into the building and confronting the creep about his phone calls, or staying out of sight and watching the place. Being a fine-arts professional, I doubted he was violent. Although, Connor packed heat. Maybe this guy did, too. In the end, I stayed in the car to see who, if anybody, showed up.

After two fruitless hours, I wanted to march in and confront the dude. Until I caught a glimpse up the street of a familiar thatch of frizzy gray hair atop a tweed jacket barreling down the sidewalk. Under his arm, Professor Sawalha carried a decent-sized package, similar in size to the one Connor picked up. With his eyes straight ahead, he hung a quick left and zipped straight into the gallery.

With my attention riveted on the building, I reviewed the case. The only major change to my earlier theory now had Thornburn as the leader, not Roger, and he used the gallery as a front to move the pieces. When a shipment arrived with a disguised artifact for Mrs. Bagley, I unwittingly put the package in Karen's bin. The following week Bagley picked it up from her and took it straight to Thornburn, who then used the gallery to complete the business transaction with the buyer, laundering the proceeds at the same time. Everything appeared legit. It was so simple. And pure genius.

Fifteen minutes later, the professor emerged. On

the sidewalk, he scanned the street to his left before taking off in the opposite direction, hustling along at the same pace as when he arrived. Only he was carrying nothing. I wanted to stay and see if anybody came for his package, but I also wanted to follow him. Unfortunately, after checking the time, I could do neither. It was four-thirty. I needed to get to the shop before Edna had a cow.

After some creative driving, and a law enforcement close call, I got to the Dauphin with five minutes to spare. With head down and hair in my face, I pounded up the steps to the front entrance.

"Sara?"

Chapter Nineteen

Kranzer—with a "K"

I stopped and brushed insubordinate hair out of my eyes. "What are you doing here?"

"I'm an Egyptologist," Connor said. "Thought I should check out the exhibits."

"You coming or going?"

"I was just leaving."

"What was your favorite?"

"Favorite?"

"Yeah, your favorite exhibit."

He scratched the back of his head. "Um, didn't have one. They were all great."

"Really? What did you think about the new papyrus collection?"

"Forgot about that one. Incredible colors."

My phone alarm chimed. "Sorry. Gotta run. Late for work."

"Oops."

I took off up the stairs. "No worries. See ya."

Connor just lied to me. There is no papyrus collection. He's definitely one of them. I've so got his number. I burst through the shop door. Edna stood behind the counter, arms folded.

"You're late."

"Sorry. I ran into my TA out front."

She smiled, but it was empty, devoid of emotion. "Don't let it happen again."

I hurried into the back room, stowed my purse, and came out to the front counter. "You have anything you want me to do if we're slow?"

Edna shook her head. "By the way, are you going to the silent auction this Saturday evening? Dr. Mitchell wants maximum employee attendance. Even from the part-timers."

The silent auction was being touted for the past several months as quite the gala. Roger was opening a new exhibit on Early Byzantine art in September, and this was one way the museum raised money for such things. There would be champagne, cocktails, and fancy-schmancy hors d'oeuvres served by, I'm sure, size-two blondes in little black-and-white outfits. So not my thing.

"Yeah, I don't know. What if I have plans? I mean, it is Saturday night."

Her bark of laughter said it all, like I was a cloistered nun whose sole entertainment on the weekends entailed escaping the hubbub of the convent to work at the shop. Which, the way my love life has been going recently, as in not, she wasn't far off. Okay, she was close. But sans the God-awful habit. I have some fashion sense.

I attempted another angle. "Besides, finals start next week."

"How's studying going?"

I grimaced. "Slow."

She fell silent for a moment. "Tell you what. I'll give you the weekend off to study, including Friday night, provided you attend the auction."

"A big shipment is coming in this weekend. Don't you need me to unpack it and get everything entered into inventory?"

Edna flipped a hand. "Not a problem. I'll get Karen to cover for you. She's been bugging me about increasing her hours. And we'll be closing early, anyway. So how about it?"

"The offer is tempting, but isn't it some big gala chic affair? Black-tie sorta thing."

"Supposed to be the event of the year."

"I'm a poor college student with nothing to wear," I whined. "No way I can go."

"Don't you have a nice dress and heels?"

I shook my head and crossed my fingers behind my back. "Uh-uh. I brought one dress down here that I wore to high school graduation. And it isn't close to chic."

"Hmmm." She drummed the counter with her fingers before brightening. "Dr. Mitchell really wants a great turnout because of the publicity and to show a strong base of support for our donors. I think I'm justified giving you up to, say, one hundred dollars to buy an outfit for the auction. I'll take it from the shop's marketing budget. How does that sound?"

I smiled politely. "Sounds like I'm going to an auction."

"Excellent. I'll make arrangements with Karen for this weekend."

Terrific. Now I needed to find a date. My chances were better at finding a fricking unicorn than landing a date not named JT Bridges.

Edna whisked into the back and came bustling out with her briefcase and purse. "I'm so happy you'll be able to attend. Have a good evening. I'll see you Saturday night. Eight o'clock."

"You, too."

With Karen filling in this weekend, I needed to make things easier for her since she doesn't make the inventory adjustments when we received shipments. That was my job. I ran a shop inventory report and printed up the order for the incoming All Things Egyptian shipment.

Sitting at the front counter, I worked through the order, hunting for new items to set up in the system. About two-thirds of the way through, I came across something peculiar. I double-checked. Yep, no mistake. The shipment included a King Tut bust while we still had thirty-three in inventory. And it had the same item number as those I kept finding discrepancies with during my review of the last three months of orders. Even if a customer ordered one through the store, we would just pull from the existing inventory rather than order from the vendor. It made no sense. Unless the Tut bust in the incoming shipment was another disguised artifact. Just like the nine others I discovered in the files. And like my mask.

On a hunch, I performed a search for the earliest order the shop placed with All Things Egyptian. As I read the screen, my head buzzed, and throat tightened. Three years ago, it received the first order, right around the time Thornburn opened his gallery. This appeared to be the missing link to the entire scheme.

The store phone's three-tone electronic ring chirped. "Good evening, Dauphin Museum Gift Shop." My tone was sickeningly pleasant. "This is Sara. How may I help you?"

A deep gravelly voice burst from the receiver. "May I speak to a...Dr. Roger Gwynne?"

"Let me see if he's still here." I put the caller on hold and punched in Roger's extension. His phone was busy. "I'm sorry, but he's on the phone. Can I put you to his voicemail?"

"Nah. Need to make sure he gets the message."

"I can take it for you and give it to Dr. Gwynne when he gets off the phone. Is that okay?" The sugary sweet taste was still in my voice. Made me want to vom.

"I s'pose. This is Frank Kranzer calling. I'm the Superintendent of General Cargo/Intermodal at the Alabama State Port Authority in Mobile."

I scribbled furiously on a pad. "Frank—"

"Kranzer. With a K."

"Got it. And you're with the Mobile Port Authority."

"Yeah. I'm the Superintendent of General Cargo/Intermodal," he repeated before spelling out Intermodal.

"Okay. And the message?" My writing hand was cramping up. 'Ole Frank better be quick.

"A shipping container from the Port of Alexandria done come through pier six. Late today customs impounded it. Had a large shipment in there for this doc fella."

"Impounded?"

"Yeah. The container," came the clipped reply.

"For what?"

"Dunno, ma'am. All's I know, it's impounded. ICE inspectors gonna be goin' over it. Probably just a paperwork thing. One little error can gum up the whole works."

"ICE? Can you tell me—"

"Immigration and Customs Enforcement."

"Yes, sir. Do you know when the shipment will be released? I'm sure Dr. Gwynne will want to know."

"Y'all should get your shipment soon. Once they finish processing the container. She's a forty-footer. Got multiple shipments. Yours is probably fine. When they find somethin' wrong with one shipment, they hold up the whole thing. Just have the doc call me if he has any questions."

"Okay. Your phone number is…"

Frankie-boy snapped off the number in rapid fire. He undoubtedly had enough of this conversation. "Okay?"

"Got it. Can I read it back, please?"

"Sure," he grumbled.

What a grump. Didn't he know if he just talked slow the first time, we wouldn't be at this juncture in our relationship? I read back the number.

"Correct."

"Great. I'll give him the message," I said with faux pleasantness.

"Thank you. Have a—nice—day," muttered a less than enthused Kranzer.

"Tha—"

Click.

I called Roger's extension again.

"Dr. Gwynne speaking."

"Sir, this is Sara Donovan. I have a message for you from Frank Kranzer of—" I deciphered my scrawl. "—General Cargo/Intermodal at the Alabama State Port Authority in Mobile."

"Who? I don't know any Frank Kranzer."

"He's the general superintendent there. He said customs impounded a container yesterday from the Port of Alexandria. It included a large shipment addressed to you."

Roger sucked in his breath. "Bloody hell. Give me his damn number."

Chapter Twenty

Hot coffee

The next morning, my jangling phone rudely jarred me into semi-consciousness. Better still, rain unapologetically pelted the side of the cottage. Between wearing no glasses or contacts and having only one eye cracked open, I couldn't read the clock too well. My right thumb and forefinger pried open the offended eye, and reality came into focus.

Awesome.

I was awake at six-thirty on a rainy Thursday morning. And no ROTC boys were scheduled for today. I laid there, my cheek jammed into the pillow. Mauzzy sitting on my head, doing the jamming.

The phone sounded again, impolitely reminding me I had a text to check. A blind hand searched and found it in a perilous position, hanging well over the edge of the tray table. I read the display.

—ALERT from the Egyptology Department. Due to a family emergency, all remaining CL201 recitation classes are canceled—

All remaining recitations canceled? Family emergency? I turned to Mauzzy, lounging on my pillow. "Mauz, I smell something."

He slid off the pillow and buried his head under the covers.

"I know it's not you," I said with a chuckle. "I meant something is suspicious."

Handsome emerged from the covers, yawned, licked his lips, and cracked into a smile. For once it was not...

A disturbing mosaic of recent events burst in my head.

Thornburn thinks I figured out their scheme and took the last artifact package for myself, knowing they couldn't say anything. Like dirty cops robbing drug dealers. It would explain why Mrs. Bagley acted strange at the gift shop, pretending not to know anything about the mask. And why Karen lied to Edna last week about Mrs. Bagley being upset. She did that to manipulate her into calling me and doing their dirty work by flushing me out. And now they planted Connor to watch me. Everything was coming together, but I needed hard proof before I went to the police. Not just vendor order histories and other stuff the perps could explain away. I was getting close, but this time I needed to make sure. No more embarrassing law enforcement incidents.

Since I already had my last recitation class for the semester, the text itself didn't impact me. But it got me thinking. My only class for the day was GBA380. In fact, it was my last class of the semester. I hit on a plan of action. I needed to get aggressive and take the fight to them before they formed a strategy and came after me in a big way. It sounded crazy, but something told me Mrs. Majelski possessed special skills. And I planned on tapping into those skills. I decided to give her the mask for safekeeping and ask her to watch my back, because I was putting the professor and Connor under surveillance. If I was right, and they belonged to a smuggling ring, they might make a mistake trying to adjust to their most recent shipment being part of an impounded container. I couldn't do anything about Mrs. Bagley because I had no clue where she lived or worked, and I was so not asking Zoe. Besides, if I got caught creeping around outside her school, they might think I was some kind of perv. And Karen was working today, so I couldn't watch her. But with those two, I had places to start. And it would be easier following them than sitting outside the gallery waiting for something to happen.

"C'mon, Handsome. You're not gonna like it outside, but Mommy's got work to do." I dragged my very unwilling roommate out from under the covers and hauled him downstairs. With umbrella in hand, out into the elements we schlepped. Me in pink princess pajamas. A bitching Mauzzy under my arm.

After five minutes of standing in the mulch, he refused to budge. All four of his stubby legs became pillars of concrete. Torrents of rain rode the blowing wind straight under the umbrella until we were getting wet.

"Sweet Handsome. Lift a leg. You don't even have to cop a squat. But I know you have to pee, so do it." A sudden gust of wind accosted the battered umbrella and almost knocked me over into the dogged dachshund. "Dude, we're not going inside until you do the deed. You're gonna keep getting wetter until you do."

He wore the most miserable, pitiful, downtrodden mug ever, begging me to go inside.

"Nope. Not 'til you pee, mister."

A door closed behind me. Connor ran off his front

steps and headed toward his car. A small overnight bag was slung over his shoulder, and he was carrying a shiny metal briefcase.

"Hey, Connor," I shouted over the storm. "Everything all right?"

He gave me a quick wave. "All good. Just gotta go out of town for a few days," he yelled. He chucked his things in the back of the car, jumped in the driver's seat, and in seconds was out onto the street.

Mauzzy put it all together and lifted his leg on a small oak tree.

"Out of town?" I said to the relieved dachshund. "Interesting. Mobile, perhaps?"

****

I slumped low in the parked hatchback facing toward the front of the Margaret Drive faculty lot, which was the closest to Garland Hall. I confirmed the professor was in his office by prank calling him there three hours ago. Since then I've eaten two packs of crackers, a granola bar, and I just finished pouring a third cup of coffee from my thermos, the latter of which contributed to the fact I had to go. Bad. And the rain outside wasn't helping things any. How did detectives pee when on a stakeout? I peered into the thermos and shuddered.

Just then a man, shielded by a crimson and white golf umbrella, rambled into the lot and down the first row of cars. I slid further into the seat.

"*Crap.*"

Coffee spilled all over my chest. But it didn't burn. Ah, right. I had a rain jacket on. That was luc...crap...coffee was streaming down the yellow slicker—onto my pants. It was a quality thermos because—*hot coffee*. My back arched as I jolted up in the seat, trying to lessen the heat in my pants, and not the good heat. I scrambled for tissues from the passenger seat to sop up the hot liquid searing my inner thigh and crotch. Soon I got the fire extinguished. The lone overt sign of the conflagration once raging in my jeans was a wet spot that could prove embarrassing if I had to exit the car. And a handful of disintegrating wet tissues scattered over the floorboard.

Fortunately, during my firefighting escapade, the target had not exited the lot. In the passenger's side mirror, a light bronze-colored sedan crept toward the exit from the rear of the lot. A head of frizzy hair sat behind the wheel. I sank back down in the seat, mindful of the remaining *hot* coffee in the travel mug now secured in the cup holder.

The car glided past and turned right onto Margaret Drive. I started up the hatchback and slipped out of the lot, staying several cars back, just like on *The Mysteries of Chance*.

When we got to McFarland, I fell in behind a minivan full of rioting children and I'm sure an under-caffeinated mom. We were heading toward I-59. If he was also off to Mobile, I couldn't follow him all the way. I had Mauzzy at home and an employer recruiting event in the evening. It wasn't urgent I attend since I was only a freshman, but my advisor suggested I build early relationships with corporate recruiters to be ahead of the game when it counted. So, Zoe and I were going, and heaven forbid if I stood her up.

We hit the I-59 interchange. He wasn't heading south to Mobile, but north toward Birmingham. It all fit. Kranzer's call alerted the ring that customs impounded their shipment. It explained why Connor left in such a hurry. He was definitely driving to Mobile. Probably to bribe someone to release the container. And the professor was off to meet with Thornburn and Roger to plot their next step. They were smart staying off their phones.

I followed the puttering sedan for forty minutes until it drifted into the parking lot of—the Dauphin. I knew it. Everything led back to the museum.

The rain mercifully stopped as I crawled into a parking spot several aisles away and observed the target get out of his car and scan the parking lot. He made a brief call, I'm sure on a burner, and took off toward the Dauphin. When he hit the first steps leading up to the entrance doors, I ducked out of the car and picked my way toward the building.

The target was about to disappear inside, but I was still tiptoeing between parked cars. I broke into a trot, dodging side mirrors and bumpers like an out-of-control belly dancer.

Splash.

But I didn't dodge that fricking puddle.

I hurtled forward. My knees and inner thighs were wet, and water seeping inside my shoes made for a nice squishy sound as I approached the marble steps. At least it camouflaged my embarrassing wet spot.

I bounded up the steps two at a time. How in the heck was this possible? Until now, I could never take two steps at a time. This was an invitation for disaster. My instincts blared at pumping legs to slow the heck down and go one step at a time. But my legs hijacked things and cut off all communications with my horrified brain. An internal battle raged as my weightless body flew up the wet steps. *Screw you brain. We're at the summit*, roared my legs. Adrenaline was my friend. My comrade. My partner. A foot landed on the top step and—shot out from under me. "Aaagh."

And now I had a fun fact for future reference. Marble floors and steps get crazy slippery when wet.

"Hey there." Something caught me around the shoulders as I reeled sideways. "I gotcha. I gotcha." It was Hank, the security guard. "I seen ya runnin' through the parking lot and figgered somethin' was all cattywampus. You okay?" He steadied me and released his arms from around my shoulders.

"I'm...fine," I said, panting like a Siberian husky in August. I would give anything for a hit of oxygen right about now. "Thanks...Hank. Do you know...where Professor Sawalha...went? I need...I need...to talk with him."

"Older feller? Crazy hair and glasses?"

I nodded several times, gulping down air.

"Doc Mitchell was waitin' when he got through them doors." He hooked a thumb over his shoulder toward the front entrance. "Dunno where they went, though. Maybe upstairs to her office."

I sucked in deep and blew out a cleansing breath. "Dr. Mitchell? Are you sure?"

"Sure as rain."

"It wasn't Dr. Gwynne or maybe a short, sturdy blonde lady?"

Hank scratched his cheek with a knobby index finger. "Sure you okay? 'Cause purdy sure I know what the Doc looks like. Been workin' here goin' on twenty-one years. Quite a ways before she got here." He bobbed his head up and down. "It was her, Sara. Bet my life on it." Alarm surged into the old man's worn face. "Why? Who's this other gal? We got a security problem?"

I hesitated before shaking my head. "No, no. There's no problem. I just thought the professor told me he was meeting with someone else. That's all. It's nothing re—"

A shrill shriek cut through the air. "What are you doing here?"

Over the security guard's shoulder, I spied Karen flying toward me with nostrils flaring.

"Oh. Hi, Karen." I attempted to act casual with a little wave of my hand. From the flinty eyes and glower on her narrow face, it wasn't working. Probably because I was standing with the security guard, resembling a drowned llama.

She stopped right in front of me, obliterating my personal space.

Hank raised his hands to shoulder level, palms out, and backed up two steps. "So long's everything's okay, I'll leave y'all gals be."

I nodded slightly to him. "Everything's fine. Thanks for saving me."

He smiled briefly, gave a quick tip of his cap, reversed direction, and hobbled back to his post at the main doors.

Karen's head swiveled back toward me. Her cast-iron eyes were popping out of her head. "It's Thursday. You're not supposed to be here."

She was no Miss Congeniality, but her reaction seeing me here signaled something was definitely up. No way I could tell her I was following the professor. I took a step back. I had to think fast. "Um, yes…but…I had some free time. I thought I could pop in and, you know, help with getting ready for inventory."

"Inventory isn't until the end of next month." She scrutinized me. "And why wouldn't you just call ahead to ask if we needed help? Driving forty minutes from Tuscaloosa isn't just popping in."

"It is if I was in the area seeing a friend."

"Well, you're not needed today." Without waiting for a response, she wheeled around and stormed back toward the museum.

This inquisition was over the top, even for Karen. What the hell did I do to get her all fired up? Unless...the professor made me tailing him. And he called her from the parking lot to get outside and run interference while he was meeting with...

Now I got it. Things were getting out of control. I needed to get with Mrs. Majelski. Fast.

Chapter Twenty-One

Looking fierce

After getting home from the employer recruiting event, the prudent thing for me to do was an online practice scenario to get ready for that dang GBA380 final. Instead, I was in front of the laptop working on my right eyebrow raise. For the last thirty minutes, I've stared in the mirror, then at the laptop, then fast back at the mirror, trying to look fierce. I needed a killer sneer like Zoe's, one I could summon on demand. Who knew why? I guess it was more important to have a ferocious scowl in my facial repertoire than passing GBA380 and keeping my GPA above three-five. This happened to be one of those moments Dad forever harped about regarding some of the "choices" I made. His deep voice resounded in my head as I worked that right eyebrow. Up. Down. Up and hold.

Sara, life is all about recognizing opportunities and making smart choices. And sometimes your choices can be questionable. Remember, the heart doesn't always make the right decisions.

Down. Now, up quick. Hold and narrow the eyes. I was nailing it.

My phone erupted in sound and vibrations, almost causing me to have an accident. I should have gone ten minutes ago, but I was too close to success to tear myself away from the mirror. I knew the ringtone. "Hi, Mom."

"Hi, honey. How did things go at Career Day? I thought about you all day and just had to call." There was even more excitement in her voice than usual.

"Great, other than feeling like a cheap hooker working a long night on the boulevard."

"*Sara.*"

"Sorry. But you know, high heels, short skirt, working hard to get noticed. I felt like—"

"Yes, you told me."

"Okay, well, it was just super crazy. There were lots of companies, and I swear half the university attended the thing."

"I know you don't like crowds. How did you do?"

I screwed my face up and looked sideways at Mauzzy. He blinked at me with disinterest and resumed licking himself. "Fine." I blew out. "And crowds don't bother me. Like I've told you and half of Maryland a thousand times, I was cheering on the team, not having an anxiety attack or seizure or whatever the paramedics said."

Boy, you freak out one time at a high school football game and nobody lets you forget it. Ever. I was only trying to show the pep band I was into it and supporting the team. When they played our fight song, I put my knitting down, stood, and let it rip. Obviously, it didn't have the effect intended when I started my festive gyrations. And ever since, I've been trying to convince Mom and others I'm cool with crowds. Okay, I hate crowds. But not because of that stupid game.

"Of course, sweetheart." Her tone sounded like a hostage negotiator trying not to rattle the perp. "Any leads?"

"I have three companies who want me to stay in touch," I said proudly.

"*Really?*"

Geez, she didn't have to sound so surprised. "H&L Bank, Masterson Financial, and Birmingham Life and Casualty."

"I've heard of Masterson. They're huge. Are the other two regional?"

"Yep, but the H&L recruiter said they planned to expand into the mid-Atlantic region, which would be great. Although, I'm not sure I want to go into banking. To me, it's just one step above retail."

Outside, multiple sirens wailed and grew louder as they approached the complex.

"That depends on what you're doing for the bank."

I stepped outside and surveyed the parking lot. Just in case. "True, but eventually it's still just glorified retail." A beat. "But hey, if they're the only one to offer me a job in three years, I'll take it."

All clear. I stepped back inside and threw the deadbolt.

"We all have to start somewhere. What else have you done today?"

I told her all about the recitation cancellations, Connor leaving for Mobile, and my decision to follow the professor.

"Sara, you need to concentrate on school." Her voice of seriousness drifted into the ether. "Finals are next week."

My stomach tightened. If I don't pass GBA380, my GPA gets dunked in the toilet. Along with my future at 'Bama. And true to form, that unholy GBA380 final sat in the last exam slot. Nothing like putting off your inevitable execution until the last minute. Anxiety wormed its merry way up my spine.

"—is nothing." Mom's voice descended from the ozone dressed as a civics lesson. "This is why we have the authorities. To serve and protect. It—"

My brain bugged out for a short walkabout, only to return to a commercial lead-in for a cop show?

"—sounds like these ICE people have it well in hand. That's their job. I'm sure they don't need help from a college student. Especially one who should be studying."

"But I'm not so sure they know what they're doing. This guy at the port sounded like he couldn't care less."

"Sara, you need—"

"I'm sure Connor is part of it," I spat out. "He lied to me and carries a gun. My neighbor is part of an international smuggling ring. What if—"

"*No more.*"

"What?"

"No. More. Following. People. Enough, okay?"

I nodded in obedience. Mom's superpowers enveloped the room, her magical hazel eyes locking on my pouting face from eight hundred miles away even as she continued her lecture. It took a lot to get her up in my grill. She sounded serious.

"I'm sure nothing's there, but if you're really concerned or notice something suspicious with this Connor, call the police and report it. But no more surveillance. Got it?"

"Got it," I grumbled.

"It's for your own good. And safety. Now I'll let you go study. I love you."

"Bye," I mumbled and ended the call.

I love Mom, but based on my track record reporting on neighbors, no way I was calling the cops. Until I had something concrete.

I returned to the mirror and laptop. Up. Down. Up and hold. Sneer.

Chapter Twenty-Two

Mums the word

It was a few minutes past six the next morning. Heavy air signaled an impending storm, and the only light spilling out came from the Student Recreation Center lobby behind me. It killed me sitting on the outside steps waiting for Mrs. Majelski to show up. The ROTC boys were in full swing, but I needed to talk with her. When I called last night, she said, *"No phones, dear. I'll find you,"* and hung up. I wanted to make things easy on the old lady, so I got here early to wait for her.

A huge pickup truck roared into the back of the parking lot and zipped into a space. Even in the darkness, its presence towered above the other vehicles.

Five minutes later, diminutive Mrs. Majelski rolled up to me, her walker scratching at the pavement with each little step she took. "Good morning, dear. I suppose you're waiting for me?" She tossed her gaze around, stopping to probe the dark expanse of the parking lot. A gentle breeze picked up, the wind attacking her soft white curls.

"Good morning. As a matter of fact, I am. I would—"

The Eighth Wonder of the World stuck a hand out. "Not here. Come with me." She pivoted the walker and rolled off toward the parking lot.

I bolted off the step and took after her. She must have turbochargers on that damn walker because the lady was making tracks. At that speed, she stood a good chance of shredding the tennis balls on the walker's rear legs. As I caught up to the galloping geriatric, a few raindrops fell.

Without breaking stride, she scanned the heavens. A flash of lightning illuminated her sweet, wizened face, followed by a low rumble. "Gotta go, dear."

Before I could process her comment, a streak of white rocketed across the tarmac, a folded walker tucked under her arm. I stood in the jet wash, mouth agape. Mrs. Majelski was—running. And not Sara-running. The old lady was sprinting.

Her voice called back, "To the truck, dear."

I lowered my head and chased after the fast fading voice. Seconds later, the skies opened, and cold rain pummeled the parked vehicles, the sound deafening. Toward the rear of the lot, a slamming car door rose above the cacophony and an unmuffled engine exploded to life.

As sheets of rain and walls of water cascaded down my face, a jacked-up pickup shot backward into the aisle. The unlit behemoth swung around, leaped forward, and barreled down on me, huge tires splashing through fast-forming puddles. Within seconds the truck skid to a stop, its massive bull bars eye level with me. The driver-side window cracked open, and a sturdy voice yelled, "Climb in."

I dashed around the hood to the passenger side, lunged upward, and wrenched open the door. Gripping the chrome grab handle with my left hand and bracing the right on the inside of the open door, I hauled my waterlogged body up and into the cab. Rain poured in as I clutched the door and yanked it closed.

My heavy panting made me sound like an enthusiastic pregnant woman in Lamaze class. Struggling to catch my breath, I lowered my head, scraping and clawing soaked hair off and out of my face. My pink Fitness Princess t-shirt had become a bodysuit three sizes too small. And so much water poured off me onto the leather seat and floorboard, I felt like the Wicked Witch of the West, melting into a gross puddle of—me. I took another big gulp of air, then blew it out.

"Quite a sudden downpour, isn't it, dear?" Sporting a broad smile sat a dry Mrs. Majelski, not a hair out of place on her gleaming white head. No heavy breathing. A picture of calm. Behind her rested a double-barreled shotgun in a black two-gun rack.

"You...you can..." Another snatch of air. "...Run?"

"I may be old, but I'm not an invalid."

"But at the gym, you—"

She waved a dismissive hand. "Pish posh. That's all just part of my cover."

My breathing and heart rate were calming down, but my mind was racing. "Cover? Are you—"

"Let's get to your car."

She gunned the truck, and we charged toward the front of the lot nearest the rec center. At the top of the aisle she casually turned the wheel while giving me a cheerful wink, the truck tearing around parked cars and blasting into the next aisle. As we neared the end of it, the truck skid to a stop right behind my hatchback. And the downpour—stopped. Completely. I faced the old lady. My mouth kept opening and closing, but no words came out. I did a double-take out my window. Yep, it was mine.

"Go on, dear. Go get it," she said with a pleasant smile, pointing with her head in the car's direction.

I wrestled open the cab door, clambered down, and popped the hatch. As I bent over and lifted the floorboard covering the spare tire, my gym shorts clung to me. All of me. Leaving nothing to the imagination. I was like a drenched sheepdog wearing plastic cling wrap.

Fumbling in the dark under the spare tire, my fingers grazed the mask. I grasped it, closed the hatch, and climbed back up into the cab, tugging the door closed. I handed it to Mrs. Majelski. "I don't know how you put it all together, but here."

Her sweetness disappeared, replaced by a set jaw and a curt nod. A gnarled finger explored where I melted the hole in the face. For a brief second, I caught the beginning of a crooked smile before she set her jaw again. "It will be safe with me." With the mask in her lap, her right hand activated the rear window defroster button on the dash while fiddling with the door's power window buttons using her left.

"What are you—"

"You'll see." She motioned toward my feet. "Hand me my purse."

I picked up a small black purse and passed it over.

"Thank you." She unzipped it. Removed a wallet. Slid out a—credit card? And winked at me. "Now, mum's the word. Okay?"

I might have made a big mistake. The poor old lady

was senile. She thought I was selling her an Egyptian souvenir, and I took credit cards? I didn't want to embarrass her, so I played along. "Sure, mum's the word."

"Good girl." She took the credit card and swiped it back and forth across an air-conditioning vent.

I was beyond embarrassed for her and didn't know what to say or do.

A mechanical whirring rose from the dash directly in front of me. Seconds later, the front of the airbag panel rose and tilted back, revealing a void. She inched forward in her seat, removed a large—handgun—from the dark space, placed the mask into the void, and replaced the gun. Sitting back, she swiped the credit card, and the panel closed.

My eyes widened as my mouth fell open.

With a grandmother's smile, she handed me her purse. "It's called a trap, dear. Now buckle up. We're going for a ride."

I was searching for the seatbelt when my head slammed into the headrest, my body flattened into the seat like a fighter pilot pulling nine G's. With cheeks plastered to the side of my face, I fought to get words out. "Where…are…we…going?"

"Around. I need to take care of some dry cleaning while we talk."

The monster truck careened onto the street, the rear fishtailing as Mrs. Majelski calmly guided the beast out of the turn. The engine responded as she hammered the accelerator to the floor, the outside scenery becoming one long blur.

I gave the cab a quick once-over. "I don't see any clothes. Are you picking stuff up?"

The old lady chuckled to herself but said nothing.

For ten minutes we drove in silence, the only sounds being the engine's roar, her foot slamming the gas pedal to the floor, and screeching tires on wet pavement.

I had no clue where she was taking us as we ripped through places of Tuscaloosa I never saw before. And never, ever wanted to see again. "What do you want to talk to me about?"

"Why the mask." She cocked her head at me, a gleam in her eye. "What else?"

"Beats me."

Mrs. Majelski turned her attention back on the road, eyes flitting between the windshield, the rearview mirror, and both side mirrors. She spun the wheel hard to the left, and the truck tore into the turn, squashing me into the side window and door as the rear fought to regain traction. "Other than your little friend, have you told anybody else about it?"

"Just my mom. And Mauzzy."

"Your little dog?"

"Uh-huh."

"I'm not worried about him."

"Ha. You don't know Mauz."

She cackled. "You're cute. That's why I like you."

A hard right sent the truck sliding sideways around a corner and me grabbing for the handle above the door. "You think...it's real?" I asked, gasping for air as she smashed the accelerator coming out of the turn, my torso compressing into the seat.

"Someone does. What's important is, you shouldn't tell anybody else." Her eyes were steel-gray hard.

"Not even the police?"

She stuck out a cautioning finger as she handled the wheel with her left palm. "Especially not the cops."

"Even if I have the evidence to prove what's going on?"

"You need to understand one thing, and never forget it. That mask is your leverage. Against everybody and anything." She faced me as we hurtled along the dark, wet road. Not a car was in sight. "Foremost, the cops." She glared at me. "Understand?"

"Yes, ma'am."

"If things go bad, you're protected so long as nobody knows I have it. Got it?"

"Uh-huh."

"That's a good girl." Her grandmotherly smile returned as she held up yet another cautioning finger. "Remember, dear. Mum's the word."

Who in the frick was this lady?

Chapter Twenty-Three

Fiona

After riding around with Mrs. Majelski this morning to places that made Sketchville look like ritzy uptown living, I ran out of time to pack a lunch. Now halfway through a sixty-four-ounce cup of soda, it was painfully obvious I should have eaten more than just instant oatmeal for breakfast. An ongoing debate raged between brain and stomach, the latter's objections making a solid argument for ditching my plan and heading straight to the food court for a veggie sub. As if on cue, my stomach registered such a loud complaint I swore it would give away my position from behind a clothes rack just inside the Flossie's Fashions store.

When I straggled home wet and bewildered from my joyride, Connor had returned from his trip to Mobile. And all day he's acted strange and suspicious. In fact, strangely suspicious. He didn't even acknowledge me when I was outside with Mauzzy channeling my inner stalker and he rushed past us to his car. I ended up following him all over the area, and halfway to Birmingham and back. His driving was erratic, but he proceeded with a purpose whenever he got out of the car. Including marching into a Doctor Mike's Sandwich Shoppe before heading straight to the shopping mall. Of course, stopping for a killer sandwich made perfect sense. I get that. But leaving there with a bag of food and going to the mall without eating anything along the way? So suspicious. I mean, it's Doctor Mike's.

I poked my head around the rack. Connor meandered about near the escalator with the still full bag of food. Mmmm, I could almost smell it. I took a deep swig of soda, hoping to silence my traitorous stomach.

"Hey, Fiona," I whispered into my phone. "Take a note."

"*I'm sorry. I don't know what you want.*"

I hissed. "Fiona, take a note."

"*I'm sorry, I can't find that. Do you want me to search the Web?*"

"Fiona, you *bitch*. Take a frigging *note.*"

Whoops. Probs shouldn't have done that. I took a gander around. Open mouths and wide eyes stared back. Connor stopped, his eyes searching in my direction.

I crouched back behind the clothes rack.

"*I can do that for you,*" Fiona chimed. "*Ready when you are.*"

Fiona. I swear that electronic skank enjoyed fricking with me. In a soft voice, I spoke into the phone. "One twenty-two. Subject is in central mall area holding Doctor Mike's bag still full of delicious food." I snuck a peek, keeping my head low. "He's looking all around. Now moseying to a trash can. He…what the…just threw out the bag of food and is strolling away. He never ate the—"

"*Here's what your note says.*"

"*Fiona.* I'm not done. I sai—"

An official sounding male voice boomed from behind me. "Ma'am?"

For an instant I was back dealing with the air marshal on a plane heading home for Spring Break.

"*Ma'am*, can I help you?"

With the sudden onslaught of authority blasting my senses, I jolted upward and fell into the rack of cute blouses. My hand lost its grip on the huge cup. The other hand instinctively shot out to catch the falling soda, at the same time ejecting my phone deep into clothes-rack oblivion. An unhealthy, protracted clatter indicated the landing didn't go too well. I caught my balance halfway into the colorful summer collection of what appeared to be very fun tops. At least I saved the soda from making me the proud owner of a complete summer collection of stained fashion wear.

I nonchalantly edged my body around, fighting off multiple tendrils of fabric clutching and grabbing at my head and shoulders. I popped my head out of the blouses, and after clearing disheveled hair from my eyes, was confronted with the no-nonsense visage of—a mall cop. On a motorized two-wheeled scooter.

From within my inner sanctum of the clothes rack, I laid on him all the cool innocence and southern sweetness I could muster. "No, but thank you for asking. Everything is okay, officer."

Marty the Mall Cop maneuvered his scooter like a cowboy getting control of a skittish horse. He dismounted, stood straight, and drew his shoulders back. Puffing his chest up, he pointed to a spot on the floor. "Ma'am, can you please…step out of the clothes?"

What a snippy attitude. His mall cop academy

training must be kicking in, which I'm sure only included two hours of orientation and a three-sizes-fits-all uniform fitting. They needed to add a few more sizes because his was at least two sizes too small, which with his body type and protruding belly was regrettable for all the patrons.

"Ma'am," he barked.

And impatient.

"Um, sure." I took one cautious step out from under the rack, working to disentangle myself as I emerged. "Ohhhhhh." My left foot caught the rack's lower frame, pitching me out of the textile tentacles and headlong into The Man. Well, the mall's version of The Man.

Marty caught the full force of me and lurched back toward a table of neatly stacked shirts. While I propelled him across the floor, the soda cup lid popped off and liquid shot out, as if my squeezing the living crap out of a soda cup could break our fall and save the day. Instead, I ended up in the soaked chest of Marty, who was bent backward onto the table. His protruding belly felt like an underinflated beach ball beneath my sprawled midsection. Shirts littered the floor. Only a few blue work shirts at the end opposite us remained on the table, right next to a sign reading, "No Food or Drink."

Behind me, a familiar voice chimed. *"I'm sorry, I can't find that. Do you want me to search the Web?"*

Chapter Twenty-Four

Officer Smirk

Pacing the floor of my cottage, which made for a lot of back and forth, I reassessed the day's strange events. As much as the heart said a reasonable explanation could be found to justify Connor's recent activities, the head overrode that emotional response and took control of the situation. He was knee-deep in it. No doubt about it. All day his actions were erratic and suspicious, with the final act of criminality being throwing a bag of food away. Without eating anything. It made no sense. Especially not a Doctor Mike's gourmet sandwich.

That bag contained something other than food, and he left it for someone in the trash can. I think it's called a dead drop. But what? An ancient statuette? Cash? A message? A veggie sub? Please, no. I hope he didn't ditch a veggie sub. That would be beyond criminal, bordering on—well—something you just didn't do. What was that—

"Mauzzy. Stop. Stop. Stop. I get it. Your butt's uncomfortable." I let out a loud, and perhaps overdramatic, huff. "Now I'm gonna have to wet-mop that spot."

He stopped and stared at me, appalled, as if I was the one caught licking my butt and dragging it across the floor.

"You heard me, mister."

Without saying a word, he stood, pointed his butt at me, and padded over to the couch. After deep contemplation, he launched up onto the cushions. Another minute of spinning, fluffing, and pawing at the upholstery, and His Highness Sweet Handsome nestled into just the right spot.

"You finished?" I asked in an annoyed tone.

I've been on edge all evening. I was about to call the police, something that could have some grave repercussions. Despite mixed emotions, I couldn't sit idly by and do nothing. And Mom kinda sorta suggested it. Since our conversation yesterday, I kept giving things a good long think, and always reached the same conclusion. Maybe she was right. As usual.

I pictured the mask in Mrs. Majelski's truck trap. The trick was saying just enough to get them to act, but not too much. Otherwise, it could sink me before everything got resolved. She stressed to me the mask was my leverage if things deteriorated. And I believed her. She had no reason to lie.

I sat at the table and took out my phone. Before I could tap in the numbers, Mauzzy whined and put on his very best "woe is me" pitiful act. "Really? Me letting you sit on the couch all by yourself isn't enough of a treat?"

More complaining and pitter-pattering of his front paws.

"Let Mommy make this one very important call. Then I'll give you my undivided attention. Five minutes. Okay?"

He licked his lips and settled back on the couch. If

I could have gotten inside that adorable little head with the knitted brows, I'm certain I would have seen him start the timer on me.

After a deep cleansing breath, I put in the numbers and waited.

A lady answered. "Nine-one-one dispatch. State your name and emergency please."

"Uh, this is Sara Donovan. It's not so much of an emergency, per se, as a very serious situation?"

"Ma'am, this line is for real emergencies only," the headless lady said firmly but professionally.

"But this is serious."

"Are you in danger or hurt?"

"Um, I guess not. But I believe there's criminal activity going on next door."

"Are any lives or property at risk?"

"Yes, well—"

"Is someone in danger?"

"No, but—"

"Ma'am, you're taking up a line dedicated to emergencies. Are any people's lives or property at risk? Or is anybody hurt?"

"Not that I know of." This wasn't going as I imagined.

"Then please hang up. Call only if there's a real emergency. One in which you are in danger or there's a serious risk to lives or property. If there's some other non-emergency problem, please call the local station." A strong tone of rebuke permeated her voice.

"But I think there's a crime going on here."

"Okay," said the unconvinced dispatcher. "I'll send an officer to your location to talk with you and take a statement. That's all I can do right now. GPS is showing you at Cypress Cottages, Number Five. Is this correct?"

"Yes," I said in astonishment.

"A unit will be there in ten minutes. Please hang up and stay at your location."

"Yes, ma'am. Thank you."

I ended the call, trudged over to the couch, and plopped down. A loving Sweet Handsome crawled over and nuzzled into my lap. Not even ten minutes passed when a loud knock on the door rattled the cottage. Putting a displeased Mauzzy to the side, I hauled myself up and peeked out the window. A police officer towered outside the front door.

Cracking open the door, I asked in a subdued voice, "Yes, officer?"

"Sara Donovan?"

"Yes, sir."

"I'm Officer Preater. Nine-one-one dispatch asked me to check things out. You called to report some criminal activity?"

I swallowed hard. "Yes, sir."

Officer Preater cast around the deck before leaning to see past me into the cottage. He straightened and set his feet apart. "Nothing appears suspicious, ma'am."

Really? Nothing suspicious in Sketchville? He obviously didn't check out the places behind the weed-propped fence. Something told me this wasn't the best idea.

"Not here. It's my next-door neighbor. Connor Reed. I believe he's part of a criminal ring along with Professor Sawalha, Henderson Thornburn, and Dr. Roger Gwynne. I've been—"

"Hold on, ma'am," interjected the officer, holding

up his hand. "You believe?"

I cleared my throat, buying a few seconds to collect myself. "Yes, sir. I believe my professor, my neigh—"

"Are you trying to file a police report on one of your professors?"

"That's right. And my TA. He's the neighbor. Dr. Gwynne is a director at the Dauphin Museum, and Thornburn was a former curator there." Even as the words escaped, I envisioned myself throwing shovelfuls of dirt out of an ever-deepening hole. And the more I did, the worse it got.

"I understand," he said with a knowing, almost disapproving, smile. "I bet finals are just around the corner. Ma'am, filing a false police report is a serious matter."

Perspiration flowed. "No. No. It's not like that. There's something going on. I've been following them and—"

"Hold on. Stop right there. Those actions sound like stalking."

Crap. There went another shovelful. One foot deeper. At this rate, I expected to be in Beijing soon.

"I'm not a stalker." Past images of me standing in the parking lot surveilling Connor's cottage, channeling my inner stalker, flooded my now very much freaking out mind. *Yes, I'll have an order of noodles, Moo Goo Gai Pan, shrimp fried rice, and two egg rolls.*

I was deep enough into it with the officer, so no stopping now. "Please. Just listen to me. I don't have firm proof, but I took a call Wednesday from the Port of Mobile that an impounded container included a shipment for the museum. And the next morning, Connor went out of town to Mobile. And the professor drove straight to the Dauphin. Oh, and Karen stopped me from going into the—"

"Who's Karen?"

"Karen Allen. She works in the gift shop, and she—"

"Okay. Okay. Just calm down. You sound very—"

"Passionate?"

"—certain about what you have seen. Although it's not a great idea to report your professor and TA to the police based on a hunch."

"Please, officer. I know it seems crazy, but there's definitely something going on."

Zoe's earlier reproach banged around somewhere in the back of my reeling head. *Every time you act on one of these feelings, you end up being wrong and create real problems for yourself. Real problems.*

Okay, so this might not have been one of my better ideas. But it wasn't some mirage or distorted reality I imagined. I was right.

Officer Preater studied me. I made out what appeared to be a slight, ever so slight, softening in his stern face.

"Sir, I'm not some whacko, nutjob stalker. Do you really think I'd call the police on my professor if I was stalking him?" A smiling, white-haired apparition burst into my head. "Wait. I know your aunt. Mrs. Majelski. I just saw her this morning. She'll vouch for me."

Officer Preater remained silent for a moment before exhaling his surrender. "My Aunt Sadie...well, she's definitely got her methods. Tell you what I'm gonna do. I'll make a report. If anything pops up later, we'll have your statement, and we can follow up with you. That's the best I can do based on what I'm hearing, despite Aunt Sadie. But I also gotta tell you. This is Tuscaloosa." He snorted. "We just don't have criminal rings here. Let alone syndicates comprising professors, teachers, and museum directors."

The guy sounded like Zoe with a gun, bulletproof vest, and a badge. Yikes. If she had those things, that would be scary. Oh, yeah. Beyond scary.

"I guess that will be fine if that's all you're able to do."

"It is. And frankly, I shouldn't even be doing this." He was smirking.

Aunt Sadie?

Chapter Twenty-Five

Newton's Third Law of Motion

It's been twenty-four hours since Officer Smirk took my report, and nothing from the police. Not a surprise, considering his attitude. And Connor was still just as nice to me when I took Mauzzy out this morning. It's such a shame someone so dorky hot and enthralled with my curves got caught up in the seedy Tuscaloosa underworld of art smuggling.

Wow. That sounded crazy. Could Zoe be right?

Or did their nefarious plan take this craziness into account? Nobody would ever tie a sophisticated art smuggling ring to Tuscaloosa. It was brilliant. And it would so be something Thornburn and his highly educated crew might cook up.

It was seven-thirty Saturday evening, and I was driving to the Dauphin for the black-tie silent auction. Because I didn't do well by myself in highfalutin social settings, I attempted to recruit Zoe as my date. I didn't get too far with her. Once she finished laughing hysterically, she yelled, "Are you fucking kidding me?" followed by more howling. None of my other friends wanted to go either, meaning I was going stag. Or was it doe? Or hind? Okay, that just sounds wrong.

After my little tête-à-tête yesterday with Marty the Mall Cop, which ended with me dodging eviction from the mall, I stuck around and shopped for tonight's outfit. I settled on a sassy little just-above-the-knee black cocktail dress with a bit of V-neck action for the Ladies. But not too much action. For fifty percent off. And with the money saved on the dress, I bought red pumps, which helped keep the legs from appearing short and stumpy because of all the curves. It's all about elongating. I topped the look off with silver earrings and a matching pendant designed to draw the eyes to the Ladies.

Not even ten minutes passed during the drive to the museum when I realized one drawback went with the outfit I purchased. One alarming drawback. The tummy tuck thing I wore to put all the curves in the right places refused to cooperate and stay up. These granny-underpants-on-crack needed to hold in the rolls—not roll down them. It was awkward enough going to a high-society cocktail party by myself. Now I had to act normal, which could be challenging enough, all the while trying to avoid breathing? I didn't need to read this contraption's operating instructions or warnings to know breathing was not an option. It was simply a function of Newton's Third Law of Motion. GBA380 may drive me away from a vaunted business degree and toward no-name college oblivion, but I could still remember high school physics. Sorta.

As Newton observed, *"When one body exerts a force on a second body, the second body simultaneously exerts a force equal in magnitude and opposite in direction to that of the first body."*

So in my particular situation, the first force was my breathing torso, with the second being the damn tummy flattening contraption. When I breathed, it rolled down, resulting in not a flat tummy but rather something more akin to a tray of sushi rolls. I wonder if Newton's wife wore a tummy tuck thing, and that's what drove him to his Third Law. Sorta like the apple and gravity thing.

Exiting the interstate, I had to decide soon because I was minutes away from the Dauphin. I spied a church on the right with an unlit empty parking lot. It hit me like one of Mauzzy's farts. I couldn't do this any longer. It just wasn't going to happen. And going solo tonight brought with it one benefit—no date to impress. Meaning no more dealing with the Tummy-Let's-Add-Another-Roll-Smoother.

I exited the road and glided into the parking lot, shutting off the headlights as the car rolled to the back of the darkened expanse. After cutting the engine, I contorted and shifted in my seat. Just gotta...*charley horse*. Pain. OMG, push through it. Yup, red pump into the door. Ouch, frigging steering wheel. Okay, almost...ah crap, crap, crap...ya...ya...holy frick, my knee. All right...c'mon baby...ah...just a bit...c'mon...aaahhh. Success.

Contraption off.

I scanned the parking lot. Nobody. Just one car parked two blocks away in front of a darkened medical office building. Mission accomplished. I stowed the rebellious underpants, started the engine, and sped out of the church lot. I was off to a posh affair full of Birmingham socialites and various wannabes. Going commando. Breezing down the road, I made a mental note to self. *Be careful when sitting. Don't let the miniskirt's little triangle of the devil betray me and make my commando secret—public.*

Since this whole sordid thing happened in a church

parking lot, did I have to fess up to Monsignor O'Brian during my next visit to the confessional? It would probably kill the old guy.

Chapter Twenty-Six

It's best to be silent at a silent auction

The museum's silent auction gala was dragging on, made even more boring by my lack of a date. A cute little perky redhead carrying a tray laden with golden champagne passed near me. I took a sip of sparkling water-and-lime as my gaze followed the tantalizing glasses of stress-busting potion around the room. I don't drink, but Mom let me have a glass of champagne last New Year's Eve after Mauzzy got excited and peed on Dad's leg as the crystal ball dropped. A very "annoyed" Dad reminded me that was precisely why I had Handsome with me in Sketchville. That glass really helped calm us. If I could just have—

A voice from behind startled me. "Sara?"

Uh-oh. I know that voice. I spotted the redhead server moving among the growing crowd of pompous wallets and checkbooks. Maybe just one glass? I twirled around and imperceptibly drew in my breath. Good thing the contraption was off because it would have rolled down in a flash. Like a cartoon character's tongue.

Standing in front of me was the most stylish, handsome man I have ever seen in my life. Debonair. Chic. Smoking. All those adjectives rolled into— mmmm, mmmm, mmmmmmm. "Wow. You clean up well, Connor." *Just breathe, Sara. The contraption is off, so breathe.*

Gone was his cute hot dorkiness. Replaced by—super-hot. The beaming hotness gazing at me, decked out in a black tuxedo—whew.

"Thanks. You look fantastic yourself."

I could only tip my head. The man had me too stunned to say anything. Or perhaps too scared to open my mouth for fear of totally fricking up this celestial moment. With me standing in a cocktail dress sans underpants. I sure could use my *Sorbet* ones right about now. With a shake of my head, I squeezed out, "Um, geez…so…what are you doing here?"

A broad smile transformed his dimples into quarter slots. "Professor Sawalha invited me. He had an extra ticket. So"—he extended his arms in a faux embrace—"here I am."

A flutter tickled my chest as a tingling warmth flooded my body. A part of me wanted to step right into those—

Officer Smirk popped into my head, the vision horrifying. Last night I called the cops on him. But he acted like he didn't know yet. Why did I feel so apprehensive?

Thud.

That was me, falling back to earth. And the reality this jaw-dropping tuxedoed guy standing in front of me was—an international criminal.

"Oh? The professor, too?" I searched over his shoulder. "He's here, too?"

Connor bobbed his head, dimples smiling away. He gestured behind me with his champagne flute. "Right over there. Why the surprise? This is a museum with

Egyptian artifacts. And he's a professor of Egyptology." He grinned even broader, if that was possible. "Kinda makes sense to me, huh?"

A short yip of embarrassment escaped from me. "I guess it's just kinda weird I'm at a cocktail party with my professor. Who I give a presentation to in just over a week from now?" With a little shrug I added, "Hey, no biggie. Just my grade for the class is riding on it."

He whispered in my ear, "Ah, c'mon. It's no big deal. He's a good guy." The man's essence was intoxicating. His warm breath caressed my ear and kick-started my heart to the point I could barely hear him over the reverberation. "Although, I wouldn't recommend you tell him about your recent activities." He straightened and winked, his blues shining beneath raised eyebrows.

My chest tightened, and ears burned. Maybe he didn't go to Mobile? Maybe he circled back to follow me, following the professor? I took a step back with a little headshake. As I did, my dress stirred ever so slightly. On my very naked butt. At that moment, I spiraled from embarrassment straight to complete and utter humiliation. *He knows I'm going commando.* Somehow, he saw my contorted activities in the church parking lot from that car outside the office building. Or he stared at my butt, thank you very much, and saw no panty lines. Or worse—both.

I opened my mouth to object when Connor said, "Shhhh, he's coming this way."

I whirled. Approaching was a thatch of frizzled gray hair sitting in secession atop a rumpled black tuxedo that enjoyed better years. Like back in the '80s, when the occupant was twenty pounds lighter. Poking out from between the two, a hooked nose and rebellious glasses.

"Hi, Professor Sawalha," I said.

His pungent cologne arrived two steps ahead of him. "Ah, Miss Donovan. What a treat to see one of my best students here. Yes, yes, my dear. What a treat, indeed."

Excuse me? One of his best students? Is that what he just said? One? Earlier in his office, he called me his best student. What's happened since then? It's only been four fricking days. Could I be slipping into the abyss of mediocrity? Or was it because during that last meeting with him I was slow on the uptake about money laundering? What a fastidious little crook.

"And my boy, I'm so delighted you came. Yes, yes. Very delighted." The old man was in his element, beaming with pride and excitement. He swept his arm around the room, the jacket sleeve riding even further up his arm, well past the shirt's cuffs. "Isn't this just a wonderful affair? Simply wonderful."

Connor nodded in appreciation. "Yes, sir. I'm very glad I came." He shot me an all-knowing smile. "Thank you for the ticket."

I burned white-hot with embarrassment. And anticipation. This breathtaking guy knew I wasn't wearing any underpants. And he was a crook. Talk about internal conflict.

The professor responded with a satisfied harrumph. "Of course. Of course. My pleasure. My pleasure." He spread his hands and tapped the fingertips in front of his face. "Are either of you planning to bid on anything?"

Connor held up a hand in mock surrender. "Nothing for me. I'm just a poor grad student here for the champagne, and"—he trained his blues on me—"the company."

A sudden buzzing filled my head, like a streetlight transformer ready to blow, as electricity surged through my prickling body. A small drop of perspiration slid along the small of my back. Not good. Moisture and electricity made for a bad combination.

"Ah, yes, yes. Struggling grad student. I remember those days," commiserated the professor with a wistful smile and several nods of wispy gray hair. "Of course, it doesn't get much better when you're on the faculty. Even with tenure. Yes, indeed, even with tenure."

I knew it. Both were poor. Motive.

Connor broke eye contact with me. "Sure makes me wonder if it's crazy chasing that doctorate."

"No, no, my boy. You need to follow your heart. Follow your passion. Things have a way of taking care of themselves. There are plenty of opportunities in our profession beyond teaching stipends. Yes, yes, plenty of opportunities." His tuxedo fought off a shrug. "You never know. Write one popular textbook or make one great discovery and..." He stopped short. "Miss Donovan, why—"

I just noticed the professor loved to talk in twos. Not just with his exclamations, like I used to think. He repeated whole phrases. *Why the heck was that in my spinning head?* I had bigger issues to worry about, like standing commando in a short tight dress in front of two art thieves. But I couldn't help myself. I revisited each time I met with him and that—a shiver ran through me—squeaking chair. And again tonight. His phrases frequently came in twos.

"Miss Donovan?"

"Yes?" I attempted to sound casual as it became apparent he had been talking to me the entire time. Right now, the least of my concerns should be wearing no underpants. "Um, I'm sorry. I didn't quite get that. It's hard for me to hear in big rooms when there's a lot of background noise."

The professor let out a subdued chuckle. "Yes, yes. I certainly can sympathize with you, my dear. Certainly sympathize. Of course"—he leaned toward me. Wisps of disobedient hair clutched at me while his cologne conducted a close-quarter assault on my tear ducts—"it only gets worse when you get to be my age." He pulled back, beaming, proud to have imparted some ancient wisdom on *one* of his best students. "I was asking, why are you here on a Saturday night with a bunch of us stodgy old people? Mr. Reed, notwithstanding."

Connor nodded his appreciation.

"I'm sure there are better places you could be. Like perhaps—the library?" the professor finished, his glee evident.

What? Could this be why I was no longer his best student? Just one of his best students. Because I wasn't studying enough? And Connor was still grinning, clearly enjoying my situation, my entire situation, way too much. I angled just enough to point my bare butt away from his ogling eyes. The lusting rapscallion. Mmmm, the lusting rapscallion. *Sara. Stop. He's a crook.*

I smiled politely. "Would you like the PC answer or the truth?"

"The truth, my dear. Most certainly, the truth." The perpetual smile vanished from his weather-beaten face. "For it shall set you free." His eyebrows rose and lips pursed.

"I'm an employee of the museum. My manager recommended I be here."

"Ah, yes. I see." The professor's eyes darted to Connor and back to me. "Makes sense. Yes, perfect sense."

"And on that note"—I motioned behind him—"there's my manager. I best say hi. Sir, see you next Monday for my presentation."

He bowed his head slightly, strands of rogue hair riding the air current his motion created.

I faced Connor and drank in his pool of blues. *Hormones—you gals are in. Head—you're out of the game. Go sit on the bench.* "See you around," I said under my breath, tingling all over. I had final confirmation my mixed emotions have run amok. And I wasn't so sure they were mixed anymore. Just amok.

I slid away from them and crossed the room toward Edna, who was engaged in conversation with Roger Gwynne and Dr. Mitchell. "Hi, everybody," I said cheerfully as I approached. An unbelievable disquiet enveloping the trio attacked my senses.

Edna sidestepped to make room for me and feigned a welcoming smile. "Sara, glad you could make it. Aren't you just lovely?" She inspected me like a grandmother sizing up her debutante granddaughter before the big event. No doubt she was calculating if I had any of the hundred dollars left over. Yeah, right.

"Mmmm, yes, Miss Donovan, good to see you. Having a nice time?" asked an unenthused Roger.

Before I could answer, Dr. Mitchell extended a welcoming hand to me. "Hi, Sara. Valerie Mitchell. I don't believe we have met."

I shook her hand. "Yes, ma'am. Pleased to meet you."

"I'm sorry, Valerie. Where are my manners?" Edna interjected. "I thought you two had met. Sara works part-time at the gift shop. This is her first year with us."

"Oh, that's wonderful."

Roger mumbled, "Mmmm, yes," and desperately motioned for a drink from one of the roaming servers.

Edna shifted her weight, an empty champagne flute in hand, while Dr. Mitchell stood there staring at me with a plastic toothy smile. An awkward pause encircled us, squeezing me like a python dressed to kill. At this precise moment, I would have given anything to be anywhere but here. Even roaming adrift through a grody parking garage. Well. Almost anything.

I forced a smile and attempted to exorcise the tension. "I love working here. And this gala is wonderful." I addressed Edna. "Thank you so much for inviting me."

She nodded with a lackluster smile.

I faced Roger. "Dr. Gwynne, did you get hold of Frank Kranzer?"

He regarded me through drooping eyelids, mimicking an indifferent tuxedoed hound dog. "Mmmm, yes."

"Did they release the shipment?" I asked.

"Shipment? Released?" Edna asked him. "You mean the one that arrived this morning?"

His eyes shifted to Dr. Mitchell, then to Edna. "Yes, customs impounded it but I took care of it." He flicked the back of his hand. "Not a problem."

"I wasn't aware," she responded.

"Just a misunderstanding. Addressed it the same

169

day I got the message. No need to inform you."

The redhead appeared and handed Roger his drink. He took a healthy gulp. Then another. Everybody fell silent.

As the intense silence dragged along, I spotted the back of a short squat lady with long blonde hair talking to Karen. "If you'll excuse me, I'll let you get back to your conversation."

I bowed out, scooting toward her and away from the Arctic Circle. Although, after our little encounter Thursday outside the museum, this cut way against my better judgment. We made eye contact. Yeah, the Arctic Circle was a tropical paradise compared to what I was wading into.

"Mrs. Bagley," I exclaimed, coming up behind her, all the while feeling Karen's freeze ray attempting to exile me to the frozen steppes of Siberia.

The blonde lady twisted around. Her brow wrinkled as she stared at me. "Excuse me?"

In a heartbeat, the lady banished me into desolate desolation. I had no idea who she was, but she sure wasn't Mrs. Bagley. Nausea swept over me as the crab puffs battled the shrimp to see who could swim to the surface first.

Chapter Twenty-Seven

The molecules are magnificent

Today was the second day of Alabama's twenty-four team Dodgeball World Cup. With Edna giving me the weekend off to study, and last night's auction debacle behind me, I should be having fun this last day before Finals Week. But I couldn't get amped up for dodgeball. The earsplitting banshee reverberated in my head. Zoe still had me miffed from her climbing room outburst. And I found myself doubting my observation skills, which I prided myself on, Zoe to the contrary. What did Mrs. Majelski mean, if things go bad, I'm protected so long as nobody knows she has the mask? She always had the answer, like some octogenarian sensei with too much time on her hands. And the old lady was as savvy as Mauzzy and crushed her workouts. But that statement kept me wondering if I made a mistake giving her the mask for safekeeping. The one constant in all this mess was Zoe, for better or worse. And Mauzzy. How far I have fallen.

On the outer trail of the Quad, a shirtless runner with easily a twelve-pack cruised past. He trained striking Caribbean-blue eyes on me and smiled cheerfully. He didn't have to do that because running can be a pain in the ass. Literally, for me. But he did. He smiled right at me. A connection. Renewed energy flowed through my exhausted body and instantly raised my spirits. I was ready to have fun.

"Hey Cap'n," a voice called to me.

I scanned the field and spotted Zoe flying toward me. She wore an ear-to-ear smile along with our team uniform, a green t-shirt with wide white-and-orange stripes and the word "Ireland" spanning the back, and black athletic shorts.

Since it was a World Cup tournament, each team chose a country to represent. We were Ireland. I wanted to be Egypt, but the rest of the team heartily voted me down. Although I was the team captain, we were a democratic dodgeball team. Good thing we didn't elect to be China.

I raised a fist high, like a fiery general rallying the troops. "Ireland," I roared, pumping my arm up and down. "Victory."

This morning our opponent was Italy. Not long into the match, it became obvious these other guys took things pretty damn seriously. They played high-velocity dodgeball, and those red rubber balls hurt. Despite taking some vicious hits, we fought hard and were able to win the second game to even the match. But in the ultimate third game we quickly fell behind when three of our players got knocked out right after the opening rush to grab the balls at the center line. That left us with three in the game to their full complement of six. And sadly, one of our three remaining players was me. The other two were Zoe and Kurt, the guy with the doppelganger I once regrettably chased and ended up in his embarrassing social media post. I called a timeout.

The team gathered around me. We were a panting, sweaty mess. "C'mon, guys, we still have a chance. All we need to do is work together and pick 'em off one at a time. If we can win this game, we win the match." For once, my passion was an asset. I made eye contact with each person. "Zoe is our best bet. We need to protect her when she attacks. And they're good at catching the ball, so shoot for their knees. *Ireland.*"

"Ireland," the team responded in unison.

We broke the huddle, and the game continued. Zoe came out so fired up she quickly blasted two of their girls, scooped up a guy's miss and promptly put him on his butt with a legal headshot when he tried to duck. The little pixie rocked. We were now tied at three players each.

After Kurt smoked a guy, I scooped up a ball by our end line and made a run for it. I cut back and forth through the backcourt on the way to the attack line, amazing myself with every feint and spin. Out front, Kurt and Zoe cleared the way, taking out the fifth opponent with a double-up attack. One person left, a big menacing guy who was by far their best player.

I crossed the attack line and closed in fast on the center line. That is, Sara-fast. I raised the ball and stared the dude down, who also had a ball raised. As I cocked my arm back, my left foot stubbed the dirt, pitching me downward. "Aahhhh." The ground rushed up as I heaved the ball with all my strength, which was considerable, thanks to all my weight work at the gym.

Crrrrrraaaaaaacccckkk.

An explosion of light blinded me. My head was a turbulence of pain, with my face buried in something—moist? I struggled to roll out of the disgusting slop, but paralysis seized me. A commotion swirled around my prone body. Little dots of intense white light floated in

173

a dizzying array of brilliance. And the molecules, simply magnificent.

Voices wafted through the smog.

"Is she out?" someone echoed from a tunnel.

"I don't know," a voice said as the words drifted by on an especially dazzling molecule.

"Sara, you okay?" It sounded like Zoe, but I couldn't be sure. Unless she was doing helium hits again.

I tried to clear my head, but I was immobile, face down with a taste of—dirt? Oh, God—dirt. In my mouth.

A nearby blowing whistle helped cut through the fog a bit. An official-sounding voice announced, "The game is over. Ireland wins the match"

"We won?" a guy asked.

"She crushed him," a girl's voice said. "The jerk is still squirming on the ground."

More footsteps. It sounded like someone just ran up to me.

"What happened?" another guy's voice asked.

"Brutal headshot."

A pair of large firm hands eased me over to my back.

"Sara," called the second guy's voice. It was calm and soothing. Like an angel. "Sara, can you hear me?"

I moaned.

"Come on, Sara. Open your eyes," coaxed the angelic voice. "You in there?"

I moaned again and cracked open my eyes. Both teams were circled around me. Everything appeared fuzzy and spinning, except for one thing. The luminous blue eyes of one Connor Reed. Wait. He wasn't playing in the game. Did I die and go to heaven? For real?

"Hey." I squinched my eyes but couldn't shake the fog. "Connor?"

A warm smile crossed his face. "You took a real shot to the head. Can you sit up?"

"Mmmm…yeah," I whimpered.

"Okay, here we go." He crouched, helped me to a sitting position, and eased a soaked do-rag off my head that hurt like—well, I don't know like what—but it really, really hurt.

"What…are you…doing here?" I asked, spitting out dirt in between words.

"I was passing through the Quad on the way back from the library. I saw these games and stopped to watch. That was quite a throw you made, right before you got whacked. You really kneecapped the guy." He gave my shoulder a gentle squeeze, his smile as dazzling as the molecules. "Not the most graceful fall, though. But still very impressive."

I rubbed my head, squinting to contain the pounding and douse his smile. "Tha…I did what?"

"You knocked out their last person. Dropped him like a rock."

I managed to get out a hoarse, "Yea."

"You want to stand?"

I spit out more dirt. Lord knows with each sputter how many germs and bacteria I ejected. "Okay."

With Connor securing one arm and Zoe managing the other, I got up on unsteady feet. After a few seconds, the remaining molecules floated away as the fog dissipated.

"You doing okay now?" he asked.

"I'm good." I grimaced. "Except for this pounding

head."

They released my arms. Both stared intently, hands at the ready to catch me.

I squished both temples with my palms to contain the heavy bass amp thumping in my waylaid head. "Thanks, guys. I'll be okay."

Zoe handed me a bottle of water and two aspirin she got from my backpack. "Here. Drink some water and take these."

"Thanks." I took the water bottle and knocked the pills back. Despite the water, dirt was still between my teeth. I took another big swig, swished the water around in my mouth, and spit it out.

Right on Connor's shoes.

My hand flew to my mouth. "I'm so sorry. I didn't—"

He waved it off. "Don't worry about it. Hey, I'm glad you'll be okay. I have to go, but if you're not doing anything tonight, how about coming over for coffee?"

I massaged the top of my head. Dang, it hurt. Did my TA, doubling as my hot neighbor and an art thief, and whose shoes were soaked with my spit, ask me over? "Coffee? Me?"

"After a head injury, the following twenty-four hours are important. You could have a concussion. Just being a good neighbor." His voice was low, silky smooth, and delicious.

"Sure, I guess." My head ached, but it had nothing to do with the headshot I took.

Chapter Twenty-Eight

Sorbet underpants voodoo magic?

After a full day of dodging red rubber balls thrown with bad intent, including one to the head, my shower felt amazing. Except for the initial stinging pain when hot water hit the scratches and scrapes on my arms and legs. But it was well worth it. Our ragtag little team advanced to the semifinals, four matches further than any of us expected. And in an hour, I was heading next door for coffee with Connor.

Following thirty minutes of intense deliberation, I opted for the low-key seductive approach. I selected my nice-ass black jeans, an easy decision, and a light-purple chiffon blouse over a plain white tank with spaghetti straps—three buttons undone. Faux amethyst earrings and a matching pendant further highlighted the sublime cleavage effect of the Ladies, put forth by my best bra working in consonance with the tank and undone buttons. And just in case, I was wearing *Sorbet*. Not only were they my good luck underpants, they were my best pair. A veritable underpants twofer.

I backed away from the mirror for a final check. My foot caught on a pile of clothes, sending me tumbling backward. Fortunately, the bed reared up to break my fall, keeping me from flipping over the loft's half wall and ending up as a chalk outline on the floor below. Like I said, good luck *Sorbet*.

I bounded down the stairs to cook a quick dinner. Mauzzy was beyond distraught, lounging with his head resting on the recliner's arm, staring off into nothingness. He knew something was up.

I took out a glass microwave bowl and dumped in two cans of green beans, one can of cream of mushroom soup, and sprinkled a half-bag of shredded yellow cheese on top. For some reason the cheese was still yellow, but I wasn't about to question my good fortune. Chucking the bowl into the microwave, I punched in two minutes, and my best non-phone technology friend jumped into action.

While the casserole concoction nuked, I got antibiotic ointment out of the drawer and dabbed some soothing salve on a nasty scrape on my arm. Next to aspirin and coffee, it was my wonder drug.

Beep. Beep. Beep.

Instant dinner. I opened the microwave and took out the bowl.

Crash.

Not even *Sorbet* underpants voodoo magic could counter the powerful ointment post-application effect. I just broke dinner. Slipped right out of my lubricated fingers. I did a quick check of my nice-ass jeans. Nothing got on them. I exhaled in relief. *Sorbet*—back on the job.

"Hey, get out of that."

Ever the nondiscriminatory food whore, Mauzzy was busy gorging himself on green bean casserole from one half of the busted dish. He sauntered away, only to circle back to the feast from another angle. As if I didn't know what he was doing.

"Stop it." I nudged him away from the mess with my foot. "Go get on your chair."

He padded a few steps away and considered me. The Little Professor was sizing me up, deciding between taking another shot at his gastronomic windfall or go recline in his chair and bide his time. He recognized I was leaving. This meant weighing a risky grab for immediate but short-lived gratification against a tactical retreat until he could lick the floor clean and scavenge the pantry at his leisure.

Decision made, he trotted over to his chair, jumped, and laid his head on the arm. He followed me out of the corner of his eye, no longer distraught, just— waiting.

I cleaned up the mess, wiped my hands of any residual ointment, and made another green bean casserole. It's the beauty of instant dinner. You make it. You break it. You make it again. All in ten minutes.

I gulped down half the mess, put the rest in the fridge, and gave myself a once-over in the bathroom mirror. What was I doing? He was my TA. Mrs. Majelski warned me about him. And he's acted way suspicious and lied to me. But he's so damn...screw it. Finals Week starts tomorrow. He won't be my teacher next Monday when I give my presentation to the professor. And hopefully not in jail, either. *Go for it, Sara.*

"See ya, Mauz," I said to the strategic genius lying in wait, pretending not to notice me getting ready to leave. "Do me a favor, Handsome. At least wait until I'm out the door before you go lick the floor. Mommy loves you."

I closed the door and took a peek back through the

window. His little pink tongue was feasting on the spill site. Dang it. Now I need to mop the rest of the floor.

****

Connor handed me a mug of steaming black coffee. "Here you go."

I took it in both hands, just in case I missed some ointment, and set it on the coffee table footlocker. "Thanks."

He placed his own mug on the footlocker and sat on the loveseat next to me. He wore faded blue jeans and a gray t-shirt, which was oh so fine with me. On all levels. Over the aroma of fresh-brewed coffee, I caught a whiff of vanilla and nutmeg. Now this man understood how to wear cologne, unlike his boss.

I took a gander around the place. Austere would be an exaggeration. Nothing changed from the first time I peeped in his window. And no gun. "Sure you live here?"

"What's the matter?" He swung his arm through the air. "You don't like what I've done with the place?"

"Shooting for the very postmodern neo-nothing look, huh?"

"I think I nailed it."

"You can count the amount of furniture on one hand. Not including the"—I gestured with air quotes toward the dented footlocker—"coffee table?"

"Nope. Two," corrected Connor, who shifted his body to face me. "You forgot the bed upstairs."

My face blazed as a surge of tingles quivered through my body. "I did."

A palpable current of anticipation electrified the narrow space between us. Glowing rays of white radiated from his pupils, giving the blue irises a captivating luminescence. They were talking to me, and I liked what they were saying.

He tipped toward me but stopped short and jerked back. "Do you know I'm doing my doctoral dissertation on the economic infrastructure of antiquities smuggling?"

What just happened? He mentioned the bed upstairs. He did the lean in. And then he brings up his dissertation? All systems were in shutdown mode, the electricity in the air short-circuited. It was about to happen, but all that remained was an expectation blackout.

"You mentioned that after recitation," I said dryly.

"Ah, right. I did. What I'd like to do is pick your brain about your research project. Sorta compare notes. Maybe we can help each other? The professor told me you still have a week left before you go in front of him."

We were back to all business. How stupid of me to think something might happen. "Sure. Pick away."

Connor spent the next hour and another cup of coffee firing questions at me. But instead of picking my brain, he vacuumed it out my ear. He wanted to know everything. After we finished, I slumped back to my cottage and took Mauzzy out for the day's final ritual. A pain in my heart overtook the pain in my head. I was an idiot to think there could have been something between us.

Mauz sensed my despair because he didn't drag things out. He was all business. When we got back inside, I made some ginger tea, hoisted him up under my arm, and marched upstairs.

"It's time for some Mr. Darcy, my Sweet

Handsome."

He extended up and gave me a kiss. At least he loved me.

Chapter Twenty-Nine

Against my better judgment

It was a warm Monday evening following last night's disappointing visit at Connor's so I was in gym shorts and a sleeveless shirt. I spent all day studying for my marketing final this Wednesday. Mauzzy displayed more confidence in me passing marketing than I did because he repeatedly let me know I needed to stop studying and show him some attention. Since it was almost dinnertime, instant noodles and a diet cola, I decided to step away from the books.

"You win, Sweet Handsome." I scrambled off the couch, crossed to the door, and picked up my keys with pepper spray, his leash, and bag dispenser. "Okay—"

He blasted off his chair, sailed across the room, and stomped on my feet with his front paws. This bode well for a quickie.

Fifteen minutes later and no results, Sweet Handsome once again reminded me that with him, nothing was ever as he made it seem. Ever.

I stood over him, my foot tapping the pavement like an overzealous drummer. "Seriously? What happened to all the whining and complaining a little while ago? The faster you take care of business, the sooner we both get dinner."

His ears lifted and eyes lit up.

A door slammed behind us, followed by the sound of running footsteps.

I spun around and caught Connor leaping over his front deck's three steps and landing on the pavement. Without stopping, he raced up the walk to his car. In a single motion he tore open the door to his rambling wreck, the rusty hinges registering their complaint. He hopped in and roared out of the parking lot. The car was moving so fast its right tires jumped the curb as it bounced out onto the street and disappeared. A cloud of gray-white smoke smelling like rotten eggs hung in the air. In the distance, an overworked engine emitted a long but retreating clamor of mistreatment.

I still had not entirely sorted out those earlier mixed feelings about this guy. Super-hot dork of a man versus international crook. I made a snap decision and grabbed Mauzzy. Although he still had to finish his business, it thrilled him to be in my arms. Either that or he concluded he once again won the test of wills, and dinner was on the way.

I rushed to the hatchback, fell into the driver's seat, and plopped Sweet Handsome into his milk crate stuffed with pink blankets featuring baby-blue doggie bones. In an instant, the car jumped backward. I slammed the shift into drive and took off after the enigma that was my neighbor. And something either very, very good. Or incredibly bad.

After thirty minutes of wild-eyed, reckless driving, he got off at exit one hundred toward Bucksville and veered onto Tannehill Parkway. Within minutes we entered Tannehill State Park, which I knew quite well from countless *Pride and Prejudice* picnics with Mauzzy.

"Why is he here this time of day?" No answer from the pile of pink blankets in the crate. "The park closes at dusk. That's in fifteen minutes."

My mouth went cotton dry. What in the hell was I thinking? This guy. This cute, dorky, super-hot guy. Was a fricking armed crook. Maybe even a murderer. And I was following him? To a soon-to-be-dark park? Alone?

To be safe, I dropped back to put a little more distance between our cars. After all, I was only armed with pepper spray and a sleeping dachshund with a *laissez-faire* attitude.

Although my brain implored me to turn around, I had to see things through. Even if it ended with my death and dismemberment.

After creeping along for about a half mile, I arrived at a darkened intersection with Confederate Parkway. There were no cars. Anywhere.

I struck the steering wheel with my palm. "Dang it."

Mauzzy's head appeared from under a cocoon of pink fleece.

"I let him get away, Handsome."

He sighed and rested his head on the edge of the crate.

Dusk was coming soon, but I didn't dare risk turning on the headlights because it would give away my position to Connor, wherever the heck he was at.

To the right, Confederate Parkway led to the Alabama Iron and Steel Museum. That risked too many people. To the left, an old secluded service road branched off from Confederate. And at some point, it had a bridge crossing Mill Creek. That's where I would set up a meet if I were an international smuggler. Or a serial killer. Or both.

I hung a left on Confederate, eased around a big curve in the road, and swung to the right after about five hundred feet. Darkness shrouded the nameless road, both from the dense canopy of trees and the fast-fading daylight.

"I don't like this."

A pitiful whimper rose from under the blankets where my little dachshund reburied himself.

"Okay, Mauz. I agree with you. Definitely not one of my better decisions." I slowed the car to a crawl. "The heck with this. It's not worth it. Here's what we'll do. I'll turn around at the creek, and we'll head home."

Whimpering became whining from the blankets, pink fluffy ripples dancing up and down.

After another minute or two, we reached the creek's bridge. There was no sign of Connor, or anybody, or anything. I cranked the wheel hard to the left, the right front tire wildly trying to grip the damp grass as I struggled to gain control coming out of the U-turn. Beside me, the passenger seat exploded in commotion, climaxing with Mauzzy popping up from the crate pitching a fit.

"Really? Now?" I slammed on the brakes, bringing the frenzied hatchback to a cool herky-jerky sliding stop, and shoved it into park. "Now?"

Hazel eyes pleaded with me. The argument, one of desperation.

"Really, dude. You should have gone before we left."

He stopped his commotion and eyeballed me. I couldn't tell if my comment pissed him off, or it

186

shocked him I had the gall to make it.

"In hindsight, not such a good plan of yours, huh? That'll teach you for dragging things out."

Staring back at the seething Mauzzy, I hit him with my fierce look. It obviously still needed work because he was unimpressed. In fact, I needed to take a lesson from him because his fierce look was—fierce. After a few more intense seconds matching wits and eyeballs, I blew out a big breath of annoyance and reluctantly gave in. I couldn't believe what I was about to do on a dark nameless road in the middle of a closed state park. Surely a psycho lurked in the nearby woods with a malevolent sneer and bloodstained chainsaw.

"You know, this is way against my better judgment."

Little paws clawed at the top of the crate, accompanied by a pitiful yelp and squeak of desperation.

"Yeah, yeah. I get it. This is all my fault. I'm the one who dognapped you before you could pee. I'm sorry, Sweet Handsome." Although I wasn't sure if my sorrow was for him or for my approaching untimely and grisly death. I took another deep breath, pure consternation and foreboding replacing my prior annoyance. "Let's go."

I put him on his retractable leash, and we got out of the car. My head was on a swivel, but it didn't matter. Suffocating black engulfed the night, ideal cover for a killer. Before we moved away from the safety of the car, I stood still and listened. My ears strained for any telltale signs of a murderer stalking in the way-too-close woods.

It was too quiet. Deathly quiet.

I had pepper spray at the ready in my left hand, the leash in my right, and phone in my pocket. Mauzzy poked and sniffed around, but no pee. He meandered toward the silhouetted bridge, sniffing up a storm. But no waterworks.

After five minutes of risking my life, I lost all patience. Rising fear and sheer irritation obliterated the need for stealth. "Mauzzy," I bellowed. "You're the one complaining you had to go. So, go already. This isn't a walk, and it's not a nighttime picnic."

All I got from him was a casual look over his shoulder at my outburst.

The sounds of a twig snapping and rustling leaves came from the woods, but I felt no breeze. A tremble attacked my voice. "Dude, you have five seconds or we're outta here. And you'll just have to hold it."

I whipped my head around. No chainsaw.

Unperturbed, he pitter-pattered over to the side corner of the bridge and sniffed around, poking his nose at something dimly white in the darkness. I dug the phone out and struggled to activate its flashlight while gripping the pepper spray and leash. For some reason, the flashlight resurrected itself over the weekend. I guess the hand sanitizer that first killed it also had some kind of latent restorative properties. Either that or my flashlight had a Lazarus moment. And whatever Mauzzy just found, he loved it. Wonderful. He was probably vandalizing some dead rabbit or something. "Hey, leave that alone."

I rushed toward him and the white thing. "Get away from it."

As I neared him and the roadkill, Handsome sauntered off and finally graced the forest with his pee.

I aimed the light at the roadkill, but it wasn't roadkill. Just a discarded Doctor Mike's takeout bag someone tossed to the side of the bridge.

"Litterbugs," I muttered, bending to pick up the bag. It was heavy. Real heavy. I shined the light into the bag.

A series of crashes erupted from the woods.

Letting out a scream, I dropped the bag and jumped back. Blinding light shot from all directions, like the Second Coming. Nothing but intense white.

An authoritative voice thundered out of the blazing brilliance. "Freeze. Hands in the air. Now."

My arms shot up in the air, pepper spray and phone tumbling to the ground.

Mauzzy finished up his pee and proudly trotted over to me, also now bathed in the unholy brilliance.

Shit.

Chapter Thirty

Following or stalking?

Why couldn't I ever let things be? Even when I knew better. With the little princess inside me imploring, *don't do it, Sara,* I did it anyway. Utter brilliance.

Nothing like clarity of thought after having the bejeezus scared out of you with blinding lights, people screaming, and ungracious hands roaming all over your person. And a little joyride in the back of a speeding police car, ingesting air replete with the *eau de parfum* of stale vomit and urine. The vom wasn't mine, although the pee could have been, considering the blinding lights and *"Freeze"* command blasted at me earlier tonight. Adding insult to injury, the cops confiscated my purse with my hand sanitizers and wipes. If there was *ever* a time for those babies, this was it.

I'd been sitting behind a small table in a windowless room for over two hours, still without my purse, answering question after question from two brusque FBI agents. Periodically, one or the other popped outside, only to return moments later. Five minutes ago, they both got up and left. Their demeanor was such I found myself missing Officers Handsy and Freeze, the Alabama state troopers who drove Mauzzy and I to the Federal Building. They seemed all too happy to hand me off to these guys right after we arrived.

I gulped down the remnants of a bottle of lukewarm water an agent gave me, taking care not to swallow my gum, the only thing they let me have from my purse before locking it away in an evidence locker. I tried for the hand sanitizers but that argument was a non-starter with them. And not that the gum was worth keeping. The taste of fresh peppermint deserted me an hour ago, leaving behind a wad the consistency of chewed paper. I checked my hair and the back of my shirt in the large mirror on the far side of the room, craning my neck like a famished giraffe on the Serengeti. But I couldn't get a good angle. Mauzzy, snoring from my lap, kept me pinned in the chair.

He was beyond his usual comatose demeanor. I think our near-death experience tonight got the best of him. At least the FBI allowed him to stay with me, but only after I called upon my experience gained from watching all those episodes of *The Mysteries of Chance*. That'll teach Zoe for pooh-poohing my choice of TV shows. They couldn't force me to talk without my lawyer. Like I even had a lawyer. But they didn't need to know that. I threatened to walk unless they let me have Mauz in the "interview" room, as one agent called it. As if I didn't know they were interrogating me. With some misgiving, they agreed. And so, it began.

The door burst open, and in strode Agent Walker, the more reserved of the two agents. He settled into a chair opposite me and rested bare muscular forearms on the table, his sleeves theatrically rolled up a long time ago. Yeah, that stunt stood no chance with me.

He let out a long, tired sigh. "Okay, Ms. Donovan. Here's the thing. In order for us to believe your story, we have to accept too many coincidences. Still, I'm not entirely sure you're lying, but—"

"I'm telling the truth."

"—you have Agent Shipton convinced you're a part of this. You're obviously not the brains behind it. Most likely the mule."

Did he just call me a dumb jackass? "That's rude."

The agent suppressed a thin smile. "We know you're not the operation's ringleader. We suspect you're a low-level courier. You—"

"But I'm not. I'm—"

"You deliver the items to dead drops and pick up the buyers' cash from other drops. Like you did tonight. Once you deliver the cash to your intermediary, you get your cut. And they contact the buyer with the item's drop location. How am I doing?" He stopped, his eyes riveted on my face, most likely waiting for me to dissolve into a confession of tears and *mea culpas*.

I composed myself and offered my explanation for like the hundredth time tonight. As I spoke, I realized he might have a point. Quite a few coincidences were sprinkled among the events. Starting with that frigging mask. Dad's voice buzzed in the back of my head. *Sara, there is no such thing as coincidence. Remember that.*

Crap. *Yep, Sara. That's what you stepped in.*

He stopped me. "Ms. Donovan, we're not interested in you. We're after the top people."

"But I've already given names to you. They're—"

"Highly unlikely suspects. Just come clean. It's

obvious you're withholding. No more obfuscation. Tell us what you know. We'll put in a strong word for you with the DA. I'm sure you'll get off lightly. Maybe with just a few years of probation." He stuck his neck out over the table and lowered his voice. "But if you don't want to help, then there's nothing we can do for you. And, well…" Without breaking eye contact, he put on a phony smile.

I tried hard not to look away. Do I tell him about the mask? Explain it wasn't my fau…wait…what? Probation? Probation. Maybe probation? The opposite of *maybe probation* was *definitely* prison time. No way I'm telling them. And if they somehow found out Mrs. Majelski had it, that ancient super-spy ninja better keep her mouth shut and not rat me out for a better deal. After all, she's the one who told *me* to keep quiet about it. She better do the same.

"Sir." My voice cracked. *Breathe. This might be your last shot before they haul you away.* "As I have repeatedly said, I was following my neighbor, but lost him when we got to the park."

My interrogator sat back and folded his monstrous arms. "You understand, under the law, I could interpret that as stalking."

I gave him a quick wiseass smile and continued pleading my undoubtedly ever-weakening case. "Following, sir. Following. Because I have good reason to believe he's part of this criminal ring that *your* Agent Shipton thinks I'm a jackass for." I glared past the G-man at the mirrored wall. "Which I'm not."

Cool it, Sara. Reel it back in. Or you'll be bunking tonight with Big Betty.

My pathetic explanation didn't sway him. He

unfolded his arms and pitched forward on his forearms. "We can also place you at University Mall the same time another drop took place. How do you explain that?"

"How should I know? I'm a college student. I go to the mall."

He nodded evenly and scrutinized me. "Let me help you remember the particular day I'm referring to, Ms. Donovan. Listen up. On the day in question, many people can place you there."

What the heck was this guy talking about? What did he...Oh. Marty the Mall Cop. That day. A disturbing vision appeared of a jiggling belly spinning on a scooter, followed by an even more disturbing vision of me—spying on Connor from behind the clothes rack. My face burned hot. And the perspiration machine, which performed an admirable job staying shut down the last two hours, flew into overdrive.

"Um...that day...I was also following my neighbor?"

"The same neighbor? Connor Reed?"

I closed my eyes and rocked my spinning head.

"Again, Ms. Donovan. Stalking. And yet another coincidence? It's too much. Let me lay it all out for you from my perspective. First"—he held out his left index finger and tapped it with his right—"you were at a shopping mall at the exact time and place where we were conducting a drop. A drop our informant arranged through a series of blind communications."

"A wha—"

The agent continued to count on his fingers. "Next. Three days later. You're over thirty miles from your home. In a state park after sundown. With a bag in your hands containing fifty thousand dollars. A bag we planted not even an hour earlier."

"But I found tha—"

He stuck out three fingers with an emphatic flourish. "And now, you expect us to believe that you, a college student, suspected a major crime syndicate included your neighbor. And you stalked him? That's not only suspicious, it's stupid. Anybody else in your shoes would have just called the police."

My head dropped.

Mauzzy groaned.

He abruptly scooted back his chair, stood, placed both hands flat on the table, and bent toward me. "Are you with me? Do you understand why we're having a real problem with your story?"

I didn't say anything. I couldn't say anything. My emotions clawed at me as the reality of the moment hit home.

The fricking FBI was interrogating me. And they think I'm lying. This wasn't some dumb TV show. This was real. And I likely gave a stolen artifact to Mrs. Majelski. They're going to send me to prison. And if I told them about everything now...

A lump formed in my parched throat. I blinked back at the hulking man, a tear swelling in the corner of my eye.

Why didn't I listen to Mom? To Zoe? Even Dad, with all his complacency and coincidence BS?

The tear slid down my cheek, followed by another. Soon, my face was a streaming mess of guilt.

But none of it was true. Why did I feel so guilty? Because I might have a stolen artifact that I didn't tell them about? Or because I let Mom and my best friend down? And what will happen to Sweet Handsome when they lock me away?

The agent sat, eased forward, and folded his arms on the table. "Sara," he said in a soft voice. "I can help you. But you have to help me. Do you want to make a statement?"

My spastic sobbing jarred Mauzzy awake. He tilted his head up at me, then confronted my tormentor with a low, guttural growl.

"Take a deep breath," he said, keeping one eye trained on the fierce-looking Mauzzy, the other on the not-so-fierce—me. "Just take your time. Whenever you're ready."

"I'm…I'm…" Trying to compose myself, I inhaled a lungful of stale air and blew out through my nose. It bubbled like the La Brea Tar Pits and whistled like a boiling teapot.

Agent Walker handed me a tissue from a box on the end of the table. "Here."

I took it from him and blew. Because they confiscated my purse, I had no access to the waste tissue baggie from my OCD Tissue System, patent pending by—Inmate #45903028. I dropped the disgusting tissue into a trashcan by my chair. He handed me another tissue, and I wiped away regret and resignation from my face.

"Okay. Feeling better?"

I nodded several times, still sniffling a bit. I really was feeling better. Never underestimate the power of a good snot blow to get back on your game.

"Ready to make a statement?"

Hold the fricking presses.

Did he ask earlier why didn't I just call the police?

Because I called the cops. I called nine-one-one and gave a statement to Officer Smirk.

What was his name? Think, Sara. It's the only thing keeping you from becoming Big Betty's bitch for the next five to ten years. Officer Pr...Pea...Prat...Prater. Preater. Officer Preater.

Uh oh. Nobody from the police department ever followed up with me. I hope he filed the report. My heart sank. This was not good. He warned me about filing a false report. I could almost see Agent No Coincidence puffing up his chest and giving a round of high fives behind the one-way mirror as his partner closed the deal.

"Ms. Donovan? Did you hear me? Are you prepared to—"

"I called the cops." My jaws hammered the stale, hard gum to the point it was about to rip out a molar.

Agent Walker pulled back and cocked his head sideways. "What?"

"Sorry. I meant to say police. But I called them. Just like you said I should've done. I told the officer about the whole thing."

Except...

He ran a hand through his hair before lunging his chest forward. His brow creased, and fists were on the table. "You called the police?"

I nodded so much I could have been a life-sized Sara Donovan bobblehead.

"Why are you just telling me this now? After almost three hours?"

I smiled uneasily. "I guess you never asked."

A pained expression washed over his face. "When did you place the call? Who did you talk to? And about

197

what whole thing?"

It was working. I had his attention. I prayed Officer Smir—Preater filed that report.

I sat up straighter. "I called nine-one-one and spoke to a dispatcher." The quaver left my voice. "A lady. I didn't get her name. She sent an officer to my place right after I called. Officer Preater." I relaxed in the chair. Sara Donovan was back from the brink.

Sorry, Big Betty. You're gonna be a lonely girl tonight.

He scribbled something in his little notepad. "Preater?"

My voice rose as I talked faster. "Yes, sir. I told him about Connor Reed going to Mobile after I got a call about a museum shipment being in an impounded container. About Professor Sawalha, Dr. Gwynne, Henderson Thornburn, Mary Bagley, and Karen Allen. And," I said with a bit of irritation, "he warned me about filing a false police report."

The agent stopped writing and glanced up. "Huh. Imagine that."

I twisted my mouth up and shot him a look.

"Was he Tuscaloosa police?"

"Yes, sir."

"When did you file the report?"

"I made the call right after I—followed—Connor to the mall. Last Friday. That report will show I've been telling the truth the whole time."

He snapped the notepad closed and shoved it in his shirt's breast pocket. "I kinda figured that out."

I took the ravaged gum from my mouth, half-expecting to yank out the entire row of lower teeth with it, and faced the empty trashcan sitting two feet from me. Leaning over, I took dead aim and—*plink*—the gnarled gum hit the lip. And stuck to it. A precarious balance between landing where it belonged and suffering a humiliating fall.

I threw a sideways look at him, who shook his head. I would say in amazement, but that was giving me way more credit than due. Way more. In fact, I think he felt sorry for me. My life in one miserable microsecond. And it gave me an idea for a closing argument.

Sitting back up, I appealed to the G-man. "You've got to believe me. If you know my life. If you understand how I'm always in the wrong place at the right time. It'll all make sense. If there's gum in the parking lot, I'll step on it. If there's dog poop in the grass, I'll step in it. If there's a nail in the road, I'll drive over it. If—"

Agent Walker put up a hand and got out of his chair. "Okay. Okay. I get it. Wait right here."

Like what am I going to do, dude, break out of a federal building? But for once I wisely kept my exhausted mouth shut and just acknowledged him with a head bob. Thank goodness for that overworked gum, which at the same instant lost its grip and dropped to the discolored tile floor.

With Mauzzy hanging on for dear life, I stood, leaving most of the skin from the back of my legs on the chair seat. Picking up the fallen gum with the tear-sodden tissue, I placed it *directly* in the trashcan.

A few minutes passed before he returned, followed by Agent Shipton, the nonbeliever. Standing together, the agents were all rumpled white shirts and bulging pecs. A second later, the door closed behind them.

A woman's voice wafted through the air.

"Gentlemen?"

The Twin Towers of Testosterone parted like the Red Sea to reveal a small refrigerator dressed in a lady's navy-blue pinstriped suit with blonde hair pulled tightly back. She squeezed forward between the beefcakes before stopping in front of me. The cramped room was so packed with humanity, if anybody else wanted to attend the Sara Donovan Revue, they needed to wait their turn outside.

"Ms. Donovan, I'm Special Agent Carol Hainsworth. I'm the FBI's supervisory agent in charge of this investigation."

"Excuse me, but you look familiar. Have we met?"

"Briefly. At the auction."

"Right. You were talking with Karen."

"We'll let you go for now while we check out your story. Please don't leave the Tuscaloosa-Birmingham area without checking with us first. Okay?"

"Yes, ma'am."

"Okay, good. Agent Walker will escort you out." She navigated back through the Red Sea and opened the door wide enough to accommodate her broad shoulders and squat frame. As she exited the room, her blonde ponytail swayed side to side.

Chapter Thirty-One

Waterboarding sucks

I just spent the last fifteen minutes of my life in the muggy garage next to the Tuscaloosa Federal Building and U.S. Courthouse. My skin was damp, and I was late for my meeting with the FBI. Fortunately, the front desk security guards had my name in their computer and didn't react to my frazzled appearance. I'm sure they dealt with all types walking through those doors.

When Agent Walker called this morning to set up today's meeting, he said I had nothing to worry about and assured me I didn't need to bring my lawyer. They just wanted to talk about the latest in the investigation and run something by me. Despite his assurances, he didn't convince me he was on the level. Less than two days ago this guy all but called me a dumb jackass, a stalker, and a liar. Although what could I say—no? That would surely piss them off and make it seem like I had something to hide.

Which I didn't.

Except for the mask.

Although technically, Mrs. Majelski was hiding it. And once things got wrapped up, I planned to turn it over to the Dauphin anonymously and let them sort it out. After I wiped it down for prints.

Geez. Who in the frick am I?

The security guard assigned to escort me stopped and opened a door to a room midway down a fifth-floor hallway. "Here you go, ma'am."

I brushed past the uniformed man and entered a small reception area reeking of sweet perfume and cigarette smoke. "Thank you, sir."

"Yes, ma'am." He poked his head inside the room. "She's all yours, Gladys," he called to a receptionist stationed behind an L-shaped desk lording over the room.

"Thanks, Mike."

I stopped in front of the desk as Mike backed out into the hallway and closed the door. It was a dark-brown monstrosity with a speckled cream-colored laminate top. Very professional. Not the crappy old government-issue battleship-gray metal desk I expected. Occupying the middle of it lay an open magazine.

The receptionist observed me over tortoise shell reading glasses perched on a pointed nose. She was probably in her mid-forties, but the way she dressed she could easily be in her sixties. She wore a dusty-blue-and-ivory dress with some kind of floral print, a large blue-beaded necklace, and a ratty black sweater draped over slumped shoulders. Thick red lipstick pulled me away from that dreadful dress to a pale bony face.

"Can I help you?" she asked in a singsong falsetto. Yellow-stained teeth peered out from cherry-red lips.

"I have a three o'clock appointment with Agent, uh…"

"Yes?" she asked, drawing out the three-letter word with her head and black hair bun angled to the side.

"Walker," I blurted out. "Agent Jackson Walker."

She rotated to her left, slid out a keyboard drawer, manipulated a mouse, and typed something. After more mouse manipulations and studying the monitor, she spun back with a frown on her painted mouth. "Are you aware it's three twenty-two?"

"I had a little problem in the parking garage."

"I see." Her snippy voice dripped with condemnation. "Still. You're late."

"Sorry." I considered her for a beat. "Two of the elevators are also out. The guard said that's always happening," I added, as if that would help make us BFFs.

She didn't respond, her close-set eyes scolding me for such a lame attempt to defend the inexcusable. After an eternity spanning way past five seconds, she picked up the phone, punched in a four-digit number and waited. "Your three o'clock is here." She listened briefly, then nodded. "She knows she's late. Mmmm hmmm. Okay. I'll tell her."

My cheeks burned. Fricking parking garage.

The receptionist placed the phone back in its cradle. "Please have a seat. He'll be here shortly. Can I get you something to drink?" Her voice was back to candy sweet. Talk about mood swings.

"No, thank you."

For the next six or seven minutes I waited in a metal armchair while she skimmed through her magazine as if I didn't exist. Finally, a soft buzz vibrated from a sturdy metal door next to her desk, followed by an electronic click. The door cracked open. A tall, dark-haired man stuck his head into the reception area. It was Agent Walker. I never thought I would be happy to see him again.

"Ms. Donovan, thanks for coming in." He flashed a never-before-seen toothy smile as he held the door open with one hand. In the other he held a thick light-blue folder with a midnight-blue binding.

I rose and headed toward the door. "Yes, sir." Nerves erupted as perspiration worked its magic in all the wrong places.

"This way, please. Thanks, Gladys."

He let me pass through the security door into a well-lit hallway. He wore black suit pants and a tailored white shirt revealing a chiseled V-shape back with broad shoulders tapering to a flat waist. I did the requisite butt-check. Now here was a guy who used a stair-stepper. A lot.

Did I just a butt-check a federal agent? *C'mon, Sara. Get a grip. Focus on the situation. Not the butt.*

I followed him and his butt through a short corridor and into a small conference room. A polished red-maple rectangular table dominated the middle of the room. A pair of wheeled armchairs cushioned with black material were on each long side. A matching chair flanked each end. No mirrors were on any walls, with the only wall adornment being a six-by-four-foot white board taking up most of the space on the far wall. The room was much better appointed than the disgusting interrogation room they had squirreled me into Monday night Tuesday morning. It even smelled better. Like warm cinnamon and apples. He motioned with a beefy hand to sit.

"Water? Coffee?"

"No, thanks."

Unless you want to serve it shirtless. One glorious

butt-check and I forgot why I was there. *Focus.*

"Okay. Let's get started." He yanked out a chair opposite mine and settled his massive frame into it, like a dad sitting in his kindergartner's chair on Back-to-School Night. Opening the folder, Agent Walker sifted through some papers, skipped back to the front, and scanned the first few pages. Without a word, he closed the folder and set it aside on the table. Motioning with his eyes to a sleek black gizmo in the middle of the table, he punched a button, sat back, and observed me closely.

"Nine-one-one dispatch. State your name and emergency please."

"Uh, this is Sara Donovan. It's not so much of an emergency, per se, as a very serious situation?"

It was the recording of my call to the cops about Connor. Like the stuff they played on those reality cop shows for the perp. Oh, God, did I get played?

"Ma'am, this line is for real emergencies only."

"But this is serious."

I was talking so fast. My voice sounded like a cross between Professor Sawalha's chair and an over-caffeinated auctioneer.

"Are you in danger or hurt?"

"Um, I guess not. But I believe there's criminal activity going on next door."

Was this one of those enhanced interrogation techniques some Washington politicians complained about a few years back because—

"Are any lives or property at risk?"

—if so, I now understood their concern. This was beyond awful.

"Yes, well—"

"*Is someone in danger?*"

"*No, but—*"

"*Ma'am, you're taking up a line dedicated to emergencies. Are any people's lives or property at risk? Or is anybody hurt?*"

"*Not that I know of.*"

"*Then please hang up. Call only if there's a real emergency. One in which you are in danger or there's a serious risk to lives or property. If there's some other non-emergency problem, please call the local station.*"

"*But I think there's a crime going on here.*"

He showed mercy on me and clicked off the recording.

I hung my head. I totally understood if he arrested me right then and there for disturbing the peace. And no need for a lawyer because what I just heard was defenseless. Even Mauzzy couldn't get me out of this one.

"Okay, Ms. Donovan. As you can see, we confirmed everything you told us about calling the police. Good for you, because I'm sure you're aware, lying to a federal agent is a crime."

"Yes, sir. I am. And I didn't lie. I have done nothing wrong. I told you that the other night. Besides, I don't lie." I was aiming for respectful with just a bit of indignation.

Make your point and don't poke the tiger. They don't know about the mask.

When his mouth curled up in a pressed smile, I realized I might have missed respectful and crossed over into indignant.

"I'm sure you don't. Let's get down to it. Okay?"

"Yes, sir."

He opened the dossier, extracted a blown-up photograph from beneath the top papers, and slid it in front of me. "Do you know this person?"

I most certainly do know, Captain Obvious. It was me. Hiding behind the clothes rack at the mall. I don't know how they got that shot, but it was so not flattering. I swallowed hard. "Yes, sir. That would be...um...me."

I had a bad feeling about this. Things were not starting out the way I imagined, with us chitchatting about the weather and getting to know each other. Maybe I should have taken him up on that coffee. It was a wonderful icebreaker for making conversation.

"Correct."

I smiled faintly.

"During our investigation, you popped up enough times to get on our radar. Initially, we just wanted to talk with you."

He slid a few more photos in front of me. I was in each one. Not always the main subject, but definitely in every pic. And many times, not at my best. Geez, my hair was awful in that one shot. Oh my God, that's me in the church parking lot. A bad feeling slithered up from the pit of my plummeting stomach. And it wasn't gas.

Agent Walker exhaled. "But things changed when you showed up at Tannehill. When we put all your activities together, as explained to you Monday night, it made for a very suspicious set of circumstances." He finished with a proud grin. "Ending with you holding the bag. Literally."

I shot back a nervous smile.

"You've been the topic of many a discussion the

last two days. We've gone back and forth on what to do with you. If anything."

I don't know about before, but no doubt I became a topic of conversation after the church parking lot. How embarra...*do with me?* That couldn't be good. What other damn photos did he have buried in his secret little folder? Hey, now who was the stalker? It cut both ways, G-man.

"Although this is an FBI satellite office, on this case we've been acting in a support role for U.S. Immigration and Customs Enforcement."

I broke in. "ICE."

"Their lead on the case is Agent Grant Doherty. He's been adamant your intentions were not malicious or criminal. And your recent actions, albeit ill-advised, were innocent. The only thing you're guilty of is exercising poor judgment. And," he trained his eyes on me, "our team, and more important, Supervisory Agent Hainsworth, support this assessment."

This could be Dad lecturing me during junior year of high school. Or the air marshal last month. I made a face. It could be a number of authority figures over the years. "Does this mean I'm clear?"

"That's correct."

I let out a big breath of relief. "Thank you."

"However—" The G-man hesitated. "—Agent Doherty knows you pretty well. He's convinced you can help the investigation."

"I don't know any Agent Doherty. Wait. Was he the guy taking all those peeping perv photos? Because if he is, I am not—"

"Whoa. Whoa. Whoa. Hold on, Ms. Donovan." Agent Walker corkscrewed around toward a camera in an upper corner of the room. "Grant? You wanna help me out here? Please."

A few seconds later, the door to the room opened and in stepped...

Chapter Thirty-Two

It can't be

"Connor?"

He bit his lower lip and settled into a chair at the end of the table. "Hi, Sara." His probing eyes searched me for a reaction. "I'm Grant Doherty."

I flopped back as my whole body fell limp. My mouth was open, but nothing came out. I tried to comprehend this new reality, and for perhaps the first time, I had nothing to say. And to make matters worse, he had on some navy-blue polyester-blend sports jacket straight out of a chain department store. So hideous. How could he think polyester trumped his worn jeans and gray t-shirts?

Connor, Grant, whatever the frick his name was, regarded me before dropping his head like a student just called into the principal's office. It could be he was ashamed I caught him wearing polyester. I would be. What a far cry from his tuxedoed hotness at the auction.

Agent Walker squirmed in his seat, most likely trying to work out an exit strategy.

My gaze wandered around the room before settling back on Grant. "I don't…I can't…"

He stretched an arm across the table to me. "Sara, I'm so sorry but—"

I recoiled. "Sorry, my ass. You—lied—to me. You

fucking lied to me. About everything. Even your name. All a lie." Dropping the F-bomb on a federal agent was not advisable, but I didn't care.

"I wanted to tell you. But I couldn't. I was undercover."

"You were *spying* on me? You *are* the peeper photographer?"

"What? No. Although—" he stopped, a pinched expression on his face. "—someone apparently spied on me."

Instant blush. I bowed my head. "Touché." I wanted to tear out of the room, right behind Agent Walker, and never see Grant again. Or Connor.

Grant's voice was calm and reassuring. "Listen, Sara."

I raised my gaze to his.

"Three months ago, my office got a call from Professor Sawalha. He told us the Dauphin received several statuettes from a collector for an authenticity assessment, and the museum called him in to conduct it. He authenticated the pieces but suspected the provenance. He didn't tell anybody about his suspicions and instead called us right away."

I frowned. "The professor? You mean he's not involved? But...just last week...I saw him meeting Mrs. Bagley and another person at Denny Chimes. It was so dark. And wet. And late. Everybody ran when I got closer. But I know it was him."

Grant shook his head. "He's been assisting us ever since his call. That's why I came to Tuscaloosa as his TA. It allowed us to confer without raising suspicions and, if necessary, I could penetrate the museum." He hesitated for a second before a revelation spread across his face. "That was you at the Quad?"

My head tipped sideways. "That was you? You were the third person?"

He let out a faint whistle, and a muted chuckle of disbelief. "Man, we thought you blew the investigation and my cover that night. I was meeting with Agent Hainsworth and the professor to discuss what he found in Cairo the week before and to plan our next steps. First, I heard someone splashing around and thought nothing of it, because who in their right mind would try to sneak up on us in wet shoes? Then, I heard someone trying to sneak up on us—in wet shoes. We agreed on one of our alternate meeting protocols and scattered. *That was really you?*"

I raised a hand. "Guilty." Oops. Bad word choice. "I wasn't following you, though," I added quickly. "I just saw something suspicious and wanted to get a closer look. Who meets in the middle of the night? After a monsoon. At the flooded Quad." I screwed up my face. "Sorry."

"It's okay. But I gotta tell you, we were on pins and needles until they contacted us about making a good faith exchange." He fell silent.

"The professor?" I prodded.

"Right. Despite the provenance, he was positive someone stole those statuettes from an Egyptian government warehouse after 1989."

"Why 1989? How could he pin it to such a specific year?"

"Because he remembered cataloguing these specific artifacts for the Egyptian government and supervising their storage in a government warehouse outside Cairo."

"In 1989," I said.

"Bingo," he said with an easy smile. "We contacted the Egyptian government, and after they got past their initial self-denials and obvious embarrassment, they performed a physical check of the warehouse and found the objects were missing. We suspect a low-paid warehouse guard stole the items and sold them to a local gang of tomb looters. Who probably then sold them to a dirty dealer or smuggler. Happens all the time."

"But how come the Egyptian government didn't notice the statuettes were missing?"

"Overstuffed warehouses and rudimentary record keeping. It was pure coincidence the professor handled the same artifacts in Cairo over twenty-five years ago." His eyes grew wide. "Imagine that. Sheer coincidence may end up busting this ring wide open."

"Who all is in this ring?"

Agent Walker swept the peeper photos off the table, returned them to his folder, and joined in. "We don't know yet. But we're certain a ring is operating in the region. Could even be right out of the museum."

Vindication. I may have been wrong about Connor/Grant and the professor being involved, but I was right about the antiquities smuggling. And technically, they had involvement. Just not as the bad guys.

"We think it's the same group that orchestrated the October looting of the Akhenaten dedication tomb," Grant said. "That was a sophisticated job. And the people we're chasing here are just as sophisticated. It's possible they compromised someone on the dig team."

"I read about that," I said. "They stole a lot of

valuable stuff."

"Sure did," he replied.

"You really think it involves some people at the Dauphin?"

"We think so. But we're not sure. This is where," he stopped, then hesitated before continuing. "We...I...would like to ask for your help."

Even though Mrs. Majelski warned me to keep quiet, and the banshee was *shrieking* at me, my heart took control of the situation. "About that. The Dauphin, I mean."

"Yes?"

"I kinda forgot to mention something." My face scrunched up. "I just *might* have an artifact I received at the Dauphin."

His eyebrows drew together as he exchanged a glance with his partner. "Sara, are you confessing to—"

"*No.* I thought you were involved. I didn't know who to trust. And then with today's waterboarding of me with that damn recording, I just forgot."

Grant's face became taut. Stern.

Was bunking with Big Betty back in my immediate future? Or worse, an amorous Roxy Rhonda? I took a few seconds to gather myself, then pressed on. "Someone in Cairo working for a company called All Things Egyptian shipped it to me at the Dauphin. Accidentally."

"Why would someone do that?" Grant asked. "Ship something to you worth maybe millions— *accidentally?*"

It sounded as bad as I envisioned when I first kept it quiet two very long weeks ago. I might need a lawyer. Or better yet, Mauzzy.

I took a deep breath. "I'm not sure. Mrs. Bagley, who I think is the ring's mule—" I shot a quick frown at Agent Walker. "—and I had both ordered souvenir funerary masks. But I think hers was an actual artifact. And their Cairo man, Mansour, might have switched hers for mine. Accidentally."

"How do you know the name of the Cairo contact?" Agent Walker asked.

"I looked in the gift shop's files for the name and contact info for the vendor that shipped that type of souvenir. And then I called them."

Grant's eyes bulged. "You *called* them?"

"Uh-huh. But he didn't tell me anything other than his name. When I asked about Mrs. Bagley's order, he pretended he didn't speak English and hung up."

"What makes you think he's involved?" Grant asked. "He could have just been an employee."

"Oh no. He knew about the mask. And a few days later I got a call with the caller ID blocked. I tracked it back to a gallery in Birmingham owned by Henderson Thornburn. He's a former art history prof who used to work at the Dauphin."

"Sounds like you've been busy," Grant said, a tone of admiration in his voice. "That's how you knew about him on Monday when we were, uh—"

"Interrogating me," I snapped.

He held up a quick hand to shush Agent Walker. "We prefer the term interviewing."

"Uh-huh. Call it what you want. Anyway, yeah, things seemed fishy. So, I investigated."

"What's the name of the gallery?" Agent Walker asked.

"Thornburn Gallery of Antiquities."

"And the Cairo vendor again?"

"All Things Egyptian."

"Okay, let's get back to this mask," Grant said.

"Two weeks ago, after I got my mask, this Thornburn dude called me. At least I'm pretty sure it was him. He said I had something of his, and he wanted it back."

"What did you tell him?"

My cheeks grew warm. "Um, I just figured he was a friend messing around so I hung up on him." I stopped and considered the absurdity of the past two weeks. "Besides, it might not be the real thing, anyway."

Grant eyebrows rose, his stoic expression softening a bit. "Because…"

"Because I melted a small hole in it. It might just be cheap metal or something the manufacturer coated in plastic and painted—but I don't think so."

"You melted it?"

"Spilled nail polish remover on it."

"Nail polish remover?" Agent Walker asked.

"I was doing my toes and knocked the bottle over when I reached for the cotton balls. The mask was on the same table." I twisted my face up. "And that's about it."

Grant considered my explanation, all the while bobbing his head with an index finger placed to his lips. "Cotton balls?" he asked, his eyes brightening more than their usual splendor.

I nodded vigorously. "They were across the table from me."

Agent Walker's eyes narrowed. "What makes you think it's an artifact?"

"There's a yellowish metal underneath the plastic coating. It could be brass. But I think it might be gold. I don't know of any other metals with that color. And why cover it in painted plastic unless you're trying to hide something?"

That got Grant's attention. "Where's the item now?"

"I gave it to Mrs. Majelski for safekeeping. She suggested it and I thought it was a good idea."

"And just who is Mrs. Maj...alski?"

"Majelski. Sadie Majelski. She's a rocking old lady who works out at the gym the same time I do. I also water her plants when she's away." I paused for a second. "Which is quite a bit."

The FBI agent hunched forward, his folded arms dropping on the table. "Why would you leave a potentially valuable item with her? Sounds like you could be putting a defenseless old lady in danger."

I cracked a smile. "Ohhhh, I think she can take care of herself. Pretty sure she owns a very—colorful—past."

Grant cocked his head. "Colorful? How colorful?"

"I'm not sure, but she told me her walker was part of her—cover? And last Friday while we drove around talking, she made some crazy maneuvers in her truck. She said she had to 'take care of some dry cleaning,' but we never even passed a dry cleaner."

The G-men made eye contact. "She specifically used that term?" Agent Walker asked.

"Yup. Dry cleaning. Why?"

"In certain circles, the term means eluding or evading surveillance," he replied.

"Certain circles?" I asked.

"It supports your conclusion regarding her colorful background," Grant said.

My brow furrowed. "All I know is, she seems to know a lot about me. Where I live. Where I go." I pointed at him. "About you. When I—"

"About me?"

"Yes, but no way—"

Agent Walker's face shared Grant's concern. "When did you give her the item?"

"Last Friday. You don't think she's involved, do you?"

"It's highly likely," Grant said.

"Didn't you just say she suggested you give it to her?"

"That doesn't make her a crook. She's just worried about me. I mean, I water this lady's plants. You guys suspect everybody about anything. You even suspected me of involvement."

"Sara," Agent Walker said, "you *are* invo—"

"Not in the way you first suspected. Hey, I know it doesn't look good. But I'm telling you. She isn't your perp."

Grant exhaled. "You're right. It doesn't look good. It's not just her suggestion you give her the item. There are other pieces you're forgetting, including her somehow knowing about me. As long—"

"But that—"

He held up a hand. "Listen, Sara. As long as she possesses that item, and until we can verify just who she is and what you gave her, we're keeping her under surveillance. Understand?"

I swallowed. "Yes."

"And whatever you do, don't tip her off," warned

Agent Walker. "Because if you do, you'll be impeding a federal investigation. That's a crime."

"He's right. Absolute silence. If she contacts you, don't give anything up. Call me immediately. This is serious. Okay?"

"Yes," I muttered.

Crap.

Chapter Thirty-Three

You got a warrant?

This Friday morning, I was back at the Federal
Building, sitting in the same well-appointed conference
room as earlier in the week. It's been two days since my
FBI meeting when Connor became Grant. The
professor became—a professor. Mrs. Majelski became
a suspected international antiquities smuggler. And I
inadvertently became a contributor to the antiquities
black market. With all these character transfigurations,
I half-expected Mauzzy to shape-shift into a bookish
academic lecturing on Freud's *The Ego and the Id*. Or a
lawyer arguing the finer points of stop-and-frisk in front
of the Supreme Court.

The door to the room opened. Grant entered
carrying a thick, light-blue folder similar to the one
from the other day. Hopefully without more photos of
me. Fortunately, he was back to wearing his gray t-shirt
and faded jeans. I wanted to tell him to burn that
hideous polyester jacket, but it would probably just
melt. Agent Walker trailed him in a black pinstripe suit,
white shirt and solid bright-red tie.

He dropped the folder on the table and took a seat
opposite me. "Good morning, Sara. I appreciate you
coming in on such short notice."

Agent Walker nodded in agreement and settled into

the chair next to him.

"You're welcome. I'm missing studying time for this meeting. You know it's Finals Week. And I have an exam Monday for my most important and difficult class."

"I understand. Before we get started, I want to apologize about Monday night at Tannehill. You shouldn't have been there and it surprised us. So—" Grant blew out. "—I had to let the process complete itself. It was my call to kill the op and have you busted."

"You had me busted? You—"

He held up a hand. "Please. Listen to me. I knew you weren't there for the drop. You followed me. For sure, bad judgment on your part. But that's it. And I couldn't let you walk away with the cash. That would have made things worse for you and us. I had to come up with an idea on the fly to save both the investigation and you."

"Seriously? Having me arrested was saving me?"

"We never arrested you," Agent Walker said through his teeth as he flipped through his notebook like he was taking an open-book exam.

"You and your pal, Agent No Coincidence, sure as hell made me feel you arrested me. You little—"

Grant jumped in. "At the time, I knew you wouldn't agree with my decision. But it was the best thing for you. Now you're cleared in the investigation and I can really use your help."

"The best thing for me, *or the best thing for you?* Sounds like you just wanna use me." I was about to unload on them when I noticed Grant. He was crestfallen.

"I would never use you. This is your decision. You can help or not. No questions asked, and no pressure."

I considered Grant, then Agent Walker, who was studying me. I scowled at him, sending the man diving for his notebook.

Grant folded his hands on the table. "Here's the problem. When you walked in on the drop at the park, that severely compromised the investigation. It was the second and final stage of a good faith exchange. The mall—"

I winced.

"—was the first stage. A small transaction for a scarab. After that successful exchange, we agreed to purchase a bronze Osiris statue for fifty thousand to show we were serious and for them to prove they could provide authentic pieces beyond minor stuff like scarabs. From what we can tell, their smuggling methods are ingeniously simplistic. They also use an elaborate sales transaction system with multiple double-blind elements. Dead drop locations they can safely monitor from a distance. Blind communications through layered intermediaries. Unwary transporters and distributors. It's why the FBI suspected you were a—"

"Dumb jackass?"

He frowned. "Mule. No disrespect. Trafficking lingo for—"

"I know what a mule is," I said as scathingly disrespectful as I could.

He cringed, took a few seconds, and continued. "After you blew the op, we made contact again with the ring and said the cops followed our courier. That the buyer didn't know the courier was running her own scheme on the side, and the feds were onto her. Not us."

"Her? You sold me as a rogue courier? That was your brilliant 'idea on the fly?' You—"

"I had limited options. Eventually we reassured them her own stupidity got her busted, and our deal remained clean."

"Rude."

He pressed his lips tight. "Our courier, as in you, was a layered intermediary so no way someone could trace her back to us. We emphasized our buyer wanted the piece they offered and was ready to move straight to the big transaction. They wanted an additional ten million. We settled on five."

My mouth fell open. "An extra five million dollars?"

"Twenty-five mill in all. These people are clever. And sophisticated. They understood the market for this piece."

"What piece is worth that much?"

Excitement exploded across his face. "It was so amazing we didn't believe them at first." He came out of the chair and paced behind the table. "Two months ago, we put the word out an anonymous collector wanted to buy a high-value piece for the crown jewel of his Egyptian collection. The message that filtered back blew us away." He stopped across from me. "Somebody offered the Pharaoh Akhenaten statue."

"What? Not *the* Akhenaten statue?"

The three-thousand-year-old statue of King Tut's father was the most valuable piece stolen from the Egyptian Museum during the Arab Spring protests that ended Hosni Mubarak's reign. Thieves rappelled into the building from the roof and made off with dozens of objects, including the Akhenaten statue.

An outsized smile radiated over Grant's dorky-cute face.

I scratched my head. "But…how…no way. That's impossible. The Antiquities Ministry said a boy found the statue in the trash and turned it in. It had some damage but they've been restoring it."

"Correct. When we heard this item was on the market, we asked the Egyptian government if Professor Sawalha could inspect the Akhenaten statue. A few weeks ago, he made a quick trip to Cairo. As it turns out, for the last several years, the Egyptian Museum was unwittingly restoring a worthless piece of limestone. As the professor put it, a brilliant fake, but nothing more."

I shook my head so much I felt like I was watching a championship ping-pong match. "That's beyond incredible."

"It sure is. And it shows we're up against some innovative people. With the protests going on in Cairo, they put their plan in motion. We believe the ring contracted the thieves to get this specific statue. Their bonus payment was they could keep anything else they stole. After the theft, the ring planted the phony piece in the trash near Tahrir Square."

"How did they know somebody would find it *plus* turn it in?"

"We don't know. But the boy's uncle was on the faculty at the University of Cairo. The uncle called the ministry. And bam. The Egyptian Museum recovered the fake." Grant clapped lightly. "Another brilliant double-blind op. We think they've been sitting on this for some time. Waiting for the right opportunity to make the big score before shutting it all down."

"Twenty million is worth waiting for," I added.

His eyes widened. "Twenty-five."

"Because of me. Sorry."

"Don't worry. We would never pay the money. Purely window dressing."

I sat back, past events and coincidences pinballing off my inner skull so fast it was like lottery balls bouncing around up there. I was wrong about Grant and the professor. What else did I get wrong? I propped my elbows on the table and cradled my head and face in outstretched fingers. "Do you know who these people are?"

"No. But we're getting close. The information you gave us Wednesday about Thornburn and the Cairo vendor has proven helpful. The Egyptian authorities are getting teams in place, waiting for our signal to take Mansour down. And we've had Majelski under surveillance since then, too. She's a cagey lady. Twice she put the slip on our teams." He shook his head in disbelief over the octogenarian super-spy ninja. "Putting her aside, last week we thought we caught a break when customs impounded a shipping container from Cairo."

I popped out from behind my hands like a mother playing peek-a-boo with her baby. "In Mobile."

He sat, considering me for a second. "Ah, that's right. You took the call for Roger Gwynne from the Mobile Port Authority."

I sat up straight, my head bobbing in excitement. "Some grump named Kranzer."

"Yep, that's him. When news of the flagged container got to us, we were convinced more artifacts were being smuggled in. Possibly even the Akhenaten statue. We planned to identify the suspected stolen items and place GPS micro-trackers on them to lead us right to the bad guys. The problem is"—he thumped the table with his fist—"nobody notified me or this office about the impoundment until the following morning. By the time I got to Mobile, customs already released the shipment."

"Why would they do that?"

"Gwynne called Kranzer, who put him in touch with the senior customs agent on duty. He threatened the guy with a phone call from the governor and worse unless he released the museum's shipment from the container. He warned that a long-promoted Early Byzantine exhibit opening the following weekend was at risk unless customs released their shipment."

"That makes no sense."

"Right. There's no exhibit slated for opening this weekend. So—" he addressed Agent Walker. "—why did he make that call?"

"At the time, twenty million reasons."

"That's what I think. Why else take such a risk?" He surveyed me, his eyes awash with contrition and vulnerability. "Sara? I could use your help. But it's your call."

Damn it. There was something about this guy. Right from the start. And now I was in this mess because I let my head overrule my heart. I sucked in a cleansing breath, puffed up my cheeks, and blew out slowly. "What kind of help?"

"At a minimum, Gwynne has some culpability. From what we can tell, for a museum director, he's pretty overextended financially. Fancy house. Big mortgage. Ever bigger spending wife. But we need more evidence."

A kaleidoscope of colors and cacophonous sound filled my head. The more he talked, the louder the banshee screeched. "I don't know how I can help."

Grant stood, ran a hand through his hair, circled the room once, then sat. "Here's the deal. We got a tip from one of our informants last night. A shipment should hit the gift shop tomorrow morning. There's supposed to be a package in it for your Mrs. Bagley. We squeezed our guy hard on the reliability of the intel. He didn't waver, said his source was beyond impeccable." His eyes locked in on me. "He emphasized, don't question it. Act on it."

"That's why you need me? To get the package?"

He hesitated and wiggled a hand. "Not exactly. We need you to place a few listening devices. And if there's a shipment in the gift shop with a package for Bagley, place a GPS micro-tracker on the items in that package. We'll give you two trackers. If there's only one item, just place one tracker."

I blew out a little snort. "I don't know how to install listening devices and trackers. I couldn't even install my printer."

"It's no big deal. They're beyond easy to install. Assuming you agree to help, the key is to get the micro-trackers placed Saturday morning when you unpack the shipment. Don't worry about the listening devices until Sunday. They're just a failsafe for us in case the trackers don't work, or somebody discovers them. The FBI will remotely activate the trackers Saturday morning and the listening devices Sunday afternoon."

Agent Walker took a clear plastic bag from his

inner jacket pocket and handed it to me. It contained two black disks, smaller than the size of a penny.

"Those"—Grant pointed at the bag in my hand—"are what the listening devices look like. They're voice activated, highly technical, and even more expensive. The micro-trackers are similar, but much smaller and thinner. Both self-adhere."

"Why me? Why don't you just have your *support team* place these things?"

Agent Walker's jaw tightened, but he wisely kept his mouth shut.

"Although we believe it involves somebody at the museum, we don't know for certain who it is or how deep the conspiracy runs. While Gwynne is a clear suspect, there are other persons of interest. Including Dr. Mitchell. We interviewed her at the beginning of the month under the pretense of a new Bureau outreach program to build relationships with people in her profession. She asked if there was a precipitating event, and we told her it was the looting of the Akhenaten dedication tomb. That answer had her eyes bouncing all around the room. Bottom line, we can't trust anyone at the Dauphin. And with its elaborate security systems, a black-bag job is out of the question."

"Black bag?"

"When the Bureau contracts technicians with particular skills to gain entry surreptitiously," the FBI agent said.

"You mean burglars," I said pointblank.

Grant shook his head and quickly interjected, apparently trying to protect Agent Walker from getting into it with me. "No. They're vetted and cleared legitimate contractors. Again, this job would be too complex for that option. Especially with the shipment arriving tomorrow. And," he paused for added emphasis, "you're already on the inside. You're above suspicion." He extended his arms across the table and clasped his hands like a pious altar boy. "Sara Donovan, will you please help me?"

I put the bag on the table and eyed him. Then Agent Walker. Then back again. "You got a warrant?"

He twisted around and pointed a finger at Agent Walker. "You owe me twenty bucks."

The agent dipped his head and forced a tight smile.

Grant turned back to me, his face triumphant. "Somehow, if we ever got to this point, I expected you to ask that question." He opened the folder on the table and took out a set of papers. "Got it late last night. Not too long after the tip came through. Gwynne's phone call getting that shipment released helped make our case. The judge wasn't happy, with it being past her bedtime and all. But she signed it."

"You knew I would say yes?"

"I had a hunch."

"I have a major final on Monday. You're asking for a huge favor."

"I know. But we have a real shot here. And"—he stared right at me—"if you had just handed the mask over to the FBI instead of hiding it with Majelski, you wouldn't have blown our op at the park. And we wouldn't be here."

My body stiffened. "Really? You want to go there? Or you want my help?"

He lowered his head and raised both hands in surrender. "I'm sorry. You're right. I need your help. It's your call. I'll understand if you don't want to help. I just want to nail these people."

With elbows on the table, I steepled my fingers and shut my eyes. My life flashed by, allowing me to relive some of my not-best moments, ending with Zoe's blazing glare and hands on hips. I opened my eyes. Grant was studying me.

"Okay. I'll do it."

Chapter Thirty-Four

It's no big deal?

I burst into the back room of the gift shop where Edna waited, standing with arms folded and wearing her perpetual frown.

"Good morning," I sang, hoping my being three minutes late went unnoticed, even though we didn't open for two hours.

She nodded and squeezed in behind a desk besieged with piles of paper, shipping manifests, and supplier invoices. "Morning. You're late."

"Sorry. The police pulled me over five miles from here."

"That's your problem. Be on time." With her head bowed, Edna snapped a folder closed and flipped it into an overflowing wire out-basket on the corner of her desk. "We got a shipment in this morning from Cairo." She motioned with her head to a wooden crate on the floor near a table so large it would fill my living room. "Make sure you get it unpacked, sorted, and into the system before we open."

"Any special orders in there I need to know about?"

"Hmmm? Oh, uh, no." She tossed a thick manila folder into the out-basket, snagged a worn overstuffed file from a different pile, and pored over the contents.

Dang it. I had a sleepless night worrying about today. And this morning, a traffic ticket. All for nothing. I schlepped over to my bin to store my purse with the high-tech gizmos. No need for them today.

After a few paper shuffles, without looking up, Edna added, "Oh, actually, yes. There's a special order in there for Mrs. Bagley."

Game on.

"Okay. I'll put it with Karen's things."

Head still buried in paperwork, a curt "thank you" was the only response.

I dropped my purse into the bin. Using my body as a screen from prying eyes, I dug out a baggie from the purse with the two micro-trackers and two *Made in Egypt* stickers to cover up the devices. I tucked the baggie in the front left pocket of my jeans as the back of my neck prickled from anxiety. How in the heck can I get those trackers on the package with the lady sitting ten feet away? One thing I knew for certain. A good plan wasn't forthcoming in my current state. First things first.

I hustled to the opposite corner of the room and a small table with a drawer and shelf underneath. On top sat the most important piece of equipment in the backroom, if not the entire museum. It may not have been the newest, and certainly not the best, but it was the linchpin to the shop's successful operation. The coffeemaker. Edna could be quite the prude, but she sure could brew some good coffee. And this morning its full-bodied smell was exhilarating.

I poured the wondrous black goodness into my large purple mug and slogged over to the unpacking table. With a deep breath, I cut the strapping and delved into the crate. Two white envelopes containing the shipment's packing lists rested on top of many white and brown boxes of varying sizes. One was thick and addressed to Dr. Roger Gwynne with the Dauphin's address. The second, thin and addressed to Mary Bagley.

I took out the thin envelope and opened it. Just one item. I rummaged around in the crate until I found a large box with *Mary Bagley* on it, lifted it out, and carried it to the table. Out of the corner of my eye, I noticed Edna watching me.

I needed cover. Returning to the crate, I unpacked the entire thing, piling all its contents on the worktable. After sorting and stacking the boxes across the table, a privacy screen soon surrounded the Bagley box. I sat and pretended to write something as my left hand worked the baggie out of my pocket.

"That's interesting, Sara."

My hand froze. I poked my head up over the wall of boxes. She remained behind her desk. "Hmmm, what's that?"

"You've never unpacked a shipment like that before."

"Like what?"

"Unloading the entire crate onto the table without working off the packing list as you go."

"Wow, you're observant," I said, my hand still glued to the pocket. "It's a new system I'm trying out."

She stood and circled out from behind her desk, my thumb frantically shoving the baggie back into the pocket. With her back to me, she poured another mug of coffee.

I took a chance and tore the baggie out of my

pocket, hiding it between two stacks of boxes.

She faced me. Her eyes narrowed. "You're coming up with a new unpacking system now when you leave next week for the summer?"

"Sure. Why not? I have a job when I return in August, right?"

Edna shrugged. "I guess."

Talk about a ringing endorsement.

"Okay then. If this new system cuts down on the time, I'll use it when I return."

She raised an eyebrow before crossing the room to her desk. "I doubt it will save any time. It seems inefficient."

I smiled, attempting to put her at ease. "You may be right, but nothing ventured, nothing gained."

"Mmmm hmmm."

I unfolded the packing list for the main shipment and worked off it, opening boxes and making check marks on the list. After ten minutes of working in silence, Edna lost interest in me because she stopped looking over every thirty seconds. I took the Bagley box, opened it, and pulled out a bust of Queen Nefertiti. It was eight inches tall and painted black with a gold headdress, necklace, and base. With one eye on her desk, I inched my hand toward the hiding place. As I took a sip of coffee, my hand grasped the baggie and slid it in front of me. I pretended to be writing while working to separate the seal with my left hand. Thank heavens I had fingernails because otherwise no way I would have been able to open that damn thing. With it finally open, my fingers pinched a tracker and eased it out into my lap.

"How's it going over there?"

I waggled my right hand, the left in my lap wrapped tightly around the device. "Slowly."

Edna studied me for a few seconds. "As I suspected."

"That's why you're the boss," I crowed.

She scowled before diving back into her paperwork. "Pick it up. You only have an hour before we open, and I can't cover the register for you."

"Picking it up," I said, the cheer in my voice belying the absolute panic tearing through me.

"Good."

Laying the bust on its side, I pretended to examine it for damage. With the tracker in my lap, I peeled off the protective backing and in one unhurried motion stuck the thing on the bottom of the bust's base. Slipping my hand back in the baggie, I repeated the motion with the label, ensuring it fully covered the tracker. After returning the bust to its box, I took out a long roll of brown paper from the shelf beneath the table.

I caught a glimpse of Edna. She had a knowing smile plastered on her face. "It just keeps getting better and better, doesn't it?"

I made space on the table to roll out enough paper to cover the bust's box. "It sure does. I'll never do it this way again." Yeah, I'm so through with law enforcement stings.

She kept watching me. "With age comes wisdom."

After cutting a big piece of paper, I wrapped the box, scrawled Bagley on the wrapper, and hoisted it. The thing easily weighed three to four pounds. Lugging it over to the storage bins, I placed it in Karen's. Crossing the room to the worktable, I closed my eyes for a brief second and breathed in deep, letting out a slow silent sigh of relief.

Chapter Thirty-Five

Seriously? It's no big deal?

Because I overslept, courtesy of an ill-advised decision to attend a game night marathon last night with my friends, the window of opportunity for placing the listening devices was closing fast when I got to the gift shop. It was ten-fifty-five Sunday morning. The museum opened at twelve, and I still had to print sales and inventory reports for the Monday morning senior management review. The reports were my excuse for roaming the executive floor today and entering various directors' offices. I couldn't print them yesterday morning because I needed Saturday's sales data included, and Edna wouldn't let me stay late to do it.

"That's why I schedule you to start at ten on Sundays," she said.

I didn't want to argue and couldn't come up with an excuse quick enough without raising suspicion. I needed thirty minutes to get ten copies of each report printed, sorted, and bound. That left me thirty minutes to install the devices before the shop opened.

I ran into the gift shop, plucked the baggie from the bottom of my purse, and dumped the purse in my bin. As instructed earlier by Grant, I stuck the first device on a corner underneath the worktable in the back room. Hurrying out to the front, I stuck the second on the bottom of the checkout counter before logging onto the system and starting the inventory reports generator. One minute later the printer whirred, spitting out reams of reports. By eleven thirty-five I was lugging an armful of reports out of the gift shop and chugging for the elevators.

As I neared the bank of three elevators, I hit the brakes.

Taped on each, a handwritten sign read, "*Out of Order. Preventive Maintenance. Should be ready by noon.*"

Seriously? The Universe couldn't have waited until Tuesday—after my GBA380 final and presentation with the professor—to screw with me?

Since the executive offices were on the fifth floor, and time was my enemy, I ran for the stairs. To be precise, ten flights of stairs. With an armful of reports. And panic tearing through me. All the ingredients for a bad ending.

Once again, the Universe didn't disappoint. On the last flight, my foot didn't clear a stair, sending me careening downward and reports flying. Everywhere.

When gravity finished with me, I lay sprawled face down in a filthy stairwell, reports scattered between the fourth and fifth floors. Fortunately, my hands broke the fall. The flip side, they ended up in something sticky, and my purse with sanitizer sat back in the shop. I scrambled to my feet and carefully went down the stairs to the fourth-floor landing. Gathering fallen reports, I climbed back up to the fifth, collecting the remaining ones along the way.

Tugging open the heavy fire door onto the fifth, I dashed through the halls, distributing reports. And thankfully, lightening my load with each delivery. In Dr. Mitchell's office, I dropped the reduced pile of reports on a visitor's chair and produced the baggie of listening devices. I fished one out, removed the backing, and stuck it under the desk in the front right corner. I buried the baggie back into my front pocket and was gathering up the remaining reports from the visitor's chair when—

"Why are you in my office?"

My stomach plunged into my shoes as my heart catapulted into my throat. "Um, just delivering the weekly reports for the Monday meeting."

Dr. Mitchell stood just inside the door, hands on hips, eyes boring into me. I would have given anything to see her plastic smile from the auction. Anything.

"Why then are there reports in my chair? What were you doing in here?"

"Oh…nothing. Really. Just resting my arms for a minute. I had to take the stairs with all those things."

"Oooh, I understand. I came from church to get caught up on paperwork. Not happy to see those elevators out." She tottered to the desk, dropped into the chair, removed black wedge sandals, and rubbed her feet. "By the third floor my calves and feet were killing me."

I winced in faux sympathy. "I'll leave you alone. I still have a few more to deliver." Before she could say anything, I scooted out of there and hurried through the hall to Roger's office, where I delivered the remaining reports and placed the fourth device in the same position under his desk. I was leaving the office and headed for the conference room when my phone chimed. The time was eleven-fifty-two.

"Zoe, can it wait?"

"Where are you?"

"I'm at the museum and I don't—"

"You're fucking working? *This* weekend?"

I looked around. Nobody. "I have to."

"No, you don't. I thought you placed those things Friday night?"

"Not possible. Look, I really—"

"We're supposed to study today for GBA380. That final is tomorrow."

"Dang it. I forgot to tell you."

"Well, you're on your own tonight. Nana is having her ninetieth birthday."

"Sorry."

"No harm here. I'll be ready. But when are you gonna take the practice case studies? You haven't done any yet."

I blew out. "I'll do them after work."

"You're playing with fire, Sara. You blow that final, you blow any chance of coming back next year."

"Shouldn't be a problem." I glanced at the phone display. Eleven-fifty-five. "I really gotta get going. I have to open in five minutes."

"Okay, good luck studying tonight. Lemme know if you have a problem."

"Thanks. Tell Nana happy b-day."

I was outside the conference room. Nobody in sight. With a final look-see up and down the hall, I bolted into the room. Until my belt loop caught the door handle, yanking my torso sideways into the door before bouncing backward, my head banging against the doorjamb. And there I was, in the final stages of wrapping up my first spy mission, stuck to the door like a hapless fly in a web. I freed myself from the deviant door handle and scoped out the hall. Still clear. Nudging the door back open, I pushed through sideways, keeping a healthy distance from the handle's clutches.

For the conference room, Grant told me to stick the bug in the center of the table, meaning I had to go all the way under the table.

I got on my knees, scooted to the center, and placed the bug. No problem. One to go. I crawled back out and stoo—*thump*.

Instantly sat.

It was dodgeball all over again. Except for the mouthful of dirt. But the molecules—magnificent.

From a sitting position half under the table, I rubbed the top of my head, trying to clear my senses before Dr. Mitchell caught me in a difficult-to-explain position.

After the molecules dissipated, I slid out from under the table and hauled myself up. I had two minutes. At the door, I stuck my head out. All clear. Shoving the door wide open to keep that damn handle away from my persecuted jeans, I popped into the hall and Sara-streaked toward the lunchroom while burrowing into my front pocket to feel for the last device.

It wasn't there.

Ducking into the ladies' room outside the lunchroom, I locked myself in a stall and pulled out the baggie. Empty. I reversed the pocket. Other than some lint and a disintegrated napkin, it was also empty.

Did he give me five or six bugs to plant? The lunchroom was my last objective, and I had no more bugs, so I must have lost one. Too late now to hunt for it. I needed to get to the shop.

Three minutes later, and elevator repairmen are liars, I stood huffing and puffing outside the shop's unlocked front door. Not good. That told me—

"Where have you been?" a gruff Edna asked from behind the front counter.

I bent over, hands on knees. "Upstairs…delivering the…reports."

Still hanging my head, I peeked up and saw her glaring at me. "It took you the entire two hours?"

"Um—" Wheeze. "—I got a kinda late…start."

"So, it would seem. Make sure your time card reflects it." She spun around and disappeared into the back.

I drew in a deep breath and let it out. After the second one, my wind slowly returned. This was shaping up to be quite the memorable last day of work.

Once behind the front counter, I thought it needed a good wipe down. I bent under the counter to get my wipes and spotted a familiar black disk smaller than the size of a penny. Sitting on the shelf. Not adhered to the counter. I picked it up, snapped off a piece of tape from the dispenser, and taped the bug to the bottom of the countertop. Then I made sure it stayed.

I spent the rest of the day wondering if Edna found the listening device on the shelf. And if a half-roll of cellophane tape was bad for bugs. Especially expensive ones.

Chapter Thirty-Six

Bad decisions, bad results?

I was beyond relieved my final day at the museum ended with no further issues as I blasted into Sketchville's parking lot and cut the wheels hard to the right. The hatchback's front tires exploded up the curb of the spot next to Grant's car. Somehow, I instinctively slammed on the brakes to keep from ending up in the living room where Mauzzy lorded over his kingdom. My head snapped forward and back like a besieged crash dummy.

If I wasn't beyond exhausted from this demanding weekend, my pain receptors would have had a few things to say. But they've been offline since late this morning because there was zero response when I tripped on those damn stairs.

I jerked the weary hatchback off the sidewalk and curb. The front end bounced down with a squeaking crunch. Grabbing purse and phone, I fell out of the car and staggered up the stairs to my cottage. No sooner did I get inside, put my purse down, and give an excited Mauzzy kisses, my phone chimed. I glanced at the caller ID.

"Yes, Grant?"

"Hey. Got a minute?"

"Sure, but that's all you'll get. I have a lot of

studying to do."

"It will only take a minute. Come on over."

"Fine." I ended the call and bent to stroke an overexcited Mauzzy. "I'm sorry, Handsome. I have to go next door for a few minutes. But I'll be back."

He stopped pitter-pattering, set his jaws firm and stamped the fiercest scowl on his face I have ever seen from him.

"I'm not happy about it either. It'll just take a minute." I dashed out the door before Mauzzy could say or do anything else.

"Hey," Grant said, standing in the open doorway. He gave me a thumbs-up sign, coupled with a half-smile and raised eyebrows.

"I think so."

I followed him into his cottage and settled onto the ratty love seat, but not before stubbing a toe on the footlocker turned coffee table.

"Ouch. You okay?" he asked with a sympathetic face.

"Pssh. I'm fine. No biggie." I was embracing the sweet serenity of numbness. The sole remaining benefit of last night's bad decision to stay out until four.

"Can I get you anything? Soda? Coffee?"

I shook my head.

"Sure you don't need a caffeine boost? I sorta heard you get in last nigh…uh, this morning. Although knowing what you had to accomplish today, I'm not sure staying out that late was the best of decisions."

I wanted to vaporize this guy after the favor I just did for him, but instead called upon my newfound sneer face.

Concern spread across his face. "You feel okay?

'Cause you suddenly look like hell."

Real nice. Just the reaction I wanted. I probably looked like a diaper-crapping newborn. Exhaustion is a bitch.

I blew out hard. "I just need some rest. Which I'll get tomorrow night."

"Okay, sounds good." He sat on the bottom step leading upstairs and faced the loveseat currently giving my lower back an impromptu acupressure massage. "How'd it go?"

I shifted around, searching in vain for any section of the loveseat not broken. "Seriously. You gotta get a new couch."

"I can't condone buying high-end furniture for a short-term assignment. Besides," he said, looking amused, "it would be out of character for my cover. Remember, I'm a poor grad student."

I made a wry face. "Thanks for reminding me. This has all been a charade."

"Not everything."

A little surge of—something—coursed through me. Was it fatigue putting words and false meanings in my head, or did he just send me a message? A wonderful message of—

"I need a quick debrief. We activated the one tracker you placed yesterday, although as of this morning the object hasn't moved. How'd things go with the listening devices?"

In a flash, I became five-hundred pounds heavier, with those fricking springs torturously poking into my back as I sank further into the depths of the worn loveseat—and despair.

Closing my eyes, I jammed a thumb into my

forehead to summon some nourishing, albeit caffeine deficient, blood flow. I was so damn tired. I didn't want to deal with him now over losing one of his expensive gizmos. I just wanted to go to sleep, and I still had studying waiting for me. "They're all in place."

"Excellent. I'll check with the guys in a bit to make sure everything is working okay. I'm indebted to you for this."

"Sure."

"We couldn't have done this without you."

I forced a smile and threw a half-hearted fist pump in the air for minimal emphasis. "Yea, me."

"Okay, well," he said, getting up from the stairstep and walking to the door. "We got it from here. I'll let you know later how it goes. Just remember, this is an active investigation. Not a word to anyone. Not your mom. Not your best friend. Okay?"

I stood, my violated lower back screaming in delight at being freed from the loveseat's clutches. "Okay," I exhaled and shuffled toward the open door. "Although I told Zoe. Friday night. After you asked for my help."

Grant stopped me at the door and placed his hand on my arm. "That's all right. Just no more until I say it's okay. And Sara—" He gazed deep into my half-open eyes. This morning before leaving for work they were bloodshot and underscored by deep black bags. I could only imagine how they looked now. His eyes were a cool blue pool of warmth. Mine, a cold—cesspool. "—thanks. Really."

Boy, this guy was great undercover. I guess I'll never know how good he was under the covers.

"No problem." I tramped out the door and slumped

down the front stairs toward my cottage and Sweet Handsome.

Chapter Thirty-Seven

Diet sodas and gummies

The last twelve hours were not my finest. I recognize that's setting the bar low. Unfortunately, there are no lifeboats on this *Titanic*.

After I left Grant's place, I took a three-hour nap and powered up the laptop to tackle some GBA380 sample case problems. Within fifteen minutes, after I realized it was a bad idea to wait so long to start them, my laptop crashed. And when I needed JT. When I was actually looking for him. I couldn't find him. Not on his phone. Not in his dorm. Not even at the mall's Geeks and Gamers Lounge.

Karma—thou art a bitch.

After I called off the geek search, I had enough time for three hours of old-school studying and another three-hour nap before leaving to take the exam. Of course, the Universe and her trusty sidekick, The Bane of My Existence, thought one last parting kill shot was in order. This morning they conjured up a grumpy old bus driver, and the bus lurch to beat all bus lurches. The result? My phone wrapped around the chrome handle of a seat back—while still in my hand.

Smart phones can do many things. Bending not one of them. With one shot, they killed both my phone and timekeeping device. Right before my

GBA380 exam, only the final arbiter of my 'Bama career.

And now. Four hours later. It was over. Totally— completely—over.

I sat on a bench outside Alston Hall, holding my head in trembling hands. I just finished dancing with the devil, and I had all the poise and balance of a rhino on crack.

A perky little Zoe broke out of a roiling sea of student humanity flowing from Alston Hall. She bounced up to me, all gleaming teeth and shining eyes. "How'd ya do?"

"I don't know," I howled. "Halfway in, my writing hand cramped up. Toward the end, my words looked more like a bad EKG than a well-supported conclusion."

"A bad EKG? What the fuck are you talking about?"

I held up a quivering hand. "Too many diet colas and gummies. Too many, too many…"

"How many did you have?"

I held out my lunch bag and shook it upside down. Nothing fell out.

She eyed the empty bag. "And how much was that?"

I squinted hard in concentration, trying to recall what I packed this morning, and drive out the killer bees raging inside me. "Um, four diet colas."

And just like that, I had to pee. Bad.

"A soda an hour? While in lockdown? Please tell me you went after the exam."

I frowned. "Nope. Not yet." Now I really had to go.

"And the gummies?"

I frowned harder. "Two pounds."

She took an arm and guided me to a standing position. "Holy shit, girl. You had breakfast, right?"

"Microwave…boom." I stood and trudged with her toward the student center everyone called the Ferg. "But two big coffees."

"Oh, Sara. You're a hot mess. Here," she said, digging in her backpack and taking out a flattened baggie. "Eat this while we walk to the Ferg to get some food in you. It's PB&J. I was too nervous to eat anything in there. Four diet colas? Gummies? *And* coffee?"

With that reminder, I squeezed my legs tighter together, got the word "thanks" out, and took the smashed sandwich. I bit off a corner of the PB&J.

"What happened since Friday? You were good then. You even sounded halfway decent on the phone yesterday."

"Connor. No sleep. Grant. Phone bro—"

"Grant. I knew it. I fucking knew it. Damn it, I warned you, Sara. This thing was way too much for you. He should have never asked you for help. The selfish shit."

I blinked back with dead eyes. My mouth wrestled with a second bite of the dry sandwich while I pinched my legs tighter together. "It's…not…his fault." Talking while trying to keep bits of sandwich and pee from escaping was like working the high-wire without a net.

"The hell it isn't. He gave you those buggy things and that—what was it—micro-tracker. He—"

I hissed, squeezing down a piece of sandwich. "Shhhh."

250

The sandwich was more PB than J, but it had the intended effect. The buzzing in my fragile body subsided to a low hum, like a whirring sewing machine. Things were much calmer than the pissed off beehive that ravaged my senses just a few minutes ago. Regrettably, the flood waters inside me continued to build. Fast.

I swiveled my head, making sure nobody was in earshot. "I told you that in confidence. You can't tell anyone, let alone shout it to all of Tuscaloosa."

Zoe dropped her voice, but not the edge to it. "He doesn't care about you. All he cares about is his career and making the big bust." She released a sharp exhale of derision. "Those fuckers are all like that."

We fell silent until we got to the Ferg. It was the longest seven-minute walk ever. Zoe was quiet because she was pissed, which resulted in her grip on my upper arm making my fingers scream for mercy. For me, I needed complete concentration to keep the Hoover Dam in my bladder from busting loose. It was all I could do during the trek to quell an overstimulated nervous system while not peeing into my shoes.

After we entered the Ferg, she released my arm, nourishing blood surging through my parched limb. "Okay, you—"

I took off. I think my earlier bee infestation imbued me with some of its powers because I made a frigging beeline straight for the ladies' room. Five minutes later, things were looking up. I even had more room in my jeans.

Zoe was waiting when I exited the ladies' room, my relieved smile the signal no mishaps occurred on the way in. At least no major mishaps. There might have been a slight minor mishap, but I couldn't be sure.

"Damn, girl. I don't think I've ever seen you move that fast. C'mon, let's get some food into you."

After hitting the food court, we found a four-chair table off to the side and settled in. I placed my tray on the table and dropped purse, backpack, and empty lunch bag on the chair next to me.

"What's that?" she asked in astonishment, staring at my food tray.

"A tuna sub and chips."

"Uh-uh," She said, shaking her head and pointing right at my tray. "*That.*"

My eyes shifted. "Diet cola."

"Are you fucking kidding me? Diet cola? Nuh-uh, dumbshit. Go get some water. No caffeine for you until next week."

"I need it. I go in front of Sawalha this afternoon at four."

She crinkled her nose and threw a little head shake at me.

"Okay, okay. I'll get some water." I took the diet cola and put it on her tray. "Here. You can have it." I took a big bite of the tuna sub and headed off in search of water.

When I returned to the table with a bottle of dull water, Zoe had reduced her chef salad to lettuce remnants. I took a few minutes to scarf down my sub before speaking. Soon I felt like myself again. "It wasn't his fault."

"Is this Sara Donovan talking, back from The Land of Enchantment?"

"I'm serious. I could have walked away and not helped. They…he…wouldn't have done anything. It was my decision."

"He shouldn't have even asked you. Not around finals. You've risked getting into the business program and staying at 'Bama just to help the feds. And for what? You gonna get a reward or something? A piece of the loot they recover or something? Nope. You got squat. And you'll get squat."

"I did it because I like him." My eyes were wet. "I really like him."

"For real? Ten days ago, you ratted him out to the cops. Last week, you followed him and it almost got you busted. But now, you like him?"

"I know. I know. It looks bad. But the entire time, even when I called the cops on him, I've had a nagging feeling I was wrong about him." My chest tightened as a tear wandered down my cheek. "I let my head get in the way of my heart." Another one slid behind the first. "If I listened to you and Mom, none of this would have happened. But I didn't. And now—" I sniffled. "—I've lost Grant and probably failed GBA380."

Zoe melted. "Ah, girl. C'mon. You're the smartest person I know. Well, the smartest person with the most questionable judgment. But hey, you don't need good judgment to ace GBA380. Just smarts. And you got that. I'm sure you'll be fine."

"I don't know about that." I hesitated, fighting back a cloudburst of regret. "I really, really like him."

Chapter Thirty-Eight

Crap—I forgot the scotch

With Finals Week officially ended, all my friends urged me to hit the Strip for celebratory pizza and barbecue. For once, I learned my lesson about bad decisions from Saturday night's game night and the ensuing aftermath, ending with this morning's GBA380 disaster. With envious regret I declined, left the Ferg, and made the trek back to my cottage to prepare for that damn one-on-one presentation.

Since finals ended at noon, the buses switched to a summer schedule and the University eased parking sticker restrictions. That meant I could drive and park near Garland Hall. Take that, campus bus system and the now former Bane of My Existence.

Now I was trying to tear through campus to get to Garland Hall on time. However, because of all those fricking damn parents. With all their damn trailers. And their damn kids. With their damn goofy smiles and dorm junk everywhere. There was no fricking damn place on campus to tear through.

After what felt like a year later, I made it to Margaret Drive and checked the dashboard clock. Frick. I held my breath and cut hard around the corner onto Capstone Drive. By chance, the Universe decreed enough was enough, because a barren street complete with my pick of parking spots stretched out before me. I screeched to a stop in a primo spot, leaving a bit of my tires' sidewalls along the raised curb. Grabbing purse and backpack, I jumped out of the car and took off running toward Garland.

Earlier this afternoon, after a second cup of coffee, I made one last dry run through my spiel. Unfortunately, that dry run mutated into a wet torrent of perspiration. It finally hit home this was one-on-one with Professor Sawalha for sixty frigging minutes. And now, as I "sprinted" with head down up the stairs into Garland Hall, that musty perspiration transformed into pure stinky fear.

I hit the inside staircase on a dead run. Although, since I was late and about to do a one-on-one, probably not the best descriptive phrase to use. By the time I crawled onto the fourth floor, my lungs ached. My sweatproof outfit was sweatproof no longer. And I forgot everything except for the opening statement.

Rebounding along the dark walls toward his office, I fought balancing the need for speed with catching my breath. It quickly proved to be an unattainable balance. I sounded like a wheezing herd of buffalo thundering through the creepy dark hallway, with the lamenting floorboards impolitely announcing my arrival long before I appeared in the doorway.

Sqqqquuuuuueeeeeeeeek.

Unbelievable.

An astonished Professor Sawalha faced me from his chair when I stumbled into the cramped office. "Miss Donovan, this is quite un—"

"Sir, I'm so...sorry I'm...late." My chest was heaving so much I worried the Ladies might get seasick. "There's no—" deep breath. "—excuse, but I got caught in all…the moving-out traffic around the dorms." I sucked in another breath, dropped my stuff on the—empty—chair and tugged a presentation folder from my backpack, taking care not to drip on it. I handed it to the bewildered man, who did not move to take it.

"Miss Donovan, I'm sorry, but—"

"Please?" I gave the folder a quick shake and extended it closer to the wide-eyed man, forcing him to take it.

I may have been late. And he was about to fail me. But I was going down fighting. People have called me stubborn my whole life. Mainly by Dad. And Zoe. But at this very moment. With my college career at 'Bama precariously hanging in the balance, GBA380 aside, I intended to put that trait to good use. No way this little man was telling me I couldn't do my presentation. If he wanted me to stop, he better call security. And good luck with that.

I took in a deep breath of aromatic air—and coughed. Another deep breath, this time through open mouth, did the trick. "According to law enforcement experts, the illicit market for stolen antiquities is the fourth largest in the world. With the amount of money being thrown around for antiquities, it's no wonder the black market for this stuff is so huge. There are teams of looters with ever increasing sophistication operating in countries all over the world, including Egypt, Peru, Mexico, China, and Japan, just to name a few."

I took a second to gauge the reaction. His glassy stare told me—not so good. I needed to step it up.

"Please, Miss Donovan. You must st—"

I persisted, my voice getting louder and rushed. "They are usually locals who go out in the dead of—"

The professor's hands went up, palms facing out. "*Miss Donovan*. Please. Stop. Just—stop."

My face burned hot. How could I have screwed up my most favorite and easiest class? If I was lucky, after graduating from some lame local college, I might carve out a little career in retail. Maybe a bookstore or bank? Tears welled up, the emotions of the last several weeks soon to spill out onto the floor in front of this very pissed off man.

He exhaled. "Thank you. Please let me speak. Okay?"

I nodded, fighting the tears. I refused to give him the satisfaction of seeing me cry. I stood there. Head bowed. Arms at my side. Waiting.

The professor muttered something, but I didn't catch it. Nobody wants to hear their executioner's final morbid command.

I sneaked a look at him.

His face was—beaming? Why was he smiling when he just flunked me? The sadistic little jerk.

I took the presentation packet back and packed my things. "I understand, sir."

"Miss Donovan?"

"Hmm?"

"Sara. Didn't you hear me? I said you got an A. You don't have to do your presentation. In fact, I'm giving you an A-plus."

For a moment I could only stand there with mouth agape. "What...how...why?" I tried to find my composure, which quickly became a difficult task. I couldn't remember where I last put it.

257

"Didn't you get my message? I called several times this morning. After the third or fourth call, I left a voicemail."

A vision from the bus ran through my head. "No, sir. My phone kinda broke this morning." My shoulders sagged as I dropped into the empty chair.

"That makes sense. Yes, definitely makes sense. No matter. I waived the need for you to give a presentation based on your recent efforts helping Mr. Doherty on the investigation." He beamed at me over the top of his glasses. "It's clear you did the research. Although, how shall I say it? You didn't quite get everything right, hmmm?"

I slid lower in the chair. "Not quite everything, I guess."

The professor clapped his hands together and held them in front of his chest. "Well, Miss Donovan, Mr. Doherty called early this afternoon to tell me they made several arrests. They're busting the entire ring."

I sat up with a start. "They…what? He what?" Grant said he would tell me when it all went down. Instead, he called this guy first?

"Yes, yes. Apparently, it was a big bust. They've even arrested someone from the Dauphin. Mr. Doherty said by the middle of the week the FBI will have the entire network dismantled. It's virtually unprecedented. He said it's all because of your help." He rose from his chair and—*squuuueeeeeekkkkk*—extended his right hand. "So, you got an A-plus. Congratulations."

My rising anger at Grant lying to me dried up any budding tears. Maybe the heart got it wrong this time, and the head was right all along about him.

"Did he tell you who they arrested from the

Dauphin?"

The professor shook his head. "No. Just that they got her cold."

Chapter Thirty-Nine

Someone's knocking at my door?

After GBA380 and my meeting with the professor, I was so exhausted I didn't remember going to sleep. I awoke with a throbbing head and a ten-alarm inferno in my chest, signaling I might have done something incredibly stupid last night.

I spied the clock across the room. Three o'clock. Last night's escapades quickly came into focus. I rolled over and scanned the floor.

Damn. It was true.

And unfortunately, there was no discarded clothing and an unknown comatose guy from a night of youthful blowing-off-steam passion. That would have been an acceptable tradeoff for last night's reckless activities.

Instead, an empty pizza box lay on the floor. Along with two empty bottles of wine that were just the end of the beginning. After Zoe got me home from an off-campus party celebrating the end of finals, which I'm sure was quite an effort on her part and I'll hear about that one later, I ordered pizza. So far, so good.

While waiting for my large deep-dish vegetarian, I ripped the place apart on a quest for alcohol. At the time, it seemed like a good idea. Only because at the party, and against my better judgment, I drank two light beers. For a non-drinker like me, that meant afterward pretty much everything was on the list of good ideas. Like guzzling two bottles of cooking wine. And not real wine used for cooking. Actual *cooking* wine sold in the grocery store solely for—well—cooking.

Bang. Bang. Bang.

Perfect. Now somebody's at my front door.

"Sara," a voice called out.

I fell out of bed, crammed a wide-brimmed floppy hat on my splitting skull, and snagged a pair of large dark sunglasses off the dresser. I ricocheted down the stairs, bouncing from wall to wall to banister to wall, feet and rubbery legs struggling to keep me upright.

"Sara."

"Hold your fricking horses," I bellowed. "Oooohhhh."

I made it to the bottom of the stairs intact, sliding along the wall toward the door. I stopped and peeked out the side window to see who in the hell had the audacity to wake me at three o'clock in the afternoon. After a few seconds, my eyes adjusted to the radiating brilliance. Things just kept getting better and better.

"Hey, Grant," I mumbled, half opening the door and leaning against its edge. "What're you doing here?"

He gave me the once-over and cracked up. "You okay?"

"Mmmm, not sure," I whispered. "Kinda long night."

He frowned. "I can see that. I guess you're done with finals and everything, huh?"

I grimaced. Definitely a good call putting on the sunglasses. "You don't know the half of it. What do you want? I need to go back to bed."

"I've got something to tell you. Can I come in?"

"Is it professional, or personal?"

"Uh...both?"

I stepped back, fully opening the door. "Make it quick."

He entered and I gently, *ever* so fricking gently, closed the door.

"Cripes, what happened last night?" he asked, surveying the wrecked living area.

I took a quick check around the room, mainly to make sure no embarrassing articles of clothing were anywhere. Destruction reigned, like a band of marauders marauded the absolute hell out of the place. "I was...looking...for something."

"Uh-huh. And did you find what you were looking for?"

"Kinda."

"Oookay. I'll leave that be."

"The professional news?" I asked with an air of impertinence. Despite my recent alcohol intake, I hadn't forgotten he told the professor about the bust before me. All I wanted was to go back to bed. In fact, he still hasn't told me about the bust yet, and he's had plenty of time to do it.

"Right. Professional news. Because of your help, we busted the smuggling ring. The entire network. We started late Sunday and should have it all finished up by tomorrow." Grant's white teeth laid siege to my beleaguered eyes, despite the sunglasses. "The micro-tracker worked great. Led us straight to them. We caught a museum employee and the ringleader together in the same room with the tracked object. Along with several other artifacts and a big pile of cash. This morning they've been singing like canaries. Both are trying to cut deals with the DA by hanging the other out to dry. We're squeezing the employee hard because we want to pin everything we can on the boss."

"Good for you. Of course"—I looked daggers at him, which was thoroughly useless on account of the dark sunglasses—"I already knew about the bust."

"What? How could..." He snapped his fingers. "Sawalha told you."

"He did," came my curt reply while searing him with my white-hot sunglasses-diffused fierce look. It was such a waste because it felt killer. But I was so not taking off those glasses.

"I called you before Sawalha, but your phone kept going to voicemail. I left three or four messages. Didn't you get any of them?"

I smiled feebly. That fricking bus driver and his Bane of My Existence continued to curse me. "Ha. Funny thing. My phone broke yesterday morning. And between my last final, and that damn presentation, and—" I swallowed hard. "—last night's party, I haven't had the time to get it replaced."

Grant unfolded an easy smile. "Don't worry about it. I just feel bad because I promised to let you know how it went. Instead, you heard it first from him." He put on the most sincere, caring face I have ever laid hung-over, light-shaded eyes on. "Please accept my apology. Do you forgive me?"

"It's not your fault. It's all mine. If I hadn't broken my phone, none of this would have happened. And if I had just—"

"Let's say it's both our faults, and we forgive each other?"

I let out a huge breath. "That's a deal I can make,"

I whispered.

"You want the personal now?"

"Uh-huh."

"I'm no longer a teaching assistant. My undercover gig is up. I'm flying home once I wrap up some administrative details on the investigation." There was a tenderness I hadn't seen since that night at his place, before he gave me the twenty-questions drill. "Technically, I'm not part of the faculty."

"Washington?"

A moment was coming, and I looked a mess. I had a floppy hat on with hair sticking out everywhere. Wearing big dark sunglasses—indoors. I stared down through the bottom of the glasses. Dang it. I had sauce stains on my jammy shirt and what appeared to be an encrusted chunk of red pepper or black olive plastered on my right boob.

He took a step toward me. "Uh-huh. My office is in D.C."

I didn't back away. Not because I couldn't. Because I didn't want to. "I live outside D.C. In Annapolis," I offered. "With my parents." Geez, that sounded really bad.

"I remember," he murmured. He took another step toward me. "We'll practically be neighbors."

My entire body prickled with anticipation. I did the lean-in as he took the last half step between us. Our bodies touched.

The room began spinning as an incessant buzzing filled my head. Suddenly I had to vom.

Push it back down, Sara. Oh yes. Do it, man. Kiss—

Crap. He's about to kiss me. Forget about the vom

suppression, which proved successful. I had morning hangover breath. The worst kind of morning breath. Well, I suspect the worst kind was morning hangover vom breath but—

His arms wrapped me up. Our lips met. A soft kiss. Then, oh my… All kinds of sensations coursed through me. And thankfully, not the recently suppressed vom.

"Sorry about the morning breath," I purred.

"Sorry about not doing this earlier," he replied.

I was on fire and tingling at the same time. We stumbled toward the couch, hands fumbling over each other like—well—two aroused people who hadn't gotten any in a long, long time. Right before we got to the couch, I emerged from my erotic haze just enough to remember I left a garbage dump there last night during my frenzied alcohol hunt. With one eye open, I swatted a junk heap off the couch, and we fell onto the cushions. All the anxiety and emotions of the last three weeks poured out of me as we—

"Oomph," Grant grunted from atop me.

I opened my eyes. "*Mauzzy.*"

While my hormones were raging, my little guardian dachshund crept downstairs to check out the commotion that woke him. Only to find Mommy in a death struggle with a man. Having none of that, he transformed himself into fifty pounds of junkyard dog and launched onto Grant's back. From his perch, he stared at me with such reproach a pang of guilt zinged me. But it passed.

"Get down," I demanded from underneath, leering over Grant's right shoulder at my disapproving dachshund.

He hung his head and whimpered.

"Oh, I'm sorry. Mommy's all right, baby."

Satisfied with the results, Mauzzy dropped the hurt act and leaped off. In three quick steps and a jump, he was in his chair. There he sat, glowering at the strange intruder and warning him with a continual low guttural growl.

I glared at my Not-So-Sweet Handsome, again the sunglasses wasting my awesome fierce look. "Mauuuzzzy."

Grant propped himself up with a little chuckle. "Talk about a mood breaker."

"He's good at it," I said with a bit of irritation directed at my jealous roommate.

His eyes worked me over. "Who says we can't get that mood back again?"

"I'm all for it. But first, I have to ask. Who got busted?"

"Not at liberty to say yet. In about thirty minutes I have to run back to the office, hopefully to wrap up a confession and plea deal. If all goes well, I can tell you over dinner tomorrow night."

"What? I have to wait a whole day?"

His smile was both knowing and lascivious.

Chapter Forty

Oops. Did it...?

Finally, Wednesday evening got off its butt and arrived. I've been waiting for tonight since Grant left yesterday. Reliving those thirty minutes with him kept me from thinking about my brief run at 'Bama coming to a miserable end after I got my grades. That first kiss, morning hangover breath and all, was just what I needed to forget my impending future as a commuter student living with her parents.

"Are we ready to order or would you like more time?" the waiter asked, his hands clasped behind a ramrod-straight back.

"I know what I want. Grant?"

"Me too," he replied with a ravenous smile at me. Maybe a bit too ravenous.

I blushed as tingles erupted throughout my body. Good thing they dimmed the lights in *Angelina's* small but elegant dining room. But who could blame him? I looked and felt great, rocking a mid-thigh solid black bandage skirt with a deep-pink ruffled layer blouse. And my *Sorbet* underpants.

Clearing his throat, the waiter said, "Very good. Miss?"

"Definitely the mahi-mahi special."

He acknowledged me with a crisp nod, hands still

clasped behind him. "Excellent decision. I guarantee it will not disappoint you. And for you, sir?"

"I'm a meat and potatoes guy. Tonight, I'll upgrade and have the filet of beef special."

The waiter signaled his approval with a click of the heels and a quick bow of the head. "I promise you. It will be a big upgrade. The reduction sauce is fantastic." With another click of the heels, he pivoted and dashed off to place our order.

I focused on my dorky-hot dinner date. "You were telling me about Roger Gwynne. I cannot believe he's innocent. I mean, he made the phone call to get that shipment released. So guilty."

Grant took a sip of sparkling water and lemon. Nodding, he said, "We all thought the same thing. But his reason for the call is kinda funny." His sparkling seas of blue were full of warmth, and goodness, and yum.

"I'm not seeing the word 'funny' and Roger going together."

"I didn't say *he* was funny. Now, remember," he cautioned me with an extended hand, "since it's still an open investigation, you can't divulge any of this to anybody. I'm able to tell you because we brought you in to assist with the case."

"So, we're colleagues?"

He returned my flirty expression with a lecherous smile. "Not quite. More of an informant-turned-consultant."

We sat for a moment, remembering, drinking each other in, feeding off the other's palpable desire and heightened anticipation.

I broke the smoldering mood. I just had to know.

"Roger?"

Grant started. "Uh, right. Gwynne. You know why he made that call to the Port Authority?"

"Don't tell me there really was an exhibit opening soon because—"

"No, no. We confirmed he lied to the customs agent. The reason was"—he leaned in toward me, his eyes alive with laughter—"to keep his wife from cutting him off."

"As in no sex?"

"Right."

I grabbed my water, suddenly in a desperate struggle to banish the nauseating picture of the staid Dr. Roger Gwynne having sex before the revulsion ruined the delicious meal I just ordered. "Really? Sex?"

"Turns out his wife was remodeling and redecorating their home. That shipment included the last element of the construction schedule. She needed the work completed in time to host a reception for the local art world the night before the silent auction." He paused, his mouth drawing into a playful smile. "And serve as an early promotion for the new Byzantine exhibit opening in September. The one the silent auction supported."

I shook my head. "What?"

"So, in a way, the shipment *did* have to do with an exhibit he was planning to open. Only it wasn't anytime soon. And it wasn't because there were pieces in it for that exhibit." He took another sip of sparkling water, trying to contain his growing amusement.

"Why would his wife threaten to, you know, withhold the goodies just for a museum exhibit?"

"She didn't give a damn about the exhibit. She

only cared about making sure her posh reception, six months in the planning, became Birmingham's social event of the year. And there were some very specific art pieces in that shipment, high-end replicas she ordered to decorate the house. All about a theme. When you told Gwynne that customs impounded the container with the museum's shipment two days before her soiree, he had no choice but to tell her."

"I take it the news didn't sit so well with the esteemed Mrs. Dr. Gwynne?"

"It sure didn't." Grant's dimples deepened. "When we tried to corroborate his story, she told us he offered to get some comparable replacements from the gift shop. As loaners. Just for the reception. Well"—he switched to an overdone haughty tone—"this impertinent and insensitive attempt at appeasement infuriated her to no end. She had no choice but to threaten him with the prospect of separate bedrooms and worse if he didn't get her artwork in time for the reception."

I took a sip of sparkling water. "So, he made the call."

"Yup. Simple as that. He was innocent." Grant caught himself. "Of the smuggling. But he made false statements to a federal agent when he placed that call. In exchange for his cooperation, we negotiated for him to receive judicial diversion."

"What's that?"

"He pleads guilty in exchange for probation and the opportunity to have his conviction expunged if he keeps his nose clean. It's a win-win in situations where someone with no record makes a bad decision that leads to a low-level offense. Gwynne's crime was more serious, but his high-priced lawyer earned his money and got the DA to relent. For the next three years, he'll be available to us on investigations as an unpaid consultant."

"Judicial diversion," I repeated, burning it into memory. I wasn't planning on any more incidents with The Man, but it was good to know.

"It's a useful tool when we need to get someone to talk who may have stepped in it but isn't a target of the investigation. And speaking of lying to a federal agent…" His mouth formed a grim twist.

Why was he staring at me like that? I didn't lie. Did I? Of course not. I don't tell lies. Well, except for the little white ones. But those don't count. I couldn't tell Dad he got a bad haircut. Or Mauzzy that he packed on a few pounds, and it went straight to his butt. I showed consideration for their feelings and redirected the truth. But certainly not—

"Sara?"

Another sip of water. I could sure use a heavenly miracle right about now regarding this damn water. "Yes?"

He lowered his voice, his eyes locking onto mine. "How many listening devices did you place in the Dauphin?"

I fidgeted with my napkin and extended for a roll in the center of the table. "Um…why would you ask? Whatever you gave me, I placed. Just like you told me."

"Mmmm. I see."

He wasn't buying it. Sure, easy to recognize *now* that telling him back *then* would have been the correct choice. But I was so damn tired. And done with everything. Yet another snap decision gone awry.

Grant continued. "Here's the thing. Five were fairly typical with the information they transmitted. You know, the things we're used to hearing. A lot of mundane matters. A few leads we followed up on. Stuff like that."

I popped a piece of roll in my mouth and nodded attentively.

He tilted his head and considered me. I stopped chewing. I didn't like the direction we were heading. I've seen this look before. Too many times. Not from Grant. From my past. And it usually preceded a reprimand about something inappropriate I did or screwed up. Emphasis on the latter.

"But from the sixth one, the FBI got all kinds of strange conversations and noises." He stopped and waited for a response.

I choked down the half-chewed roll with a big gulp of water. *Seriously God, where's the fricking miracle? I could kinda use some help here.* "Like what *kind* of strange conversations and noises?"

Grant turned his head and looked off into the air. He turned back, smiling. "Hmmm. Let's just say while the other five all had a fixed location, which they should since you stuck them on objects in targeted rooms, this sixth one seemed very—mobile."

"Oh?"

He nodded and took another sip of water. "Initially, it had everyone confused. First, we heard the sounds of someone driving. You know, talking to other cars and singing—country music, I believe—with the radio."

I swallowed and poured another glass of water. Yeah, I still hoped God was listening in and decided to pull off the miraculous transformation I so desperately

272

needed. It's not like He hasn't done it before.

"Then, someone had a meltdown over a computer issue. Finally, right before we figured it out, that person had a rambling—interesting—soliloquy about an upcoming exam. A certain GBA380 final?"

I dropped my head in my hands. I was beyond humiliated.

He eased my hands away from my face. "I didn't mean to upset you."

I winced. "I wanted to tell you. But when you asked if all the devices were in place, I didn't want to hear anything about losing one of your expensive gizmos. Your 'no big deal op' exhausted me and I made a snap decision. And—" I took a healthy gulp of, damn, still water. "—my snap decisions are usually not such good ones."

"It's okay. I was just having a little fun with you."

"I sorta lied to you." I dropped my voice. "You're a federal agent. Can I get judicial, um, division?"

"Diversion. And no, you're—"

"*No?*"

Heads whipped around our way.

"*Am I going to jail?*" I whispered loudly. An image of a lounging Roxy Rhonda waiting in my jail cell popped in my head.

He shook his head. "You're not in trouble. You're not guilty of anything."

I breathed out. "Thank, God." I guess that's better than the old water-wine miracle. Although I would have appreciated both. I took a few seconds to compose myself. "Where was the missing one?"

"We think"—he pointed to my purse hanging on the chair—"it somehow fell back inside your purse

273

when you took the devices out of the bag."

I took the purse off the chair and peered inside. Picking up the new phone I got this afternoon, I pointed it inside the purse and activated the flashlight. There were hand sanitizers. A toothbrush and toothpaste. Wallet. My OCD Tissue System, patent pending by Sara Donovan. A handful of old fuel and grocery store receipts. Keys with pepper spray. Makeup. And— among the gross sticky stuff, crumbs, and dirt at the bottom of every purse—was a small black disc.

I produced the sixth listening device. "Oops?"

Grant took it from me, wrapped it in his handkerchief, and placed it in his jacket pocket. "Thanks. This would be number six," he said with a wink. "And these babies aren't cheap."

I swallowed. "I've heard that."

As I tore off another piece of roll, a vision struck me so humiliating, so totally embarrassing, I sat there aghast. I could only gawk at Grant with wild eyes. Open-mouthed. My stomach tightened. I squeaked out, "Did it—"

He shook his head. "Once we figured out what happened, I asked the FBI to deactivate it Monday afternoon. It wasn't—" A quick clear of the throat. "—operable...when we...uh...you know." He clutched his water glass.

I heaved a sigh. "If not Roger, who was it at the Dauphin?"

"You haven't figured it out yet?"

I ran through my list of remaining suspects. "Dr. Mitchell sure acted suspicious when she caught me in her office. And she has an art history background. It can't be... Wait. I bet it was that bitch, Karen."

274

"Nope. Thornburn and—your boss."

"*What?* Edna? No way."

His eyes widened. "Big time way. She came clean today after we gave her a onetime offer. The DA liked her proffer letter. Said it will hang Thornburn. So, we cut a deal. She's still facing prison time, but not near as long as him."

The news stunned me. Edna wasn't my favorite person in the world, but she never did anything to hurt me. "But she was so plain. Unassuming. All about the rules. How can she be an international criminal?"

"That's the point. She didn't want to attract attention."

"How? I mean, why the Dauphin?"

"Ah," he wagged a finger for emphasis. "Yet another imaginatively simple approach. It just took a little planning. They were a couple. He—"

"Eeeewwww, you mean, like—a couple?" I felt nauseous all over again. First Roger and now Edna having…

"Now former couple."

"So gross."

"He was the brains. Four years ago, he came across an opportunity during a business trip to Cairo when he met Mansour and learned about his extensive network of tomb looters. A few months later he cooked up the smuggling scheme with Mansour. She went along with it."

"Because she loved him."

"Didn't ask. Not important."

"It is to me." We fell silent for a moment before I spoke up. "I was right about him though."

"You sure were. Your tracking that call to his

gallery was brilliant. And discovering their front company really helped us get out in front of things. The Egyptian authorities were ready to arrest Mansour and shut down All Things Egyptian as soon as we gave them confirmation he was complicit."

"Why did Thornburn call me?"

"He wasn't sure you had his mask. Mansour insisted you received one of the souvenir versions and thought maybe you switched it out for the disguised one. But no paperwork was in the gift shop showing you even received a souvenir mask."

"That's because mine came in the shipment in a separate envelope addressed to me, which I took home."

"Makes sense," Grant said, bobbing his head. "So, after you hung up on him, Edna called to smoke you out. And it worked. When you told her about your mask, that was all they needed to know."

"They thought I had the real one?"

"They weren't sure. She admitted they searched your place and couldn't find it. This caused Thornburn to consider a double-cross. He worried Mansour kept the piece when he saw an opportunity to blame you. After they searched your place, they didn't know how to proceed. Other than to monitor both of you. Remember, this guy is an art history type. Not a violent criminal."

"What a brilliant plan, disguising artifacts as souvenirs."

"Sure was." Grant took a sip of water. "He had Mansour set up a souvenir front company in Cairo and buy artifacts from his local network. Each time he acquired an item, he dipped it in liquid plastic and painted it to look like the countless souvenirs coming out of Egypt. Nobody along the way gave these items a second look because they were cheap souvenirs that were a dime a dozen."

"Which explains the gift shop."

"Exactly. With Mansour executing the Egyptian side of the operation, all Thornburn needed to do was get his girlfriend a job as a buyer for the gift shop. Since—"

"*Please*, don't call her his girlfriend. Unless you want to ruin my dinner."

Grant held up a hand. "Sorry. So, since Thornburn once worked for Gwynne, he was able to get her the job as the assistant manager. Once hired, she searched for a customer to use as a virtual blind mule and found Bagley's extensive order history and tendency to pick them up during the week. She was perfect."

My hand flew to my mouth. "I put those packages in Karen's bin, at—Edna's direction. Was Karen involved?"

"She had no clue. On the days you put an artifact package in her bin, Edna waited until you left Sunday evening before removing the package and taking it over to the gallery."

I frowned. "Once they dipped the objects in plastic, they're ruined. Aren't they? I mean, they're plastic coated."

"Once she got the items to the gallery, Thornburn dipped them in acetone to remove the plastic. Since they made a point to only deal with stone and gold, it didn't harm the piece. And a cheap souvenir instantly transformed back to being a valuable piece of Egyptian culture."

"Ingenious."

"Sure is. And simple."

"What about Mrs. Majelski and my mask?"

Grant nodded. "You were right. She wields a unique skill set. With quite the background. Although you should have given us the item when you first suspected something, giving it to her turned out to be a wise decision. She drove everybody nuts. Nobody could keep up with her."

I giggled. "I can just imagine."

"That little old lady could teach us a few things about running a covert op, that's for sure." He shook his head and chuckled. "In fact, I'm certain she was our informant's impeccable source. As it turns out, you're the granddaughter she never had. She's been watching out for you all year. Or as she told us, 'for her protection, dear.' She's better than any lawyer you could ever have—or bodyguard. That little old lady threatened us with…well…just know if we didn't clear you, she would be *very* unhappy. Her stare made sure there was no misunderstanding." Grant shuddered, obviously trying to shake off the icy visage of one dangerous super-ninja bodyguard granny.

"That's sweet. I know that stare. She's okay?"

"More than okay. We sent her name up the chain as a possible consultant for the FBI."

"Protection, dear," I said, smiling.

"You've got nothing to worry about with her around."

"And my mask?"

"It's real."

My mouth fell slack. "Real? I was right?"

"We melted off the plastic and found a simple gold

funerary mask. Sawalha puts it from the Eighteenth Dynasty. Possibly from the looted Akhenaten dedication tomb. He figures the black-market value is easily two million. We'll be turning it over to the Egyptian government once we no longer need it as evidence."

"Million?"

"Millions."

Chapter Forty-One

Sweet home—Alabama?

Today was it. The day my life crumbled around me. I sat slumped on the couch amid stacks of boxes and large plastic storage containers. I've been contemplating the veritable certainty I failed GBA380 and will return home to live with my parents forever as a professional commuter student.

I tried logging into the University system late last night to check if they posted my GBA380 grade. Per usual, the website was down for unscheduled maintenance. And as of five minutes ago, it remained down. Just the Universe taking one last shot.

After I took that fricking exam, my confidence jumped ship, leaving me alone to navigate the high seas of despair. And in less than three hours, it was all over. Assuming the system ever got back up. Regardless, I knew how this was going to end.

A sharp knock on the door startled me. It couldn't be Mom and Dad. They weren't due for another two or three hours. I gave the couch and surrounding floor a quick once-over. Mauzzy leaped off his chair and assisted with the inspection, but I knew what he was searching for. The food whore.

Inspection complete, he jumped back in his chair as I dragged myself up off the couch and shuffled across the crowded floor. My GBA380 shackles jingled with each scuffed step. *Dead woman walking.*

I checked outside before swinging the door open. "*Grant.*"

He took one step through the doorway when I propelled myself forward, wrapping him up in a tight hug.

In keeping with the story of my life, any good gesture or action on my part usually results in unintended consequences. In this specific instance, I knocked him off-balance. He stumbled backward, struggling to catch himself while I had his arms pinned and my head buried in his chest. His heel caught the doorjamb, and we fell out onto the front deck.

"Oh," Grant grunted as he hit the deck and absorbed the force of my landing on top of him.

I raised my head from his chest. "Sorry."

His eyes had a mischievous glint as he wriggled his arms out from underneath me. "I see we're starting right where we left off last night."

There we were. Prone on the front deck. Kissing madly like high school kids behind the public library.

Mauzzy whined from the front door. But I didn't care.

Cars whizzed by on the road outside the complex. But I didn't care.

A truck rattled past, its heavy engine chugging and choking to a stop somewhere nearby. But I didn't care.

Oh, my God. He smelled so damn good. Like a fresh ocean breeze. I didn't give a *frick* about anything but the present moment. Not even with what was coming later today with my grades. All I cared about was—not stopping.

"Sara?"

A heavy car door slammed.

"*Sara.*"

Suddenly, I cared.

I rolled off Grant, stood, straightened my shirt and shorts, and raked hair out of my face. "Mom," I cried out, skipping down the stairs to intercept her. "You're early."

We met on the sidewalk and hugged. She whispered in my ear, "What on earth are you doing?" as I desperately searched over her shoulder for Dad.

I didn't see him.

Heartfelt greeting complete, we stepped back from each other. Mom was so attractive she could be a model, even now in her fifties with her short salt-and-pepper perfectly coiffed hair. She wore a cute pink-and-white tennis outfit, the short skirt showing off long bronzed legs.

"I…uh…did Dad…"

She barely shook her head. "I don't think so. He was too busy grumbling about parking the truck to notice anything else."

"You're sure?"

A truck's rear door rolling up clattered in the background.

"You're fine," she said with a flip of her hand. "Just be more careful." Her attention shifted to something behind me. "Who's he? You never mentioned you had a boyfriend. He *is* your boyfriend, right?"

I squinted back toward the cottage. "I don't know. He's my neighbor. And we just—started dating?"

"Have you—"

"*No*. We'll talk later. Not now." I pirouetted and held an arm out toward an approaching Grant.

Grating metal and Dad wrenching out the truck's ramp punctuated the air.

"You must be Mrs. Donovan," Grant said as he neared, hand extended with a welcoming smile. "I'm Grant Doherty."

"Lucy Donovan. Pleased to meet you," she said, gently shaking his hand. "Sara said you're neighbors."

He yanked a thumb back toward his cottage. "Live right next door."

"Mom, you guys are here way early."

She sucked in a deep breath and let it go. "That's your father. He was up at six this morning banging around the motel room, making coffee, and packing things up."

A deep male voice thundered behind us. "Sara."

I spun around.

The moment of truth just arrived.

Funny how fast things can change. Fifteen minutes ago, the moment of truth was not for three hours. Now it stared me in the face from a fast-moving Dad on a mission. He had on a ratty old t-shirt, black shorts, and tennis shoes with ankle socks. He was already a tall burly man with an intimidating physicality, and this outfit just emphasized his presence. Thick, long legs swallowed up the parking lot in a matter of five or six quick strides.

I acted casual. "Hi, Daddy."

He marched up the walkway, only stopping to wrap me in a massive bear hug and kiss my cheek. "Hi, honey." He leaned back and fixed on my face. "You okay? You look tired. Finals go well?"

"Yes, but I'm not—"

"*Great*. You all packed?"

"Pretty much."

"That's my girl." His hands smacked together in a resounding thunderclap. "Okay, let's get moving. We're burning daylight." He took two steps toward my cottage but froze when he caught sight of Grant, who stood to the side with hands in his front pockets. His exuberance evaporated. "Who are you?"

Grant was unfazed. He put out a hand. "Hi, Mr. Donovan. I'm Grant Doherty. Your daughter's neighbor. Very pleased to meet you, sir."

Dad enveloped the hand in his massive paw and crushed the crap out of it, like he does with every handshake. Something about making strong impressions. "Jack Donovan. Likewise." He eyeballed him. "You here to help?"

"Absolutely, sir."

"*Great*. Let's get a move on." He wheeled around and charged off to the front deck, roaring over his shoulder, "That truck isn't going to load itself. I want to get at least to Chattanooga before we have to stop."

"We're heading back today?" I called out.

Seconds later, Dad faced us atop the deck steps like a ship captain addressing his crew. "That's right. I wanna be on the road by five. Let's go, people. We're burning daylight."

The rest of us straggled toward my cottage. It was just a matter of time before Dad asked. Meaning, within five steps of getting inside.

When I got to the door, he was inside shaking his leg. "Get away from me. *Sara?*"

"Mauzzy, leave him alone."

284

He stopped, considered me, and lifted his leg.

"*Sara?*"

"Mauzzy," I scolded. "Get in your chair."

The little guy understood the situation and knew all the right buttons to push. Always did. And he was hitting all the high notes in his manipulative repertoire to accomplish the objective—staying with me next year at 'Bama. That's why he peed on Dad last year during our negotiations to come here. He wanted to make sure nobody left him out of the discussion. Little did the Crafty One know, we were moving back home where the two could match wits for the entire school year. And then some.

With his mission accomplished, he broke off the assault and padded over to the recliner. When he jumped on his chair and made his way around to face us, I could see pride etched all over his smug little face. Sometimes the little dude scared me.

"Have you got your grades?" Dad asked.

In my head, Denny Chimes bonged my death knell.

"All but my last final."

"Why's that?"

Bong.

"The system was down all day yesterday."

"Haven't you checked today?"

Bong.

Grant wisely picked up a big box by the door and left for the truck.

Mom took a shot at running interference for me. "Jack, let it be. Sara can check once we get home. It doesn't need to be right this second."

"It really does because we have a decision to make. Put her things in a mini-storage here for three months and save fifteen hundred dollars. Or—"

Bong.

"—move her home for next year."

Oh, God.

Come on Universe, let's get it over with. Time for the kill shot. Do it.

I maneuvered around stacked boxes to get to the couch where my laptop sat on the coffee table. "Let me see if the system is back up."

Dad sat next to me, shoulder to shoulder, before I could even get to the sign-in page. His excitement at saving fifty-thousand a year was clear. He elbowed in front of me, staring at the screen. "Is it up?"

Bong.

I angled sideways so I could see the screen around his head. My fingers typed furiously as I logged in. "I don't know yet."

The screen changed. I was in.

Bong.

"What's that? Looks like—"

"Yes, I'm in."

"Well? I don't see anything."

"*Jack.*"

"What?"

"Just hang on," I said. Three mouse clicks later, I was on my transcript page.

Bong.

Dad bent forward, his face inches from the screen.

I jostled him to the side with my shoulder and hunched in toward the laptop, my eyes scanning the screen as I searched for GBA380.

Bong.

The cottage fell silent. My heart raced. Ears rang.

Scalp tingled. Perspiration—well, cranked up.

"Well?" he said, trying to nudge me out of the way. "I can't see anything from here."

"That's the point," I said, fighting him off.

Grant returned. I caught his eye and frowned. He gave me an encouraging nod and a wink.

A thick finger pointed at the screen, drawing me back to my cyber firing squad. "There. Right there. What's that say?"

I concentrated on the screen. "It says—ninety-five. For—"

"Where's your GPA?"

"—GBA380. My GPA is a three-point-seven-five."

"*Really?*" Dad exclaimed. "Are you sure?"

"*Really?*" Mom asked, excitement in her voice.

"I knew you could do it," Grant sang. Pride and—love?—filled his voice.

"Double-check it," Dad said.

I backed out of the way, beaming. "See for yourself."

After studying the screen for several seconds, he said under his breath, "Son of a bitch." He pulled back from the screen and gave me a big, big hug. "I had faith in you. I just needed to keep the pressure on because otherwise…"

With a laugh of relief over his shoulder, I said, "Yeah, sometimes I don't make the best decisions."

Dad pulled back, grinned, and squeezed me again. "Exactly." He gave me a peck on the check and stood, his eyes casting about the room, no doubt in a desperate search for Mauzzy.

I jumped up, ran over to Grant, and he wrapped me up in a loving embrace.

"I'll see you this summer?" I asked.

"Count on it. I'm so proud of you," he whispered in my ear.

With a thunderous clap of his hands, Dad bellowed, "Okay, people, let's get that truck loaded. We have a mini-storage to fill. And we're burning daylight."

From over Grant's shoulder, I located the ever-dangerous Mauzzy, sitting tall in his recliner.

Watching.

Thinking.

Planning.

He was my Sweet Handsome. And I loved him.

A word about the author...

B.T. Polcari is a graduate of Rutgers College of Rutgers University and is a retired executive of an international government contractor loving life as an empty nester in Chattanooga, Tennessee. If not in the office trying to churn out wondrous words of fun, then he's either on the tennis court trying to smash the fuzz off that little green ball, in a bowling center trying to bowl perfect games, or out on the lake trying not to capsize. But always trying.

bt@btpolcari.com